THE
CRIME
BRÛLÉE
BAKE OFF

A
CLAIRE WALKER
MYSTERY

THE CRIME BRÛLÉE
BAKE OFF

REBECCA CONNOLLY

SHADOW
MOUNTAIN
PUBLISHING

Library of Congress Cataloging-in-Publication Data

Names: Connolly, Rebecca, author.
Title: The crime brûlée bake off / Rebecca Connolly.
Description: [Salt Lake City] : Shadow Mountain Publishing, 2025. | Series: A Claire Walker mystery | Summary: "Amateur baker Claire Walker gets caught up in a murder mystery while competing on a baking show in Blackfirth Park in England, where she also falls in love with the viscount Jonathan Ainsley." —Provided by publisher.
Identifiers: LCCN 2024024427 (print) | LCCN 2024024428 (ebook) | ISBN 9781639933044 (trade paperback) | ISBN 9781649333025 (ebook)
Subjects: LCSH: Television cooking shows—Fiction. | Baking—Fiction. | Man-woman relationships—Fiction. | BISAC: FICTION / Mystery & Detective / Women Sleuths | FICTION / Romance / Clean & Wholesome | LCGFT: Detective and mystery fiction. | Romance fiction.
Classification: LCC PS3603.054728 C75 2025 (print) | LCC PS3603.054728 (ebook) | DDC 813/.6—dc23/eng/20240708
LC record available at https://lccn.loc.gov/2024024427
LC ebook record available at https://lccn.loc.gov/2024024428

Printed in the United States of America
University Press

10 9 8 7 6 5 4 3 2 1

To Great-Grandma Motes,
who taught my mother how to make and
shape rolls and has therefore
changed all of our lives for the better.
Generations and their friends
will call you blessed, Eliza.
And not just because of carbs.

And to Paul Hollywood,
who I hope will give me a handshake for this one.

CHAPTER 1

"All right, class, that is time. Please place your exams on the corner of my desk, then return to your seats and wait quietly for the bell."

With their usual obedience, Claire Walker's Year 7 students filed up to her desk and did so, turning their exam papers face down without her needing to ask. There were no groans of distress at the exam ending when it did, no sighs of exasperation or frustration, no telltale signs of pride or glee.

Basically, it appeared that none of her students cared about this exam one way or the other.

Not that studying for her exams ought to delight them, but there was not the slightest spark of interest or appreciation for history. It was just another subject, just another course, just another exam, none of which excited them in any way.

She was not particularly excited either and hadn't been for some time.

She enjoyed teaching, for the most part, which was why she had chosen the field as her degree. She enjoyed history more, which was why she had added it as a minor to her undergraduate degree.

But neither teaching nor history were truly what she had hoped to do with her life. It was simply the most practical course. The more secure path. The more certain way.

But Claire would have given it all up in a heartbeat if she could have been the one thing she had been dreaming of since the age of ten.

A baker.

And it was that dream that had her stomach clenching, her heart racing, and her eyes darting to the clock with the eagerness of a teenager about to depart for summer holidays.

Her watch had buzzed during the exam she was proctoring, alerting her to a notification on her phone.

She hoped it would be the answer to the question she had been asking herself for three months now.

Would she be a contestant on *Britain's Battle of the Bakers*?

It was the biggest amateur baking competition in the United Kingdom, if not all of Europe, and somehow, she had been naive enough to think herself qualified enough to apply. What was even more confusing was . . . it was working.

She'd sweat her way through the online application about her signature bake, focused her breathing through the phone interview about her baking strengths and weaknesses, silently panicked through a sweet and savory test bake for the off-camera panel of judges, worried as her work was examined by an actual food technician, then proceeded to shake through another round comprised wholly of bread.

After having survived each of those death-defying tasks, she'd done the most terrifying thing known to baker-kind.

She'd done a test episode, tackling a technical challenge while being asked rapid-fire questions about herself, her life, her profession, and her bake.

She'd shed actual tears when she'd been released from that task.

Two weeks ago, she'd met with a psychologist tasked with weeding out applicants who weren't quite "show ready," though what exactly that meant had never been expressly stated. The lady asked Claire what she did for fun, aside from baking. How she coped with stresses in her life. How excessive pressure manifested for her. Any history with anxiety, depression, or other mental health issues? Did she bake to forget?

It felt like an interrogation of her very existence, if not testing the limits of her love of baking.

There had been no indication of the results of the interview; she'd only been told that she would be contacted in a few weeks with an answer.

Pairing her phone notifications with her Fitbit had seemed like a good idea at the time, but today it was utter misery. She couldn't check her phone during an exam, but what if . . . what if she'd made it? What if it had worked?

Or, more realistically, what if it was her dad asking her to pick up a shift at the White Fox when she was in town next weekend so they could have a family workday at the pub?

Claire would seriously consider telling him no just out of spite.

And then she would probably spend the evening frantically working her way through Dame Sophie Layton-Hughes's newest cookbook in order to calm herself down and prove to herself that she was a baker no matter what the show's answer was. She was on page 197 as of last night, which was game pie. As she was fresh out of game in her place—no commentary on her social life or status, thank you very much—it would have to wait while she moved on to Richmond Maids of Honour.

Crepes alive, she was memorizing the bakes of the book.

She really needed to get on the show. Her sanity might depend on it.

She'd been at university when *Britian's Battle of the Bakers* aired its first series—the theme had been Original Bakes—and the show had become an instant hit, not only for her, but the entire British public.

It had been around series five, the literature-themed series, when Claire had decided to bake along with the contestants. Not exactly with them, given the rapidity of the tasks and the abbreviated timeline of the episodes, but when they had a Classic Bake with a particular theme, she would assign herself the same and work to figure out how to fulfill the brief set by the judges within the time frame given. She'd make the bake again and again until she got it perfect. It took days each and every time, but she always managed to get it done.

It might have helped her social life to not bake so intently quite so often, but she swore to her mother that her bakes went to social occasions.

Unless they were terrible, and then they went to the bin or the neighbor's dogs.

The only trouble she had was with the Occasion Bakes, where multiple dishes were expected within an impossible time limit. It wasn't just Claire who thought so; the contestants on the show seemed to always struggle. She rarely saw an array of perfectly finished items for the Occasion Bakes.

She knew the show inside and out, series by series, and bake by bake. But she hated competition and had since her mother forced her to play hockey. Hours and hours of trying to keep up on the pitch with her teammates and opponents

THE CRIME BRÛLÉE BAKE OFF

had not only solidified her lack of athleticism in Claire's mind, but it had also spoiled her appetite for competition.

Yet there was something about baking that made her want to compete. That told her to risk losing on a visible stage. That told her to dare. That told her to try.

It was madness. Utter madness.

She wouldn't make it to the show. The entire field would be full of amateurs, but not all amateurs were created equal, and she was not creative enough to inspire the judges, even if she did have plenty of other skills. All she could do was bake what she had practiced and hope it would be good enough.

The bell rang, and the students hustled out of the classroom, a handful shouting their goodbyes to Claire as they left.

Alone at last, Claire exhaled roughly and closed the classroom door. School would not be dismissed for another period of classes, but she had no students for this last session. If she started grading the exams now, she wouldn't have as many to correct at home before working on her Richmond Maids of Honour.

But first, she needed to check her phone.

She moved around her desk, her right hand almost flying to the handle of the top drawer and pulling hard. Her phone was in her hand before she remembered reaching for it, and she stared at the blank, black screen for a moment.

There was no guarantee there would even be a call today. It could be another week or two before any calls were made one way or the other. There was no reason for her to be holding her breath right now.

"Don't be daft," she muttered to herself, tapping the screen with her thumb.

One missed call. One voicemail.

She felt her eyes widen, a newfound strain rippling around the edges of her vision. All she had to do was relax and blink, and everything would feel better, but between her eyes and her breath, she felt thin around the edges.

Something shook in her chest as she swiped the screen up and accessed her voicemail. She pressed play, holding the phone to her ear while her fingers began to tingle.

"Hello, Miss Walker," a polite, prim voice chirped. "This is Anne Fulton with *Britain's Battle of the Bakers*. I am pleased to inform you that, after successfully completing and passing all portions of the application, you have been selected as one of the contestants for series twelve. Please contact our office as soon as possible to confirm your place at . . ."

The rest of the message faded and became garbled in Claire's ears, her breathing growing frantic, her lungs constricting hard and fast, the air barely escaping her body before she was gasping for more. She gripped the edge of her desk, her phone clattering to its surface, and sank onto her chair as her wobbly knees gave out.

She couldn't breathe, and yet she was breathing. Her eyes began to water, and she wasn't sure why.

She was panicking, but that didn't make sense. How could she be panicking about something that was actually a dream come true? Where was the burst of joy and the thrill of excitement? Where was the warmth and delight?

Why was there only panic?

This was a new and terrifying development, and absolutely a sign that she should not have applied, which meant the phone call was a mistake she needed to correct.

She was never going to survive this.

She picked up her phone, her thumb darting across the screen to dial her sister, her gasping breaths growing louder and louder to her own ears.

"Why are you calling during the school day?" Ellie greeted.

"I think . . . I'm having . . . a panic attack?" Claire managed, splaying her hand on the desk as her hairline began to tingle ominously.

She heard her sister drop something on her side of the phone. "Okay," Ellie said slowly, "welcome to the club. Stay calm, Claire. Inhale for four counts, exhale for five. Can you do that?"

"Uh-huh . . ." Claire tried to do as her older sister instructed, her breath stuttering, resisting her attempt at control.

Impossibly, it began to work, and there wasn't as much desperation to her breathing. She could feel sensation returning to normal in her extremities, and the tears streaming from her eyes slowed to a faint trickle. Her hearing was restored, and she could swallow without feeling like she was choking.

Which only left her state of mind, such as it was.

"Okay, duckie," her sister's voice soothed, using the nickname their father had bestowed upon Claire. "That's not like you. What happened?"

Claire allowed herself another two long, slow breaths before she even tried to speak. And then she said the words she didn't quite believe:

"I'm going to be on *Britain's Battle of the Bakers*."

CHAPTER 2

8 WEEKS LATER

This was the dumbest thing that had ever happened to the estate of Blackfirth Park.

In the history of seventeen viscounts, that was saying something.

But Jonathan Ainsley was certain he was right as he watched the trucks parking along the gravel lot that had been created on a portion of the green.

Who had ever thought of allowing a television series to use a family home, protected by Historic Houses, as its setting?

He paused in his thoughts as he considered the actual number of places that had done just that, and quite successfully so, and amended his statement.

Who had ever thought of allowing a reality television baking competition series to use a family estate, heritage, and holdings, all protected by Historic Houses, as its setting?

It would appear that he did.

The contract had been examined by no fewer than five attorneys, and every paragraph amended to his every demand. The money coming from the contract was exceptional, and his property managers assured him that the amount of publicity for the estate would generate more popularity in summer visits, which should increase their ability to maintain the property.

Money. Publicity. Popularity.

None of those things were particularly tasteful motivations, but he was a man of business and a man of sense. He could not, in good conscience, turn down the opportunity to improve the house and estate just because he would have preferred to keep the walls up, the doors closed, and the deluded home bakers in their own kitchens instead of invading his.

Well, the estate's kitchens.

His own kitchens were off-limits.

In fact, his entire house was off-limits. The show would be allowed access to the historical kitchens and the mill, neither of which were connected to the main house at all anymore. The renovations of 1913 had taken care of that, but the preservation of those kitchens had remained paramount.

Unfortunately, Jonny still had to be at the estate throughout filming to ensure compliance and continuity, or something of the sort. He didn't mind being at his home, of course, but he tended to keep to himself during popular seasons to avoid being noticed as Viscount Colburn by the tourists.

American women, mostly, who still thought a titled man was worth something in England.

Vulgar, delusional, nonsensical idiots.

At least he wouldn't have to do any interviews about the estate or its history, thank heavens. The show had its own historical advisers, as well as some local ones, who would take care of the entire thing.

Historical, indeed.

How could the producers of the show possibly hope to do an entire series of bakes with a historical theme? That was their entire purpose in choosing his estate—the perfectly preserved historic kitchens and mill were exactly what they were looking for. But the kitchens were preserved from the eighteenth century, and bakes from any other century would probably require equipment that the Blackfirth Park historic kitchens would not have. Were all the bakes going to be from the eighteenth century?

He did the math quickly in his head. Eight bakers, two rounds an episode, with the second round of each episode requiring multiple bakes. And, if his estate manager was to be believed, there would be different subthemes for each episode. How many different historic delicacies could be made in a kitchen limited by time and space, no matter how impressive?

No wonder the show was on its last leg. No fewer than three people had told him that the last two series had been disappointing and the show was on the brink of cancellation.

And the producers thought a *historic* theme would improve the situation?

Not likely.

Jonny scoffed to himself as he watched the crew begin to unload, knowing well enough that the irritating green-and-white-striped tarps he was seeing would form the awning of their makeshift workspace, which was entirely un-historical, he noted. He'd only given the plans a cursory glance after his manager had approved them, so he couldn't recall how large, how stable, or how unsightly the construction work would be while it was on his land, but that awning . . .

It was as though a bakery from the sixties had been

resurrected and insisted on keeping the same mold-infested and mildew-ridden color scheme it had died with.

Security from the show would take care of any trespassers, but how could anyone make his estate look picturesque with that monstrosity near it?

His mobile buzzed in his pocket, diverting his attention from the horrors of the canopy. He glanced at the screen, his smile turning wry as he answered. "Trixie, I don't have any news yet."

"You've got to know *something*, Jonny," his cousin insisted in her determined way, the background sound of traffic telling him that she was in her car. "The trucks arrive today, don't they? And the setup begins?"

"Yes, they have, and yes, they are," he sighed, resting his arm on the window. "The awning is hideous."

Trixie coughed in distress. "I very much beg your pardon, Jonathan. That is a *classic*."

"You haven't seen it, Beatrix," he shot back. "It is a monstrosity."

"Just think of it as one of your blessed exotic plants in the greenhouse. Then it'll be lovely and unusual shades."

Her mockery was unnecessary, but she did have a point.

"Trix," Jonny groaned almost plaintively. "Cut me some slack. I'm stuck here for six weeks minimum."

"Trapped at your very large and gorgeous house, oh, poor you." She snorted. "You don't have to do anything, Jonny. You don't have to be social, although Gabi would die for a signed cookbook from one of the judges if you feel like doing something kind for your sister. You can be a Scrooge, but since you're a control freak and going to be watching them in case you can spring a potential lawsuit on them, you might as well come off your perch a time or two and see what's going on for yourself."

Jonny was used to his cousin's sharpness, but he wasn't prepared for the intensity behind it. "Since when do you bake, Trix? Or Gabi, for that matter."

"We don't," she retorted. "You're missing the point."

"You love a baking show, but you don't bake? You seem to be missing the point."

Incoherent grumbling met his ears, making him grin. "It's a great show, Jonny. Better than all the other trash out there. And maybe I will bake once I meet the contestants!"

"How are you going to meet them?" Jonny asked with a laugh. "No one outside of the show's team is allowed on set except me. And I'm only allowed because I live here."

"Tell them to make an exception for your favorite cousin," Trixie informed him. "I'm coming up next week."

Jonny closed his eyes and tapped his brow to the glass. "Thanks for the notice. At least you're not coming up right this minute."

"Don't be ridiculous, I'm doing the school pickup at the moment, how could I possibly drive to Oxfordshire?" There was a slight break and rustling through the phone. "Hello, Ava! Thanks very much! All right, kids? Get in, get in, there's a line behind me."

Jonny looked toward the ceiling of his study, debating if he should hang up instead of allowing his cousin any further conversation on the subject.

Hmm. The crown molding needed to be cleaned. He'd have to ask Mrs. Clyde to bring in some help one of these days.

"Right, say hello to Cousin Jonny, kids."

"Hello, Jonny!" three young voices chanted.

"Hello, Wynken, Blynken, and Nod," he replied dryly.

The kids groaned at his usual joke. "Jonny," the youngest droned in disapproval. "It's Charlotte, Peter, and Amy!"

"Oh, that's right." He cleared his throat. "Hey, Trix, I've gotta go. The cars just pulled up, which means I have to play host."

"Tell Alan I love him," Trixie insisted.

"Who's Alan?" one of the kids demanded. "Daddy's name is Darrin!"

Jonny shook his head as he hung up the phone and turned from the window. He straightened his collar and wondered if he ought to put on a suit jacket for the added professionalism.

Oh, why not?

He pulled it from the hook on the back of the door and slipped it on as he left the room. He didn't normally dress formally when he was here, but there was something about meeting people as the viscount that made him rethink his wardrobe. At least he hadn't bothered with a tie. He might be the man who owned the property, but it wasn't as though his status really meant something nowadays.

It was usually more of a hindrance than anything else.

And yet, there was something inherently ennobling about being the seventeenth of anything, something that made him stand a little taller, live to a higher standard, and feel the weight of expectation passed down through the sixteen generations before him. But he was in no hurry to do anything about an eighteenth viscount any time soon.

His mother, rest her soul, wouldn't have haggled him on the subject, though his father would probably have wanted him to have a son instead of letting the title go to a cousin. The thirteenth viscount had had only daughters for the longest time, until finally a son was born when his wife was thought past bearing years, so they hadn't needed to let the title fall from the direct line.

In modern times, they could have just made one of the daughters a viscountess in her own right, but that was neither here nor there.

Jonny cared about the estate more than the title, and he was determined to do whatever it took to make his estate profitable instead of hobbling along.

The Historic Houses were after him to turn over the entire estate, and he was sure the National Trust would be sniffing around as well, but he couldn't let the place go yet.

There was the argument about so much space for just one man but considering how small the place was where he actually lived, he ignored that particular argument.

He was an investment banker. He knew when things were worth time, effort, and money, and when they were not. There was still something to be had in this old place, and until his mind and his heart agreed on the heritage, he would stay the course.

His colleagues thought he was unbelievably stupid, but they were also jealous that he occasionally got invited to some of the most exclusive events in the UK due to his title alone. Besides, he still had an idea of romping about the south green with his kids, just as his father had done with him and his sister.

It was the only remotely sentimental notion he had.

Well, other than revamping the holiday ball at Blackfirth. The last party had occurred long before the Great War, but the accounts of the events in family diaries had always captured his imagination. There was something very Victorian about it in his mind, though the tradition had been started by the eighth viscount in 1731. But there was a rumor that Queen Victoria and Prince Albert had had the Blackfirth Park Holiday Ball on their annual schedule.

It was a grand legend, though.

Sadly, it was not the only legend surrounding Blackfirth—a fact he was quite certain would be brought up repeatedly throughout the filming of the show. Perhaps it was even why the producers had chosen this place out of all the other historic estates with preserved kitchens.

Whatever would up their ratings, he supposed.

"My lord," greeted his head butler as he met him on the landing. "The producers and the hosts of the show have arrived. We've set up a luncheon for them in the dining nook, though you certainly do not have to attend. Once you have made your greetings, we can make excuses for you."

Mr. Clyde and his wife had been at Blackfirth since before Jonny had been born, and they ran the private aspect as expertly as any traditional butler and housekeeper could have wished. They knew Jonny's tastes, knew his schedule, and knew when and how they could act as parental figures without making him feel in any way babied or coddled. And when Jonny traveled to London for company meetings every quarter, he often returned to find Blackfirth in better condition than when he'd left it.

It was entirely possible that Clyde knew the place better than Jonny could ever hope to learn. Perhaps he ought to have been the one talking with the media about the place.

"Thanks, Clyde," Jonny told him, clapping him fondly on the arm. "How do they seem?"

Clyde shrugged. "Respectful enough, and eager to be here.

I don't imagine we'll see much of them once things get underway."

"One can only hope." Jonny nodded, giving his butler a slight smile before moving down to the entry to greet their guests.

There were eight of them, all told, and a few seemed vaguely familiar, though he would have struggled to name any of them. Being entirely uninterested in television or social media would do that.

"Hello," he greeted as he reached the bottom of the stairs. "Welcome to Blackfirth Park. Jonathan Ainsley, Viscount Colburn." He held out his hand rather generally, waiting to see who would step forward.

A man in his fifties with a slight gut and a balding head stepped forward and took his hand. "My lord. Grant Sybil, showrunner. Thanks so much for giving us permission to shoot at Blackfirth. It will be absolutely perfect for this series. Let me introduce you to the rest."

He turned to the others. "This is Chelsea Corrigan, our casting coordinator. And next to her, Eamon Phipps, story producer. On the far side, with the mustache, is Bill Dean, director."

Jonny nodded to them all, wondering how he was going to remember everyone's names, when he realized that each last name started with the same letter as their job. That would help immensely. He was also pleased to see that the staff of the show appeared to have sense and dignity about them.

"The elegant lady in blue, as I am certain you know," Mr. Sybil went on, "is Dame Sophie Layton-Hughes, one of the judges."

Jonny didn't know, but he did her the courtesy of a full nod before extending his hand to her. "Madam, a pleasure."

"Charmed, my lord," she chirped, her voice more gravelly and crisper than he'd expected.

"Beside her is another familiar face, fellow judge Mr. Alan Gables."

The man looked as though he had never smiled in his entire life, his neatly trimmed goatee and mustache giving his face more angles than it already had. His mouth, such as it was, formed a tight line, and he reached out a thin hand, giving Jonny's a firm shake. "Sir."

This was who his cousin loved on the show? She'd have to explain that one.

"Finally, we have our show hosts," Mr. Sybil explained, pointing to the two figures at the back. "Actress Lindsay Potter, whom you may recognize from her role in *Endleigh Castle*, and comedian and actor Charlie McCoy, who was most recently in his one-man show on the West End, *Heads and Tales*."

The hosts waved at him, both grinning widely.

Jonny nodded at them. "Pleasure to have you all," he said, not quite willing to smile in return. "I noticed the construction beginning on your pavilion."

"Yes, yes," Mr. Sybil replied with several nods. "We hope to get it finished while the weather is good so we can get plenty of B-roll and establishing shots. Would it very much disrupt anyone if we were to do our footage of the house in the meantime?"

"Not at all," Jonny told him. "We are not presently open for tours, so there shouldn't be anything standing in your way. Mr. Clyde will make sure you have access where needed."

"Lord Colburn," Miss Potter asked from the back of the

group, "can you confirm if the legend of the tenth viscount's wife is true?"

Jonny fought the urge to glare and instead clasped his hands behind his back. "Are you also a reporter, Miss Potter?"

She laughed, both her smile and her hair perfectly in place. "No, my lord, only thorough. I wanted to know about the estate we were going to be at, and that story is the first that came up."

He nodded at that, struggling to place her accent. "Where are you from, Miss Potter?"

"Chorley, sir. Near Preston and Blackburn. Why do you ask?"

Jonny raised a brow. "If we are delving into deeply personal family history on so short an acquaintance, I thought I would take my turn as well." He sniffed and looked at Mr. Sybil. "The historical advisers you hired for the show ought to be able to give you all the known information on the legend, but we will not permit any questioning of any members of the family on the subject, nor anything else relating directly to the family. Now, I have been told that luncheon is prepared for you all, but I unfortunately have a business call I have already put off. Please enjoy the dining nook, and help yourselves to a tour of the gardens, which are directly beyond the door there. Harry will show you the way."

He indicated the footman, standing nearby with a smile and a name badge, then nodded to the group and quickly exited the area. Hopefully that would be the last interaction Jonny would have to endure with anyone from the show, and, more especially, the last question he would have to endure about that stupid legend.

With all that Blackfirth had to offer, *that* was what they were known for?

Perhaps, if handled correctly, the show could change that.

But if Jonny's instincts were correct, it would do exactly the opposite.

The show would capitalize on the legend and solidify its legitimacy, turning the house and the family into nothing more than talking points in a horror story that had never found a satisfactory ending.

CHAPTER 3

"Oh my days, there it is. There it is! Can you see the awning? Can you see it?"

"Yes, Kerri, we can see the stupid awning. It's bleeding green-and-white, how d'you think we'd miss it?"

"Leave her alone, mate. If she can't be excited, why are we here?"

Claire ignored everything and everyone in her car as they made their way onto the grounds of Blackfirth Park. It felt exactly like that moment in the *Pride and Prejudice* miniseries when Elizabeth suddenly sees Pemberley through the break in the trees and her whole world gets spun on its top.

But this house wasn't Pemberley. It was far more terrifying. Gorgeous, historical, elegant, towering, resplendent—all the positive and glorious things. But it was also the site of her impending doom, so there was that to consider. If the sky had been dark instead of light, cloudy instead of clear, and crackling with lightning instead of glowing with rays of sunshine, she'd have a very different idea of the place.

It didn't take away from the impressive sight; she simply was not Elizabeth Bennet at this moment. Anything she had ever learned about historical architecture on her tours of National Trust houses flew out of her head as she stared at this unbelievable edifice.

Somebody still lived here? And they were letting them come in and bake for a show? Maybe they were big fans of *Britain's Battle of the Bakers*, and it was a treat for them. How fun would that be?

"I don't see any gargoyles," Anthony mentioned in his thick Scouse accent as their car made a turn onto another gravel drive.

"There aren't any," Benji muttered darkly, folding his beefy arms. "For all its airs, the place is practically a mausoleum. The viscount never meets anyone or does anything; he just holes up in the place whenever he's in town. All there really is to recommend it is the murder legend."

Claire looked at Benji with wide eyes. "Murder legend?"

"How do you know?" Kerri demanded, clutching at actual pearls she had worn.

Benji gave her a sardonic look. "I'm actually from Blackfirth? The village, not the estate. And I still live here because I'm a firefighter. And the murder legend of Lady Colburn is our big thing."

"How old a legend?" Anthony asked, turning away from the window to give his full attention to Benji.

"I dunno, she was the wife of the tenth viscount, so however long ago that was." He scratched the back of his head, making a slight face. "I think Viscount Grumps is number seventeen, but he could be eighteen."

"What's the legend say?" Kerri inquired with a whimper.

Claire's own curiosity was tingling like the dickens. Years of reading Agatha Christie, Dorothy Sayers, and the Maisie

Dobbs series had given her a love of mystery that was only surpassed by baking. It would be unseemly to ask too many questions about an *actual* murder, especially when it took place generations ago.

Benji rolled his eyes. "Look, I'm not a tour guide. I'm sure they're going to tell us all about the thing when we get there and have a look around. Assuming Viscount High-and-Mighty lets us."

"Then why'd you even bring it up, mate?" Anthony shook his head, sitting back against his seat roughly. "Dunno why we're even here today. We're not even baking."

"I imagine Mrs. Comer wanted her kitchens back," Claire offered in a small voice. "We have all rather taken over."

"We're the only ones staying there," Kerri pointed out. "She's getting well paid for letting us run rampant."

Claire shrugged, feeling bad all the same for the rotating schedule the contestants had set up in their hostess's kitchen. The Ivy House was the cutest bed-and-breakfast Claire had ever seen, and Mrs. Comer was the perfect country hostess. She was cheerful, giving, and keen to learn any baking tips, if they could spare the time. Claire wasn't sure if anyone else was letting her watch them practice, but she certainly was. And Mrs. Comer had given her some helpful advice on a few of her bakes.

She would take all the help she could get.

She said nothing else as they continued up the drive toward their destination, trying to focus her thoughts on her purpose for being here: baking.

The theme of the series had been revealed to the bakers only after all the contracts had been signed, and Claire could see the reason for that now.

Historic bakes. What in the world were the producers planning on having them do with that? She knew that Blackfirth Park had perfectly preserved working kitchens as well as a mill, thanks to the introductory packet all the contestants had received, so she knew that they would be using them, but what else? Surely they could not all do their bakes in the same kitchen at the same time. Or endure the same challenges for each and every bake. However the show decided to let this play out, Claire had spent the last two months learning everything she could about baking without modern conveniences and practicing the oldest recipes she could find.

It had helped make Claire a little less terrified of the prospect of her bakes, and maybe that would be enough. Maybe they would ask for exactly the sort of bakes she had been practicing.

If the pattern of the show continued as it had for the past eleven series, there would be a Classic Bake and an Occasion Bake each episode, so those would probably be historically themed as well. But what historic occasions could they dream up for the requisite number of episodes?

"Claire."

She snapped out of her reverie and looked at the door. Anthony gave her a curious glance and gestured for her to get out.

"Right, sorry," she muttered, clambering out of the car and feeling her trainers skid slightly on the gravel of the drive. "Just thinking about, you know, baking and . . . history." She winced and made a face at Anthony. "I sound like a right idiot, don't I?"

Anthony chuckled and put a brotherly arm around her

shoulder. "Don't worry, we're all nerves at the moment. But remember: you wouldn't be here if you weren't a boss, yeah?"

Claire smiled, trying to nod. "I guess so. I still think I'll be the first one out."

"Nah," Anthony insisted as they followed the trail of other bakers toward the now ominous green-and-white-topped pavilion, awning gaping open like a mouth ready to devour them.

"I think Denis is gonna be out first," Anthony whispered with a laugh. "Man's got the attention span of a gnat."

Claire snorted a soft laugh, knowing he was right but also knowing that Denis was the nicest, most jovial man of the group. He was a lorry driver from Derry in Northern Ireland, and every story he told was epic, mostly because he told them with the most creative voices.

Anthony was a fitness instructor from Liverpool who was all about healthy bakes, which meant the historic aspect of the baking could prove a challenge for him. He was younger than Claire, and yet he had become a sort of big brother for her.

His impressive size might have had something to do with that.

He'd also been particularly watchful over Freya, who was the youngest here. She was a university student from Bristol and was proverbially stressed out about everything. Claire had been trying to help her find time for studying as well as her baking and was trying to tutor her where she could. Freya was a bubbly, creative girl, and could usually be seen sporting her bright red glasses no matter what outfit she had on.

Claire didn't know the others in the competition as well yet, but she supposed that would change once the show got underway. The previous series had portrayed the contestants as having a tight-knit friendship, some even calling it a family, but there was no telling how sincere any of that was. It was entirely possible they were pretending for the cameras, but Claire didn't want to believe it was entirely fake.

She wanted lifelong friends who were also bakers. She wanted to take holidays with Freya or venture out to Wales to visit Lesley. It would be fun to explore Northern Ireland with Denis or Yorkshire with Kerri. She definitely wanted to become friends with Mathias, who was quiet, serious, and in possession of a fabulous mustache. He was also Belgian, and she shamelessly wanted to spend as much time visiting Belgium as she could. She doubted she would enjoy seeing Oxfordshire with Benji the fireman, as he seemed perpetually irritated about something, but maybe he was nervous, just as Anthony had said.

Maybe they were all incredibly nervous.

It was surreal, walking under the awning and into the baking pavilion. The arrangement was exactly as she had seen it on television, the baking stations in shades of green and equidistant from each other, the counters perfectly clean and uncovered, but the decor on the inside of the pavilion changed from series to series.

Last series, the almost disastrous futuristic theme had sleek, minimalist decor, the color scheme black, white, and silver, plus a few splashes of green that had become the brand of the show. There had been attempts at including space travel and other worlds in the theme as well, but all of it had failed.

This series, however, they were certainly not failing.

The white ceiling of the pavilion had been textured to look like plaster, and placed in occasional rows were dark wooden beams, though Claire doubted they were the real thing. One side of the pavilion had an actual brick fireplace, arched and looming just as one might expect to find in a large estate kitchen. Copper pots and pans hung from hooks on the walls, and wooden cabinets were everywhere.

It was as though the show had made this space into the historic kitchen rather than allowing them to use the real ones.

Oh crumpets—was that what they were going to do?

"Welcome, bakers."

The tone was far less enthusiastic than she had heard it on the telly, but she'd know that brogue anywhere.

Alan Gables was in the pavilion.

Claire put a hand to her heart and turned toward the sound of his voice, as did everyone else.

He was as serious in person as he appeared to be on the show, but there was a semi-relaxed air about him that was never conveyed across the screen. He had shown himself to be less of a grump in the recent series, mostly when contestants were struggling or growing emotional, but his standards had never slackened. He was certainly more relaxed in his appearance than Claire expected, wearing a simple T-shirt under an open flannel, both haphazardly tucked into jeans.

The bakers had been warned not to freak out over the judges, and certainly not to ask for autographs or the like, so they all stood relatively at attention where they were.

Waiting.

"You all look . . . rather terrified," Alan said simply, his mouth twitching into a slight smile amid his dark, neatly trimmed facial hair. "Relax. I'm not judging you now."

The entire room seemed to release a collective breath, a few bakers quietly laughing at his pinpoint accuracy of their feelings.

THE CRIME BRÛLÉE BAKE OFF

"Have a look around," Alan encouraged them. "Get comfortable in this space. The kitchens and the mill are just out that door there. You won't need to worry about the mill—we won't have you mill your own flour—but you should become familiar with the historic kitchens." He raised his brows, making his point clear.

Claire, for one, nodded obediently. She had wanted to look at the kitchens closely for her own curiosity, and now she would also do so with baking in mind.

Her own baking, that is, not that of the industrious few who might have worked their lives away in professional kitchens.

Then again, perhaps she ought to think more like them if she was going to be expected to use those kitchens in a similar way.

"Your first episode," Alan went on, clasping his hands behind his back, his wide, dark eyes surveying them all knowingly, "will have the theme of tea. Your Classic Bake will be a traditional tea cake, and the Occasion Bake is, naturally, afternoon tea. Minimum of three bakes for that one. If you did not know how the episodes worked, this is it. You have a week to plan and prepare your bakes, and then you must bake and present them for us within the time we allow. The presentations of the bakes will take place in the historic kitchens, so you will have to transport your bakes there. Walk carefully. You will find out in a few days the time allotment for this episode."

The timing was more or less what Claire had anticipated, so no great surprises there, but the theme of tea was interesting. What was so historical about that? Other than that teatime had been around the UK probably from its birth, of course.

"The catch," Alan continued, "is that you will only be allowed to use ingredients available before 1900 for any of these bakes." He offered a rather devious smile, making him look like a cartoon villain rather than a world-renowned baking expert. "Enjoy your prep."

He nodded and exited the pavilion with a fairly light step. As though he rather enjoyed the bomb he'd just dropped on them all. As though he couldn't wait to begin tearing into their bakes with his usual Glaswegian-accented criticisms. As though he knew some secret and was delighted that he didn't have to share it.

"Well, that's delightful," Lesley announced from her position at the furthest baking station in the back. She fidgeted with the bright blue silk scarf at her neck. "Anybody know what sort of yeast they used prior to 1900?"

That broke them up with a bit of laughter, tense though it was, and all of them began to do their own thing, whether that was exploring the pavilion or making their way out to the historic kitchens.

Claire decided to go to the historic kitchens, hoping it would give her the inspiration she'd need for the first episode, if not the entire series.

It was a short walk down a slight hill to the simple, unobtrusive brick building with an impressive set of chimneys atop the roof. There was nothing about the building that said it held kitchens. Not even a sign, really, until she got close enough to the front door of the building.

Honestly, she fully expected to see one of the kind workers

with a name tag that read Madge standing there, asking her to wait for the tour time to begin.

But no one was there. Not a worker, not a volunteer, not a servant. It was simply open for her and the others to go through. To explore. To experience.

And, at some point, to use.

What world was she even living in right now?

Shaking her head, Claire went in and started looking around the rooms that lined each side of the long corridor. The fact that there were multiple rooms was a surprise in and of itself, but each room also had a specific purpose: a room for cold things, a room for bread, a room for scrubbing, a room for kneading, a room for meat preparation, a room for spices and their preparation, and a massive room at the end of the building for the full meal preparation and assembly.

It was the most incredible collection of rooms she had ever seen, and everything had all been cleaned and ready for their use.

"Right," Claire said to the empty space of the bread room. "Let's see what we can make of you."

"I was just thinking the same thing over here!" a Welsh voice called out.

Claire would not have said she believed in ghosts, but in that moment, she jumped and yelped as though she knew there were some in this place.

There was that legend, after all.

Lesley appeared in the bread room with an apologetic expression, silk scarf still in place. "Sorry, love. Only me. Are you well?"

Still half expecting a ghost to follow Lesley into the room, Claire nodded. "Fine, yeah."

"What do you make of this place?" Lesley asked, coming to her side and wearing a warm smile. "I reckon I'd be running mad all over it trying to manage everything. This room and then that, backward and forward . . . Can you imagine?"

There was a maternal air about Lesley, but with a splash of fun and spunk that was more like the mischievous auntie everybody loved. It was impossible to be uncomfortable in her presence, which must have made her the perfect nurse with the National Health Service in her career. She was retired now, according to the cast bios, and Claire had the sudden desire to sit beside Lesley on a sofa with blankets and talk about life.

Or stand here and talk about kitchens.

That might be better, considering.

"I suppose it would depend on the size of the staff the cook had," Claire replied. She returned Lesley's smile. "Maybe we should have come earlier and taken the tour so we'd have a better idea."

Lesley erupted into loud laughter, gripping Claire's arm. "Can you imagine us taking that tour? Among regular folk, and asking questions like, 'How do they keep the yeast they've got from the brewer?' and 'Could you demonstrate boiling a proper pud in here?' They'd think we'd lost the plot!"

"Maybe we have," Claire suggested with a grin. "But I love history, so I'm not sure I mind much."

"I don't mind either," Lesley admitted with a wink. "Come on, chick. Let's get our inner nerds sorted and figure this place out. I'm going to need every spare minute to make over my recipes to pre-1900 ingredients."

"Right?" Claire shook her head as they started looking over the stone ovens and water heaters. "We have to let the staff know what we need for our bakes, and I hadn't even thought about yeast before 1900. I'd been focusing on trying to decipher my historic recipe's description of the dough before rising."

Lesley chuckled and stooped to look at the ash oven. "What does it say, then?"

"Light and lithe," Claire recited, widening her eyes with the exasperation she had been feeling for days. "What in the world is a lithe dough? A gazelle is lithe, a cheetah is lithe, the man of my dreams is lithe . . ."

That brought a cackle of delighted laughter from Lesley and she straightened. "Oh my days, give me a *cwtch*, chick. That was the best thing." She pulled Claire in for a quick hug, which must have been the Welsh word she used. "I have no idea what lithe dough means either, but I think you can trust your instincts. You know what a good dough looks like, right?"

Claire nodded, stooping to check out the ash oven herself. "Of course, in theory."

"So go with that. It'll be fine, trust me. Well, maybe not me, but trust yourself." Lesley pushed a lock of her dark, gray-tinged hair behind her ear. "Lithe. What a load of toss. If anyone used that word to describe dough other than who wrote it, I'll be blown away."

Feeling marginally better, Claire smiled and let herself try to relax as she explored the kitchens they would one day have to use for their bakes, and do it successfully to boot.

No pressure.

CHAPTER 4

Well, they were filming now, and there was nothing Jonny could change about anything now.

To be perfectly honest, he didn't need anything to change. Yet.

Other than the drones buzzing about like the most persistent and annoying dragonflies he had ever known, taking aerial shots of the landscape, house, and estate, Jonny really hadn't noticed much of a disturbance in having the show on his land. The contestants, whoever they were, had respected the boundaries he'd set up, and he'd been remarkably unperturbed by any of the crew at all.

Though he hated having to see the monstrous green-and-white-striped pavilion out of all his favorite windows.

He had managed to avoid interacting with anyone from the show for a week now, and it was exactly as he would wish it to be. Of course, he hadn't really left the house in a week, other than to go into the gardens or meet with tenants and the like, all of which he could do without going near the filming sites.

Today, however, the weather was gorgeous, and he wanted

THE CRIME BRÛLÉE BAKE OFF

to get out. Perhaps he could venture into other parts of the estate or possibly even go for a drive. It might be his last opportunity to have peace and quiet within the walls of his own home. Trixie was slated to join him at the weekend, and he would not put it past the woman to remain for the rest of the filming schedule, children and husband notwithstanding.

She would encourage everyone to come inside his home, inject herself into the melee, and thrust Jonny into the mix of it without taking any consideration for his own tastes and ideas.

She was pushy that way, but he loved her all the same.

Whistling to himself, Jonny started down the stairs and to the left for his usual exit to the grounds, only to find Clyde suddenly sliding into his path.

"No, my lord," he said firmly, shaking his slightly balding head, his large eyes almost severe. "You don't want to go out that way. The film crew is having a meeting and will then be coming into the house itself. Try the southwest doors. You should be able to get to the grotto before cutting back over to the garage via the gamekeeper's cottage. Or, if you prefer, you can take the northwest doors and walk to the mill, cut over to the Victoria Garden and Fountain, then meet up with the Blackfirth trail, which will meet up with the car park."

Jonny blinked at his butler, wondering if the strain of additional people on the estate was taking its toll on the man. "That is so far out of the way, Clyde."

Clyde shrugged his stooped shoulders. "Just trying to keep your social interactions to a minimum, sir. For all our sakes."

Jonny gave him a rather flat look. "Thank you, Clyde."

"Of course, sir." He nodded but stayed in his position.

Clearly, Jonny was not going out these doors.

Why was he so determined to keep Jonny from talking to anyone? Granted, that was Jonny's way and preference, but he was perfectly capable of being polite and respectful. Cordial, even, when the circumstances were right. This was a film crew, not some mob of paparazzi. He was not going to be roped into a tour or an interview, and they were hardly going to hound him for information.

Jonny narrowed his eyes at his long-standing, long-suffering butler. "They're talking about the legend, aren't they?"

"They might be, my lord," Clyde all but affirmed. "There was no dissuading them."

"And someone told them I don't like the legend?"

Clyde's mouth tightened. "As I recall, sir, you were heard to quite adamantly refuse to discuss the legend in any way and to forbid asking questions of any members of the family on the subject. As well as any other family details. We have been going to great lengths to keep that from happening, and the show has been accommodating with the changes in schedule we have had to implement from time to time."

That didn't sound good.

Jonny frowned. "Are you telling me that my week of blissful quiet and privacy has been a carefully orchestrated scheme rather than a naturally occurring phenomenon?"

"That . . . would sum it up correctly, my lord."

Clyde could stand there without shame and admit this to him? Jonny hadn't asked anybody to stay out of his way or to avoid him, even though that was how he preferred things. He had simply addressed impertinence and thought that was that. And because of that, entire maneuvers had been taken up to stay away from him?

Jonny shook his head. "Blimey, don't tell me I offended that actress . . ."

"I couldn't say, sir," Clyde informed him stiffly. "I've had no conversations with the lady, only with Mr. Sybil, and he was keen enough to agree to my suggestions."

"Uh-huh," Jonny said slowly. "And what did you tell him about me?"

One of Clyde's bushy brows rose just a touch. "Tell him, sir?"

"You have opinions, Clyde. What did you tell him?"

"Only that you are set in your ways, my lord, and it would be more amicable for all if certain interactions were avoided."

Jonny ran a hand over his face. "You're making it sound like a divorce."

"Not at all, my lord. There are no emotions involved here, and hardly a division of assets." Clyde smiled so tightly his lips almost disappeared. "I have also been informed that the mill repairs are complete, so the team will be by in a few days to finish this year's flour."

"Fine, fine, whatever," Jonny said with a wave. "I can't believe people still want to purchase the stuff, quite honestly; you can get flour at the store for less money, but fine. Right, I'm going out." He jammed his thumb behind him. "This way."

Clyde almost managed to avoid showing amusement. Almost. "Very good, my lord."

Sputtering to himself, Jonny turned on his heel and headed toward the northwest doors, which he almost never used, but he could certainly exit his own house from whichever doors he chose. Ridiculous that he couldn't go his usual way because someone was uncomfortable about something he'd said.

Something he was perfectly right in saying, by the way, as it was his own family history.

Granted, he could probably have said it in a better way, and perhaps without as much snark, but he wasn't dependable in that regard when taken by surprise.

Things just came out of his mouth on those occasions, and he could not be held responsible.

He stepped out of the house and inhaled deeply, taking in the token fragrance of wisteria on this side of the house.

Today it also bore a distinct note of yeast and bread, which wasn't unpleasant but certainly added a strange edge to anything delicately floral.

"Bakers," he muttered, glaring at the monstrosity taking up a good portion of the green in front of the house. He started walking in the opposite direction of that impending fiasco of a location and headed toward the mill, just as Clyde had suggested he could. He doubted he would go all the way to the Blackfirth trail, and he certainly didn't need to get all the way to the car park or the garage. He didn't need to leave the estate grounds at all.

He just wanted to be *out*.

Alone and out. Was that really too much to ask?

The sound of rushing water made Jonny smile, and the steady paddling sound told him the mill wheel was working, though no one would be grinding anything at the moment. Still, he enjoyed the sound of nature and industry harnessed in one and working together.

It was one of the sounds of home.

He walked along the brook toward the mill, smiling further when he caught sight of the wrought iron wheel turning steadily; the waterfalls it created in tiny bursts had always fascinated him as a child. They were fortunate here at Black-firth that the natural Oxwyn Brook flowed directly through the estate on its break from the Evenlode River, and which the eighth viscount had capitalized on by creating a millpond while still ensuring that the brook continued on its merry way toward the rest of the village.

They wouldn't have been much of an estate without a village to support, would they?

Details, the peerage and landowner thing.

Jonny moved over the stone bridge that crossed the brook, sliding his hands into his trouser pockets. Ambling, that's what this was. A gentleman ambling across the grounds of his estate. Surely the viscounts before him had taken the chance to do that. He knew his father had from time to time, though he doubted the man had ever thought about it in that way. What was the point of being a viscount with an estate if you couldn't amble among your lands once in a while?

He headed to the mill, rolling his sleeves to his elbows and grinning up at the sun peeking through the trees. It was the perfect day to be out and about on his estate, and he might even request lunch out on the veranda just for the sake of it. Why not? He never requested lunch; it simply appeared. How many plans would go awry if he changed the schedule and routine?

It would be interesting to get back at Clyde for his machinations, however well-intended they might have been, though Mrs. Clyde was certainly a force to be reckoned with, and Greta in the kitchens didn't care one way or the other. She knew Jonny was easygoing about his meals and the menu, so she did as she pleased most of the time. It would only be the

Clydes who could possibly get their noses out of joint, and every now and again, that was a delightful undertaking.

He usually left such antics to Gabi, but maybe this time . . .

He ducked into the mill and stopped in surprise.

A woman was inside the building, reading the informative placard about the history, a notebook and pen in hand, glasses on her face. She was maybe in her early thirties, and she was short. Regular clothes, minimal makeup, hair pulled back, but long and spotted with white dust of some sort.

Jonny bit back a grimace. Baker.

He cleared his throat, not wanting to be rude, but also wanting to get her attention.

She jumped as though he had sprung out from behind a door. "Crepes alive!" she yelped, clutching her notebook to her chest and staring at him with wide green eyes, made even greener by the frames of her glasses.

Very green.

Jonny found himself smiling, not entirely sure why. "Sorry. Didn't want to scare you."

"Failed that," she said, swallowing quickly and pushing her glasses up onto her head. "Sorry, didn't mean . . . I'm a bit jumpy. All these empty historical places that we're allowed to look at. I pretty much expect to be abducted by ghosts at any minute. Except you caught me being a nerd, so I forgot to be on my guard."

It was the most utter nonsense he had heard in quite some time, but he found himself more amused than annoyed. He cocked his head. "Do ghosts usually abduct?"

"I've heard stranger things," she told him with a shrug. "Are you with the crew or the estate?"

Jonny loved it when he wasn't recognized. Always far more

fun, and it meant that the person wasn't husband hunting. "Estate."

"Oh good!" Her eyes lit up, her full lips curving into a smile. "Then maybe you can tell me about the mill. I mean really tell me about it, not just what's on the placards. Although they are nicely done, I must say. Very informative."

"Are you one of the bakers for the show?" Jonny asked her, gesturing in the general direction of the pavilion.

She nodded, her lips closing on her smile this time. "Yep. Dunno how I made it in, really. We had our first task this morning, and it seemed to be okay. I just don't want to get out first, you know? That's always the rough spot. But we're not really competing with each other, you know? It's more . . . competing for the right attention. Which is weird. Like some bizarre speed dating where you're analyzed by your performance." She shuddered. "Forget I said that. The baking is way more comfortable a thought."

"Fair enough," Jonny replied, his mind spinning from the rapid-fire words she was spewing in his direction. "And your name is?"

Her eyes widened perceptibly. "Sugar, I forgot that, didn't I? Claire Walker. I'm a schoolteacher from Surrey. When I'm not baking, that is."

Her name suited her. Jonny wasn't sure why the thought occurred to him, or why he had noticed it, but it was true. She was completely mad, that much was clear, but she was also, he sensed, perfectly real at any given moment.

There was something rather fascinating about that.

"Jonathan Ainsley." He put a hand to his heart and gave the slightest bow. "Pleased to meet you."

REBECCA CONNOLLY

Claire's high brow furrowed slightly. "Ainsley. Ainsley, Ainsley—why do I know that name?"

Ah, he loved this. It really was the most delicious fun. And he wasn't about to help her.

Instead, he folded his arms and leaned against the nearest beam, waiting for her to figure it out. If she figured it out.

"Ainsley," she said again. "I know I know it . . ." She fell silent, then her eyes suddenly widened and fixed directly on him.

"There it is," Jonny announced, pointing at her with a finger and clicking his tongue.

"Oh, sugar, Viscount Colburn. Ainsley family house. Oh, cake and a custard . . ." Claire brushed at her hair and her shirt, then her hips, almost like she was looking for something.

Jonny watched her, utterly lost by her actions and words. "What are you doing, Miss Walker?"

"Claire," she told him absently. "My students call me Miss Walker. And I'm checking to make sure I don't look as ridiculous as I think I do in meeting a viscount."

"You look like a person," Jonny offered. "And I assume you were filming this morning, so what you're wearing is fit enough for the camera."

Claire groaned, shaking her head. "But not enough to meet a viscount!" She gave him a concerned look. "Do I need to curtsy?"

Jonny chuckled entirely against his will. "You've been watching too many period dramas, Claire. Trust me, being a viscount is not all it once was."

"Says the viscount living in a huge historic house on massive acres with preserved kitchens and a working water mill."

40

"Point taken," he allowed with a nod. "But it's just a title, and all it means is that I have to keep a very expensive property running or I let generations of the family down. And that occasionally, family relations will ask me for money because surely the viscount has some. I'm actually an investment banker, and you can call me Jonny."

"Well, that isn't going to work," Claire told him with a snort of disbelief. "You're the boss of the place. I can't call you anything, and I'm going to go back to the pavilion now."

Jonny surprised himself by stepping into her way. "Come on, you don't have to do that. Look, you're interested in the mill, right?"

Her lips pressed together, her jaw tightening. "Yes," she said slowly, tightly.

"Let me show you," he offered, gesturing to the mill. "I came here to look at the place myself, and you don't need to leave just because I showed up."

Claire twisted her mouth to one side. "You sure you don't mind? We're under strict instructions not to disturb the family."

Jonny scratched the back of his neck. "Technically, the family disturbed you this time, so I think it's okay." He leaned closer and winked. "Being the head of the family, I can safely say that."

She smiled, a bright dimple appearing in each cheek. "Fair enough. Do I need to call you 'my lord' or something?"

He shook his head. "Only on very formal occasions, which, clearly, this isn't. I never wear jeans on formal occasions."

"Good to know, I guess." She turned to look at the turning gears of the mill, then back at him. "I know we don't have to use the mill or anything for the show, but . . . *can* I have a look around? It's fascinating, and I love history, which makes me a bit of a nerd, I know, but I may never get to see something like this again. It's entirely possible I won't make it past the first round of the show, especially after the mediocrity I gave them on the first challenge."

Jonny raised his brows at her rambling and waited until he was certain she'd stopped, sensing that interrupting might not actually help the situation, before replying. "I literally just said I would show you around, Claire. It's fine. I'm not a historian, so I can't give you all the details, but I may be able to answer one or two questions for you."

"That'll do fine," she insisted, almost skipping in place in her black-and-white trainers. "Let me finish reading this first placard. I'd just gotten to the part about the eleventh viscount's renovation." She darted back a few paces to stand directly in front of the sign. She tapped her glasses back into place, her lips moving slightly as she read.

Jonny pushed off the beam and started toward her, trying to time his approach to coincide with her finishing the reading so as not to disturb her.

Claire made a soft sound of consideration, then looked at him with a smile. "Fascinating. Absolutely fascinating."

"Is it?" Jonny shrugged. "I'm so used to it that it really isn't all that special anymore. I was just telling Clyde up at the house that I can't believe we still actually produce flour here, considering you can buy it cheaper at the store. But there's a sentimental market or something."

"Are you kidding? Of course, people will buy it!" Claire raised her hand like an eager student. "I want a bag of Blackfirth flour just for the sake of it, but I also want to bake with it." Her eyes narrowed suddenly, her head tilting slightly to the side. "Have you suggested the show use your flour for our bakes?"

Jonny reared back, surprised by the question. "No, why would I? Don't you need specific kinds of flour for different things? Strong flour and bread flour and the like?"

"Typically, sure, but these are historical bakes. We can't use anything that wasn't available before 1900, but this mill has been here much longer than that. So depending on how specific they get with wheat treatments . . ." Claire bit her lip, nodding slowly. "You should think about it, Jonny. Might be a boost in sales and publicity."

Jonny groaned. "Not you too. Everybody wants publicity."

Claire barked a laugh. "I *hate* publicity. But I'm not the one whose estate is hosting the most popular baking show in Britain."

"*Touché.*" He made a face and indicated the stairs. "Feel like going up?"

"Is it safe?" she asked in return, shaking the railing a little.

Jonny found himself smiling. "Safe enough for the milling team to do it every day they're here. The wheat is still ground the old-fashioned way, which is part of the charm. Head on up if you want to."

Like a giddy child, she did so, leaving him to wonder how anyone had so much enthusiasm for anything when in the midst of a competition.

"You seem pretty accepting for someone who baked up 'mediocrity,' as you put it," he commented as he followed. "What was so mediocre about it?"

"Oh, it was fine," Claire replied with a dismissive wave.

"But that was the problem. Fine won't cut it. I should be grateful it wasn't a disaster. Poor Freya's tea cakes barely rose at all, and Benji's apparently weren't fully baked. Lesley's were extraordinary, and Denis would have matched if he'd had five more minutes. Anthony had a good bake, but the flavors were bad. It's not so bad having a boring bake, I guess, but I really hoped it would stand out. Which is funny, since I hate standing out."

"I'm sorry I asked," Jonny muttered. "Sounds like utter madness."

Claire scoffed loudly. "It is. Do you know, they made us do reaction shots this morning before we even baked? As if I didn't have enough going on in my head, I had to react to fake things. I'm not an actress, I'm a teacher. I mean, a baker. Whatever I am, an actor is not one of them."

Jonny made a face at the very idea. It sounded awful, which is exactly what he had predicted a TV set would be like. He'd had no interest in any of it from the beginning, and planned to continue that.

Except now he was curious. Not about the show, but about . . . baking. Of all things.

"So what's your next thing?" he heard himself ask, finding an anticipatory smile crossing his lips as they walked toward the grinder. "And how will you keep it from mediocrity?"

CHAPTER 5

"I am so tired, I think I could sleep for weeks."

Claire laughed from her slouched position on the sofa and looked over at Freya. The girl certainly looked exhausted and ready for bed as well, with her hair piled atop her head, her feet tucked beneath her comfy sweats, and her eyes closed as she rested her head on the hand she'd propped on the sofa's armrest.

"You did so well in the Occasion Bake, Freya," Claire praised, tossing a throw blanket to her from the folded pile next to her. "Those cherry madeleines were astonishing. It was absolutely genius to pair them with cucumber and dill sandwiches, and the delicacies of your macarons . . . Crepes alive, you should win the episode."

Freya giggled and glanced over at her. "Did you just say, 'Crepes alive,' Claire? Baking nerd alert."

Claire shrugged, still grinning. "I was raised in a pub, and my parents wanted to keep us from using the kind of language that might be overheard at the White Fox, so we had to make up all kinds of expressions. Mine just happen to be baking related—son of a biscuit, sugar, crepes alive, cake and a custard."

"You might be the biggest dork ever," Freya told her, still laughing. "But your rhubarb crème brûlée tartlets were awesome. Daring to do the mushroom vol-au-vents, but it worked out. I thought Alan was going to burst when he bit into it."

Claire exhaled through puffed cheeks, shaking her head. "I needed something to make them remember me after my boring bake yesterday. I wish my wild raspberry scones had been a bigger hit, but that's fine."

Freya let her head loll back to rest on the edge of the sofa, sighing heavily. "At least you did scones. Remember what Sophie said to me? Tea can't be all cakes." She yawned, covering her mouth. "I don't know why they couldn't make their decision today, there was plenty of time. What's the point in having us come back wearing the same clothes for the third day in a row?"

"Continuity," Claire said in a deep voice, mimicking the script supervisor, Stan. "We must have continuity."

Freya rolled her eyes. "I can't believe he made Lesley go back and get her scarf for stupid continuity. Everybody knows the episode takes more than one day, but we have to look the same so they can use shots from one day to the next without anybody noticing the difference."

"Do you expect that they'll ask us to do various shots of saying goodbye to each other for the possibility of any one of us losing?" Claire snickered at the thought. "Just going down the line so they have footage of everyone losing, in case they need it?"

"I bet Kerri can cry on cue," Freya suggested with a laugh. "Although Mathias might surprise us by being really emotional underneath his bristles. Won't be me crying, anyway. I look terrible when I cry, so I avoid it when I can."

Claire raised her hand for a weak high five. "Same here. The waterworks turn on everything else. Eyes puff, snot runs, face goes red. I am not a delicate crier."

Freya gave her a disbelieving look. "Come off it. You're gorgeous. You could pull off the one-tear trick easy."

"The what?"

"You know." Freya sat up and put on a somber face, then slowly drew one finger down her cheek from her eye. "That one-tear shot every movie gets in the dramatic scene. You'd rock that. All we need are eye drops."

"Who needs eye drops?" Kerri asked, suddenly bursting into the room, bathrobe open over her pajamas, sash ends flying. "I have eye drops! Is everyone okay? What's wrong?"

Claire and Freya looked at Kerri in surprise, then at each other, which was a bad idea, as Freya seemed as close to laughter as Claire was. Claire quickly looked away, clamping down on her lip hard, laughs beginning to shake her shoulders.

"What?" Kerri demanded. "What is it?"

"Nothing," Freya told her, faking a yawn to cover her own laughter. "We were just chatting. What's up, Kerri? You look frazzled."

Kerri huffed. "I am. Lesley promised to talk to me about how she managed the balance of flavors in her loaf today, and she is nowhere to be found. I've finished my good night call to my girls, my night care routine, my reading, everything I can possibly do before bed, and she is still not in her room. I know because the door is wide open, and she's not in it." She tutted and put her hands on her hips, shaking her head. "I just want to go to bed and forget all about today's miserable bakes, but until I know how her lemon and lavender loaf was as magical as Sophie claimed, I won't be able to sleep a wink. I have tried that flavor combination for *years*, and it's never been good."

Claire looked at the clock above the mantel, frowning. "It's half ten already. Lesley's like clockwork. She should be in her room or down here with a cup of tea and an Agatha Christie. Strange. Is everyone else here?"

"No, but I've asked everyone who is," Kerri insisted. "The only one who was any help was Mathias. He saw her go out for a walk after supper, but he didn't think to ask her where she was going or when she'd be back." She threw her hands up, rolling her eyes. "What am I supposed to do?"

Freya blinked slowly, which made Claire laugh. "Go to bed? And ask her tomorrow?"

Kerri threw the girl a dark look. "Thanks, Freya. Really, so helpful."

Well, there was no need for a woman of Kerri's age throwing that level of snark at a teenager, though Freya would be turning twenty soon.

Claire cleared her throat, sitting up. "Is it concerning you enough to want to go out and look for her? I'll help you look, if it is."

"Would you?" Kerri asked brightly. "I don't mean to be so neurotic, but I'll toss and turn all night, and it's going to drive me batty. I just . . . I want to get these flavors right. My mother-in-law hates me, but I might be able to win her over if I can do this. It's silly, I know it's silly—"

"I get it," Claire admitted, though truthfully, she had never cared enough about the flavors in a loaf to be kept awake all night. But then, she also didn't have a mother-in-law to impress. Or who might judge her by her baking skills.

And Kerri's girls were fairly young, so she might use

baking as her own personal outlet amid the chaos of mother-hood.

Maybe Claire shouldn't laugh too much about Kerri's frazzled state. That could very easily become Claire's frazzled state, if not her natural one. She could easily become so fo-cused, so obsessed, so frantic about the balance of lavender and lemon that it kept her awake.

"Let me just go grab a jumper," Claire said as she pushed up from the sofa. "She won't have gone too far this late." She hurried up to her room and pulled her knitted Aran sweater from the closet, slipping her arms into the sleeves as she tucked her toes into her trainers, which were still tied from earlier. It was an awkward shuffle to get down the hall like that, but she managed to get her heels down into the shoes before she reached the great room.

Kerri had traded her robe for a jacket, and Freya looked just as comfortable as before. "Have fun, you two," Freya said with a wave. "I'll be dreaming of the perfect Victoria sponge by the time you get back."

Claire gave her a half-hearted smile as she and Kerri headed out the door.

"Where should we go?" Kerri demanded as soon as they were out in the night air. "I don't want to pound on doors in Blackfirth. We'll make awful enemies waking people at this hour."

"I wasn't thinking about doing that," Claire assured her. "And why would Lesley be in the village anyway? No, I think she might be on the estate. I ran into her at the kitchens yes-terday, and we toured them together, talking about how we would use them ourselves. She might have gone back there."

Kerri shook her head and folded her arms. "Looking

around old kitchens in the dark. That might be the most mental thing I have ever heard. Haven't you two heard anything the locals have said about the ghost?"

Claire shrugged. "Might be mental, but if it'll help her in the next challenge, it might be worth it, ghosts and all. Come on, it's a short walk."

They started along the block, then up the paved path that directed them toward Blackfirth Park. Claire made this walk every morning and evening herself, finding wandering the estate grounds an excellent way to get fresh air, exercise, and a healthy dose of reality. There was nothing so humbling as tripping over one's own feet on a perfectly level path.

As long as she didn't fall on her face, which would give the cameras a lovely glimpse of road rash to accompany her blush, tripping was fine.

"They really ought to light this path better," Kerri muttered as she shuffled along beside Claire. "It's ridiculously difficult to see."

"I doubt they expect people to walk up to the estate in the dark," Claire offered in what she hoped was a conciliatory tone. "I can turn on the torch on my phone if you like."

Kerri waved a sharp hand. "Don't worry about it. I can see fine for now. It's just annoying to have to pay so much attention."

Sensing Kerri wasn't in the mood either for distracting conversation or opposing opinions, Claire keep quiet as they walked.

"I can't believe I gave them half-raw pastry," Kerri grumbled, wiping a hand across her face. "I know what fully baked pastry looks like, and I still took it out early. Stupid, stupid, stupid."

Claire looked at her in surprise. "It happens, Kerri. None of us were perfect today."

"Lesley was," Kerri countered. "Denis was close. Mathias and Freya . . . I'm going to be out, Claire. I know it. I haven't done anything worth keeping me here, and then what am I going to tell my girls? Mummy can bake, but she can't bake when it matters? No, no, something drastic has to happen for me to not go home. And then my husband will leave me because of the shame of it, and I'll be a single mum with two girls who know their father is a successful businessman and their mother is a washed-up would-be baker. I wonder if I can sue the show for libel if things get to that point."

Oh, now this was getting entirely ridiculous.

"Your tea cake was excellent," Claire reminded her, trying to keep her voice helpful as they approached the line of trees that indicated the official estate boundaries. "Alan couldn't find a flaw in it."

Limited lighting or not, she could tell that Kerri rolled her eyes by the way she huffed. "No one is going to be saved by a tea cake, Claire. It's the grandness of the Occasion Bakes they want. And I failed. Why else do you think I need to question Lesley about her flavors? How can I compete with her if I don't get the inside scoop?"

Claire rolled her own eyes heavenward, wondering when that wholesome family feeling she had been half expecting from the show would kick in, if it ever would. Kerri seemed to be more invested in the competition than anything else, and it had Claire wondering if any of the others felt the same.

A torchlight hit their faces, making both of them freeze in place. "Stop! No trespassing!"

"We come in peace!" Kerri squeaked, throwing her hands up in surrender.

Claire shielded her eyes and looked ahead. "Are you security for the baking show?"

"I might be," the young man's voice retorted defiantly. "Who's asking?"

Claire moved forward, pulling her badge out of her pocket, grateful she hadn't removed it from earlier. "Two of the bakers." She held it up for him to see.

He moved his torchlight to the card, allowing her to see him better. He was maybe nineteen, ginger-haired, freckled, wiry, and entirely too small for his uniform. This was the show's night security?

"All right," he mumbled, gesturing toward the path with his torchlight. "You can pass."

Claire nodded. "Thanks very much." She took Kerri's arm and tugged her forward, shoving her badge into her back pocket.

"That was terrifying," Kerri whimpered. "We need to find Lesley fast. I just want to go back to the inn."

It was all Claire could do to not snap at her companion for the complete and utterly ridiculous behavior she was displaying. Claire was doing her a favor by being out here at this hour looking for Lesley when Claire could not have cared less about the balance of flavors between lemon and lavender in a loaf, and Kerri was doing nothing but complaining, freaking out, and being a dramatic and utter fatalist, none of which was helpful or entertaining.

It was simply annoying.

Huh. It usually took a lot more for Claire to feel truly annoyed by a person, but Kerri had managed to accomplish it in record time. Was it the pressure of the day, the lateness of the hour, or the manic behavior that had done it? Probably a mixture of all three, truth be told.

"What's that sound?" Kerri asked in a small voice.

Forcing a careful breath, Claire smiled, though Kerri wouldn't see it in the dark. "It's the waterwheel at the mill. It's on a brook, so it's always running."

"It's so creepy."

Claire inhaled deeply, intentionally taking in the faintest scent of fresh water nearby. "I love it. The sound of the water, the spinning of the wheel, the freshness in the air . . . Listen, you can even hear the birds and the bugs and the frogs."

"I don't want to hear any of it," Kerri said as she shook her head. "I just want to find Lesley and get back. Do we have to go by the creepy mill before we get to the kitchens?"

"Yes, we do," Claire took great pleasure in saying. "It's just right up here, though. There are lanterns around the mill, and maybe they're on a timer."

Kerri mumbled something that was probably unflattering about Claire's attitude or the mill or the estate, or possibly Oxfordshire in general since she was from Yorkshire.

Still, Claire found herself smiling as the lights of the mill grew brighter as they neared, though it appeared that they were not on a timer, or even electric, by the way they were flickering. Were those actual flames on candles in those lanterns? Jonny hadn't mentioned that detail when he had shown her around the day before.

Then again, why would Claire have thought to ask Viscount Colburn about the sort of lighting used at the mill?

Why would she ask a ruddy viscount anything?

Worst of all, he was an attractive viscount, so being caught unawares by him had been even worse, and snooping around his own property . . .

Claire stared at the mill for a moment, remembering the awkward yet sort of exciting moments spent with Jonny the day before, when her eyes caught on something on the ground before the mill, just alongside the bank of the water.

Something was there, a bundle or heap of something, but the shadows it cast were unnerving. It was too solid for a mass of tarps or blankets, too misshapen to be bags of flour, and too flat to be sacks of grain. But it hadn't been there yesterday when she had been at the mill, and it hadn't been there when she had walked this path earlier.

Why she had to know what it was, she couldn't say. It was the same feeling she had when she saw a stick on the ground that could have been a worm or a snake; it didn't matter which of the things it was, she simply had to know.

And she had to know.

She headed toward the mill and the lump.

"Claire!" Kerri hissed. "The kitchens are this way, aren't they?"

"I'll be right back!" Claire said over her shoulder, her eyes fixed on that massive lump on the gravel.

Images of an abandoned bag of kittens or a box of puppies popped into her mind, but the lump wasn't moving or making any sound.

At all.

The closer she got, the slower she moved, and a sudden tension began to form in her chest as she started to make out details of the shape. She could have stopped, could have turned back, could have pretended she saw nothing and let nature take its course.

But she didn't.

Claire half gasped, half groaned when there could no longer be any question about what she had stumbled upon.

It was a woman. Face up, arms spread out at awkward angles by her side, legs splayed. Fully clothed, shoes on, hair streaming.

She was also soaking wet.

Claire moved into a better light to see the face, then stumbled backward with a startled yelp.

Lesley Kemble lay on the ground before her, eyes wide open, lips parted, unmoving.

"Lesley!" Claire dropped to her knees and crawled forward, grabbing her friend's arm. "Lesley, no, don't . . . don't be . . ."

But the coldness and stiffness of the arm confirmed Claire's fears, her stomach plummeting as the realization set in.

"Is that Lesley?" Kerri shrieked from her place on the path.

Ignoring her, Claire reached out to attempt to find a pulse on Lesley's neck, just to be sure, and her eyes widened as her fingers touched something soft and tight around her throat, almost hidden by the high-necked jumper Lesley had worn.

"What in the . . .?" she murmured to herself, feeling around it, not wanting to disturb anything too much. "Oh my toast . . ."

Her scarf. The one she'd had to go back for earlier in the day. Knotted so tightly, it wasn't giving at all for her fingers. Tightly enough to have suffocated her.

"Oh, Lesley," Claire whispered, sitting back on her heels and taking Lesley's hand in her own. She closed her eyes, then reached into her back pocket and pulled out her mobile.

Dialing quickly, she held the phone to her ear and waited for the answer.

"Hello, emergency? I'm at the Blackfirth Mill on the estate of Blackfirth Park, and I've found a dead body. And I know who it is."

CHAPTER 6

"If this is a joke, Detective, it's a grotesque one."

The stout man with pale stubble and buzzed hair was not laughing, his blue eyes showing a somberness that Jonny had to respect. "I can assure you, my lord, I am entirely serious."

Jonny ran a hand through his hair, turning away and intentionally opening his eyes as wide as they could go. It was the only thing he could think of to wake himself up besides the tea Mrs. Clyde had said she would bring out.

"Why would it be a joke?"

Claire's soft question was one Jonny hadn't expected, having forgotten anyone else was in the room. He shook his head and turned, looking over at the sofa where two women sat, one with her arm around the other who was shaking, hyperventilating.

"Because, Claire, the details of Ms. Kemble's demise are very similar to the death of the wife of the tenth Viscount Colburn. Legend has it that her ghost still haunts the place, her murder never having been solved and her soul being unable to rest. Apparently, Blackfirth Park gets to play host to another mysterious death and a new potential ghost."

He hadn't meant for his tone to grow sharp at the end, particularly with Claire, as there was no way she could have known that, but the situation was already threatening to grow legs of its own, and he couldn't bear the thought of his family and estate being enshrouded in a current scandal that mirrored an ancient one.

Claire's eyes were nearly round as she stared at him, her hand still moving back and forth across the back of her companion, and she looked at the detective in shock.

"I'm afraid he's right, miss," the detective said. "I never joke about death, it's too gristly, and I'd never make a joke about the Blackfirth legend to his lordship. I'm a local man, and I know what it has done to the family."

"That's enough," Jonny snapped, not wanting to get into the details at this particular moment with this particular group.

Claire wasn't the problem, but her hysterical counterpart might have blabbed it to all the world.

She was the reason Mrs. Clyde was bringing tea, though Jonny thought a sedative might be a better idea.

He doubted Mrs. Clyde actually stored those in her office, but there was always reason to hope.

"Here we go, Mrs. Martin," Mrs. Clyde said calmly as she entered, bearing a tray with one of the finer tea sets on it. She set it down on a table and poured some tea into a cup. "I've made it extra strong. And I've added a splash of brandy for your nerves. It's an old wives' tale, but it has always worked for me."

Mrs. Martin only nodded, still shaking as she took the cup from Mrs. Clyde.

"Miss Walker? A cuppa?"

"Please. Thank you, Mrs. Clyde."

"Brandy?"

"No, thank you. None for me."

It was the strangest conversation to follow a discussion of murder. So polite and superficial, so very British, that it might have happened on any given Wednesday.

"How certain are you about the details?" Jonny asked in a low voice, turning back to the detective. "Are you thinking murder, or an accident, or . . . " He glanced at the women, then stepped closer to the policeman and whispered, "Suicide?"

"Well, sir," the detective admitted, "we're not certain of anything yet. Not until we have the official ruling from the coroner. But I tend to believe the worst until someone can prove otherwise."

That made sense, and Jonny wouldn't fault him for that. He nodded in thought, folding his arms. "And how many suspicious deaths have you investigated, Detective?"

The detective looked almost sheepish. "This will be my first, my lord."

Oh, marvelous. A middle-aged detective who had never so much as seen a dead body outside of a morgue was going to try to crack a case that echoed one from centuries ago that had no answers.

Just what the family and the estate needed.

"Jonny? What's going on?" his sister's voice called from the hall. Moments later, she appeared in the room, a jumper pulled over her pajamas, her hair in a rumpled plait that hung over a shoulder. "What's all this?"

"Gabi, it's nothing, go to bed," Jonny said automatically, shooing her away. She'd surprised him by arriving late last night, and now, the timing could not have felt worse. A murder on his estate with his sister in residence? Ludicrous.

She gave him a dark look, then marched over to the detective. "Gabriella Ainsley, sister of the viscount. And you are?"

"Detective Sergeant Jim Watson, at your service," the detective greeted, shaking her hand. "I'm here about the body found on the estate."

"Body?" Gabi looked at Jonny. "Nothing, you said? Come on, Jon."

He heaved a sigh. "Fine, whatever, Gabs. Mrs. Clyde, some tea?"

"Right here, my lord." She handed over a cup, nodding at him sympathetically. "And Mr. Clyde has contacted the show executives. They should be arriving shortly."

"That couldn't wait until morning?" Jonny tried not to grind his teeth as he took a sip of the hot tea. "It's already nearly one."

DS Watson cleared his throat. "Erm, it's a simple matter of needing to notify the family, my lord. I'm afraid I asked Mr. Clyde if he would oblige me there."

Jonny winced in self-castigation. "Right, yeah, of course. Her family. We'll pay for them to come up here, funeral expenses, whatever they need."

"That's very good of you, my lord."

Another throat clearing took place, this one a touch higher in pitch. "Sorry, but Lesley didn't have any immediate family."

Jonny looked at Claire in surprise. "None?"

She shook her head, her expression pale and drawn, but clear. "No children, she wasn't married, no significant other. She'd recently retired from the NHS. She was a nurse." Claire bit down on her lip and looked away, focusing on soothing Mrs. Martin.

It was the first sign of real emotion he had seen from Claire since he'd been woken up, and, if he was understanding things right, she had been the one to discover the body.

He had no idea how he would have responded under the circumstances, but she was holding up incredibly well.

The tear he saw roll down her cheek made him swallow, but she swiped it away quickly and reached for her tea with a free hand.

"Gabi," Jonny said quickly, holding an arm out.

She came to him, expression earnest as she draped her arm about his waist. "What's up?"

"Just quick intros," he assured her. "While we're waiting." He pointed at the ladies on the sofa. "Mrs. Martin and Miss Walker, both baking contestants on the show."

Mrs. Martin remained silent, staring off into space with her tea in hand.

Claire sniffed and stood, holding out a hand. "Claire, please."

"You don't have to stand—" Jonny started.

"Oh, sit down, for heaven's sake," Gabi told her at the same time, giving her hand a quick shake. "Politeness goes to bed at eleven."

Claire smiled at that, and Jonny could have hugged his little sister for bringing that out. "Sounds about right."

Gabi stepped away from him and moved to the couch. "Strange time for us to have a chat, but seeing as how neither of us are going anywhere, we might as well, yeah?"

"Might as well," Claire echoed softly, her smile still in place.

Well, at least Gabi would keep her from crying more, which would help him to not be distracted. There was something about silent tears that unnerved him, but also, he was fascinated by Claire Walker, and the fact that she had discovered a body on his estate, and that it was someone she knew and had cared about . . .

He did not need the added distraction of her emotions at the moment, and that was all.

Jonny dropped himself in the nearest chair and sipped his tea, letting his mind mull over things while they waited for the others to arrive. He'd have to explain everything about the legend, if only so they would understand the significance of how Ms. Kemble died, and then, hopefully, he'd never have to talk about it again.

It was a vain hope since they'd likely talk about it all the time until the murder was solved.

"What's happened?" Mr. Sybil demanded as he entered the room, hair in complete disarray, his suit coat rumpled. Mr. Phipps and Mr. Dean followed him into the room, but the hosts and the judges, Jonny noted, were not in attendance.

Jonny looked at DS Watson and waited for him to begin. Though this was his house, he was not the person to lead this meeting, nor the one to provide the information they were seeking.

"And who are you, sir?" Detective Watson asked, sighing a little.

"Sybil. I'm the showrunner. That's Phipps, the producer, and Dean, the director," Sybil rambled. "Now tell us why we were woken up and brought here."

"A body was found near the Blackfirth Mill roughly two hours ago," Detective Watson began. "The body was identified as that of Ms. Lesley Kemble. Time of death has not been established yet, but the manner in which it appears the body was found and treated bears a striking resemblance to the manner in which the body of the wife of the tenth Viscount Colburn was killed and treated."

Mr. Sybil blinked, then looked at Phipps and Dean. "Do either of you know what he's talking about?"

Both men shook their heads. "We have the historical advisers for that," Phipps said without apology. He looked at Watson. "You may want to talk to them, Detective. If there is a real resemblance, perhaps our historians could provide some context that would be helpful to the investigation."

Jonny glanced at Mr. Phipps with interest. The man had not shown a single ounce of concern over the identity of the victim, only for solving the case.

"Interesting," he mused, rubbing at his jaw. "You believe that talking to historians, none of whom have found a firm solution to a two-hundred-and-fifty-year-old murder, would be able to provide insight into a death that looks similar to it?"

Phipps didn't even spare him a look. "The victim must have been snooping around where she shouldn't have. It's a mysterious place; that's why we chose it for filming. Who knows what the victim was doing when she met her death."

"Her name," Claire said firmly, looking around Gabi at the executives, "was Lesley. Lesley Kemble. Which you should know, as she was competing on *your* TV show. And she was probably going to win this round, at least. She deserves some respect."

"And how dare you suggest that a murder is more likely to be committed on my estate," Jonny added, rising from his chair. "Might help your ratings, huh? Get your investment back, Mr. Producer."

Phipps looked startled. "Surely you aren't suggesting . . . I would never have—"

"Then maybe," Jonny went on, keeping his tone as condescending but calm as possible, "you should remember who the victim is, who is investigating, and who can shut down your little show at any given time."

Phipps glared at Jonny as though he would spit, but he averted his gaze and said nothing further.

"Mr. Sybil," DS Watson pleaded, his voice carrying an edge of impatience, "we need to contact next of kin. Emergency contact. Anyone for poor Ms. Kemble."

"Of course, of course," Mr. Sybil muttered distractedly. "Poor Ms. Kemble."

Jonny looked at the detective, then back at the showrunner. "I think he means now, Mr. Sybil."

Mr. Sybil jerked in response. "Oh! Right, yes. I shall . . . Let me make a call." He hurried out of the room, pulling his phone out.

Watson turned his attention to the other two executives in the room. "I realize the lateness of the hour will hinder much progress tonight, but I will need to meet with anyone associated with the show in the morning. Particularly, anyone who worked with Ms. Kemble or interacted with her yesterday."

"That would be just about everyone on site," Mr. Dean told him. "We can arrange it first thing in the morning."

Gabi cleared her throat. "I think it might help Claire and Kerri if they knew the details of the original murder. They have a lot of questions about their friend."

Jonny looked at the women with interest. "Really?"

Claire shrugged. "I've never known anyone who died suspiciously. The idea that it mirrors some old crime . . . I don't know . . . all I can see is Lesley."

Kerri started hiccupping tears, dropping her head. "Lemon and lavender," she whispered. "I was worried about lemon and lavender."

"It's all right," Claire whispered, rubbing her back once more. "You couldn't have known."

Jonny suddenly wished he was anywhere else.

And that settled everything for him.

"All right," he murmured as he sank down into his chair. "The legend goes back to the tenth viscount and his wife. She was the daughter of a French aristocrat living here right before the Revolution was taking place, which some speculate could be a reason for her death. At any rate, one night, in 1786, Lady Colburn could not be found. A search was instigated, and her body was found on the ground in front of the mill. A noose had been tied around her neck, but she was soaking wet."

"Oh my days . . ." Kerri breathed, staring at him with round eyes. "It's exactly like Lesley. I mean, without the rope."

Jonny nodded, rubbing his hands together. "There was some debate as to if she had been drowned, hanged, or strangled. And how exactly the mill was involved, if it was. The murderer was never found, no motive was ever identified, and the reward the viscount posted was never claimed. There are records of interviews with scads and scads of people, but there were never any leads to pursue."

Kerri shook her head in disbelief. "And now they've killed Lesley."

Jonny bit down on his lip to keep from pointing out that whoever had killed the tenth Lady Colburn was long dead, and therefore, could not have killed Lesley. He'd give the poor woman the benefit of the doubt, as she was clearly overcome by the evening's events.

"Well," Claire pointed out softly, "someone has." She frowned and looked at Gabi, then Jonny. "Could this all be an accident?"

"I don't want to know," Kerri insisted tearfully. "Lesley's dead! Unthinkable!" She buried her face into her hands and began to shake.

Claire pulled her into her side, rubbing her arm. "Can I get Kerri back to the inn? She's done for."

DS Watson smiled in understanding. "Did she give her statement to the officers at the scene?"

Claire nodded. "We both did, yes."

"Then, yes, of course. I'll have some officers take you both back." He gestured for them to follow him and started out the doors of the room.

Kerri and Claire rose almost as one, arm in arm, and followed the detective, not saying anything to anyone else.

Jonny went with them, feeling responsible for these women, and, more particularly, for Claire. "Detective."

Watson turned. "My lord?"

"Are there enough officers to post some at the inn for the contestants?" He indicated Kerri, who looked like she might collapse at any moment. "For their peace of mind, if nothing else."

Watson looked at Kerri and Claire, frowning and shaking his head. "Unfortunately not. We have a very small force, sir. And until we know more, we have no reason to think this is about any of the other bakers. But I think we can arrange for a police escort up here for the meeting in the morning. Maybe the show can increase security?"

Jonny gave him a brisk nod. "I'll speak to them about it. If they can't fund it, we can."

Claire smiled a little at that. "Perks of being a viscount, right?"

Was that a joke or a jab? He couldn't tell, not this late and not with the night they'd had, but Claire didn't seem the vindictive or bitter sort, so he could only go with the joke and hope he was right.

He shrugged, returning the smile. "There have to be some, or no one would keep the title." He turned to DS Watson, sobering. "I'll be there for the meeting in the morning, Detective. Anything you need from me or from the estate, consider it done."

Watson nodded and gestured for the women to continue toward the door. "Let me see these ladies to a patrol car, my lord, and we can talk about that further. I might need your help."

Claire offered Jonny a small wave, then ushered Kerri out of the door, continuing to console the woman as though she had been the one to find the body.

There was something unnerving about watching Claire leave when one of the bakers had just been found dead. Like he might stumble upon her body in the morning just as she had stumbled upon Lesley's. But he couldn't ask her to stay. Couldn't ask any of them to stay, really. Didn't want to ask any of the rest of them.

Just Claire.

But he'd see her in the morning. He was sure of it.

Sort of.

CHAPTER 7

"Does anybody know what this meeting is about?"

"Beats me. Maybe it's a bonus task."

Claire ignored the conversation of the others as they were driven up to the estate, her head throbbing from the lack of quality sleep. She'd managed to fall asleep around three, and now it was half eight.

All the tea in the world wasn't going to make this morning bearable.

Kerri had a migraine and already knew the details, so she had begged off this morning's meeting. The executives didn't mind, and nothing baking related would be happening, so, according to their contracts, she didn't have to attend.

Claire couldn't tell the others any of that without explaining what had happened the night before, which she was not permitted to do.

She didn't want to talk about it anyway. It was a lot to take in, even now. Perhaps especially now, as there had been time and distance away from the experience, and it was harder to comprehend after she'd had some sleep.

Why Lesley? Why did her death look like what had

happened to the mysterious Lady Colburn? Was it all simply a baffling coincidence, or had there been other suspicious deaths in Blackfirth since Lady Colburn's?

Maybe Detective Watson would have some additional information at their meeting. Claire had so many questions, but there was no reason anyone should answer them for her. She wasn't part of the investigation, nor should she be. But Lesley had no family, and someone ought to stand in for her.

She likely wouldn't have the opportunity. The show would have to shut down, and they would probably recast everyone for a fresh start. The press would be all over every detail, which would mean more nondisclosure agreements this morning. The public would be distressed when the news came out, so the show would probably be moved from Blackfirth, which would be unfortunate for Jonny and his estate.

He didn't deserve to have this kind of publicity. No one did.

They pulled into their usual car park and were let out. Claire folded her arms over her jumper as she made her way to the pavilion without any sort of energy or enthusiasm, which was certainly a first for her. Every day, the pavilion had given her mingled feelings of anxiety and elation, but today . . .

"Coffee?"

Claire felt a nudge at her arm and looked toward it, following the cup of coffee to the hand holding it and up the arm, directly into Jonny's haggard face.

He looked remarkably casual in a jacket and T-shirt over dark blue jeans, but given the night that had passed and the earliness of the hour, that might be expected. After all, Claire was in joggers and a jumper. Crepes alive, had she even done her hair?

Why did that matter now?

"Morning," Jonny all but growled, nudging her with the coffee again. "I needed one of these to even get out of the house, so I'm on my second. I have no idea how you're even upright."

"I'm not altogether sure that I am," Claire admitted, taking the cup from him. "Did you happen to add anything to this coffee?"

"Afraid not. Black as the preferred color of the inside of my eyelids, which I am eager to see again." Jonny took a sip of his own coffee and inclined his head toward a table. "Might be some stuff over there, though."

Claire felt the side of her mouth lift in a smile. "You provided coffee for everyone? That was nice of you."

"Honestly?" Jonny offered her a tired smile. "I thought you would need some, and I didn't think it would be a good idea for either of us if I showed up with coffee just for you."

That was unexpected, but Claire was far too worn out to feel flattered, modest, or even intrigued. "Seriously?"

Jonny shrugged, his olive jacket crinkling as he did so. "I'm not in the right state of mind to be coy, Claire, and I'm not in the habit of showing off. Yes, I thought we would both need coffee, so I finagled a way for both of us to get some without anybody caring."

"Black is fine for me anyway," Claire murmured, shifting the subject back to the coffee while she had a mind to. "How much sleep did you get?"

"Four hours? Maybe less?" He stifled a yawn behind his coffee cup. "You?"

"Same. Four, tops." Claire watched the other bakers enter the pavilion, followed by the hosts, the judges, and the remaining members of the crew. "Anything relevant come out after I left last night?"

Jonny shook his head. "Not really. Ms. Kemble's emergency contact was a neighbor. So there really is no family to mourn her, which is a tragedy." He sipped his coffee and narrowed his eyes at DS Watson. "I really hope this is short and doesn't go into speculation."

Claire rolled her eyes. "Calm down. He's probably just going to inform everybody about what happened. We all know you don't want to talk about the rest of it."

He reared back, giving her a dark look. "What's that supposed to mean?"

"Just that," Claire replied, startled by his reaction. "We were all told from the beginning of shooting not to talk to the family about it. That you didn't want to discuss it."

Jonny's blue eyes searched hers for a moment, then he seemed to sag. "I'm sorry, Claire. I shouldn't snap, especially at you. I barely know you, but I already know you don't have a rough bone in your body, so you wouldn't bait anybody."

Claire sputtered loudly, surprising herself. "I might, given the right provocation. I was a schoolteacher, after all."

"Was?" Jonny repeated, looking rather interested. "Are you not going back to that after this?"

"No idea," Claire admitted with a wrinkle of her nose. "I had to take a leave of absence to be here, and they couldn't promise to hold my place at the school. But that's fine, there are always teaching positions. I just had to take this chance. I had to." Her throat tightened, and she tried to swallow, failing and looking down at her coffee cup instead. "Meeting Lesley was worth it, even if I had to be the one to find her last night."

"I wish to heaven it had been me instead." Jonny turned

to lean against the post of the pavilion, looking at her closely. "Are you all right? Really?"

Claire could only lift her shoulder. "I don't know. I slept, sort of. I got out of bed, sort of. I got here, sort of. Now I have coffee, thanks to you."

"Sort of," Jonny added with a quick flick of a smile.

"And we're about to hear all the details about the death I encountered, which may or may not have more of an impact now than it did last night." Claire cradled her coffee with both hands, hoping some of its heat might transfer into her suddenly chilled frame. "I don't know if I'm all right, Jonny. I might not know until all this is over. But I'm standing, and that's a decent sign."

"Fair enough," came his low reply. "But, please, do let me know. You seem to be one of the few normal people around this insanity, and I may find myself rooting for you on this show."

Now *that* she was not immune to, if the heat in her cheeks was any indication. "Don't be silly. They're clearly going to end the show and recast and restart when all of this is over."

Jonny cleared his throat and tipped his chin toward the producers. "I think you may overestimate their concern for their fellow man."

"Ladies and gentlemen," DS Watson announced from the unofficial front of the pavilion and gestured to the rows of chairs, "please, take a seat. We have a lot to get through, and we need to get started."

Claire opted to stay where she was, feeling the detective wouldn't mind so much, as Claire already knew the situation, and she wasn't about to be taking a seat in shock from the revelations about to come.

"What is this all about?" Benji demanded, sitting down with a thump. He tossed a white pill in his mouth and took a long drink from his cup. "Why are we out here this early? I'm having to take my chuffing aspirin with barely any breakfast in my gut."

It was all Claire could do not to roll her eyes. Benji took aspirin for an old shoulder injury or something, and he whined about an empty stomach almost every morning. For someone who made a career out of helping others, he certainly seemed to complain a lot.

DS Watson barely spared Benji a look. He cleared his throat. "My name is Detective Sergeant Watson, and it is my duty to inform you all that there was a death on the estate last night."

The entire pavilion fell silent, even those who already knew.

"Ms. Lesley Kemble was found dead last evening around eleven at the mill," DS Watson went on. "Her emergency contact has been informed, and my superiors are certain, based on the condition of the body, that this was an accidental death."

"They're what?" Claire muttered for Jonny only, unsure she'd heard right. She'd felt how tight the scarf was around Lesley's throat. There was no way anything got that tight by accident. Was there?

He only shook his head.

"We will need statements from everyone to corroborate comings and goings and to put together a suitable timeline of Ms. Kemble's activity for our reports," Watson went on. "All standard and routine, nothing to be concerned about."

"But how did she die? Are the rest of us in danger?" Denis asked in a surprisingly high-pitched voice.

Detective Watson pressed his lips together firmly. "There is no reason to think so. As I said, it has been ruled an accidental death."

Mr. Sybil stepped forward, loudly and unnecessarily clearing his throat. "This means that the show can continue, so it is good news for all of us."

"Wait," Freya said loudly, holding her hand up like a student. "The show is still happening? Without Lesley?"

Claire straightened, staring at Mr. Sybil intently, wondering the same thing. It sounded like insanity, disrespect, and manipulation all in one.

"Well, yes," Sybil hedged with a slight wince. "You see . . . Well, to be perfectly frank, we can't afford to shut down. The show's viewing numbers have been declining for a while, and this is our last chance. If we shut down, or even postpone, for any reason, they'll not only cancel this series but the entire show itself. Every crew member will lose their jobs. We simply cannot take that risk. We are already secluded from the press and the public, so there's no reason why an unfortunate accident cannot quietly stay within our little community here."

It was a rehearsed explanation, and from the expressions on every face in the pavilion, everyone knew it.

"Detective?" Freya demanded like a woman twice her age instead of the young woman she was.

Watson held up his hands in surrender. "There is no reason to suspect foul play, miss. The show may proceed. I am only tying up loose ends for reports."

Freya frowned and returned her attention to Sybil. "How

are you going to explain Lesley's disappearance? There was no way she would have lost and gone home after the first episode."

"Yes, how indeed?" Claire murmured, folding her arms.

"Was she good?" Jonny whispered.

Claire nodded once. "She was piping brilliant. Could have won."

"We will record an episode soon," Mr. Sybil said with apparent patience, and a little too much condescension, "that will appear to be the judging. But it will be announced that Lesley had to leave unexpectedly due to a medical issue, so no one will be going home. Then in a few days, we will record the second episode with the seven remaining bakers."

"Nice and neat, just like that?" Anthony made a loud sputtering noise. "Blimey, glad it wasn't me who chuffed it with the way you lot are sweeping it under the rug. Just gonna pretend Lesley didn't exist, right?"

That caused a rumble among the gathering, and Claire found herself nodding along with him. That was exactly how it felt, and her stomach curdled at the thought.

She didn't want to leave the show, since it sounded like it was going to continue, but she would have a hard time baking with the knowledge that they were covering up a death to keep filming.

"No, no, that isn't it at all," Sybil said quickly. "No, we've discussed it, and it is best not to spread a panic about this. It was an accidental drowning, right, Detective?"

"Well, I—"

"And then," Sybil continued without stopping, "at the end of the series, we will have a lovely 'In Memorium' tribute to Lesley, who will have lost her life related to the medical issue she returned home with. We've talked to Dame Sophie, and she is going to include Lesley's lemon and lavender loaf cake in her next cookbook."

"I'm sure Lesley's ghost will be thrilled with that," Mathias muttered, his mustache twitching as he stirred his coffee.

Claire glanced over at Dame Sophie, who seemed to be hearing this for the first time, if her widened eyes and strained neck were any indication.

"How *did* Lesley die?" Denis asked in a quiet voice, looking at the detective with concern.

"That is the question," Jonny muttered, probably only for himself, but Claire caught it.

What did he know?

Detective Watson cleared his throat awkwardly. "The preliminary ruling is accidental drowning."

Denis frowned, looked at the other bakers, then pressed, "Meaning what?"

"Meaning that, until we know more, that is the cause of death." Watson nodded once, clearly thinking that was the end of it.

"That's not good enough for me," Anthony announced. "Accidental drowning? Lesley drowned in the brook over there? Seriously? She could have stood up, man. We're gonna need to know more."

Others agreed with him, and Claire felt a gnawing sense of unease claw at her stomach. And it wasn't the coffee.

Watson looked as though he'd rather be anywhere else. "We believe that she slipped and fell into the brook, and then her scarf got caught. This would have cut off her airway, and—"

"Strangulation," an older voice called out. "Strangulation and drowning, is that what you are telling us?"

Claire tried to see who had spoken, but since everyone looked concerned, it was hard to tell.

"In a word, yes," Watson said simply.

Someone stood—Dr. Adams, one of the historical advisors. Petite in frame and vocal in her opinions, she was as spiky in nature as her short gray hair was in style. Her eyes fixed on DS Watson with fierce intensity. "Just like the tenth viscountess, then."

Jonny groaned beside Claire. "No . . ."

Claire winced in sympathy—both for Jonny and for Watson—as every eye in the pavilion darted between Dr. Adams and the detective.

Watson sucked his teeth a moment, then said, "We have no reason to draw similarities between the two, madam. As I said, Miss Kemble's death has been ruled accidental at this time."

"And an autopsy may show otherwise," Dr. Adams pointed out. "Not to mention that one might have initially drawn the same conclusion about Lady Colburn in 1786. Are the police really going to ignore the parallels to help the show cover this up?

"Ouch," Claire whispered, wondering when the producers were going to step in.

Next to never, she supposed, based on the complete lack of movement from any of them. They all looked pale and panicked, which failed to inspire confidence in anyone.

Watson stared at Dr. Adams with a neutral expression. "I do not intend to ignore anything, madam. All I can tell you is what I know now, which is the preliminary ruling."

Freya turned in her chair. "Dr. Adams, what else can you tell us about the death of the viscountess? Was it suspicious?"

"And is her ghost really haunting this place?" one of the younger production assistants asked in a small voice, causing some murmuring to spread among the group.

"Oh, for the love of . . ." Jonny rubbed a hand over his face, the rest of his words remaining unsaid.

Probably for the best.

Dr. Adams cast a questioning look at DS Watson and gestured toward where he stood.

Sighing, he waved for her to join him in front of the group. "Fine, Dr. Adams. You can give them some insight. Meanwhile, the officers here and I will begin conducting interviews. Thanks very much, cheers."

He stepped away, heading directly for Jonny and Claire.

"Can I have a word?" DS Watson said when he reached them.

Claire looked at Jonny, who was looking at her, his expression reflecting her utter bewilderment. "Sure, I guess," she replied.

"Right, yeah," Jonny echoed just after her.

"I only need his lordship," DS Watson said politely.

"I don't care if Claire comes," Jonny shot back, nudging his head toward the path.

DS Watson left the pavilion, and they followed, walking a few paces away as the historical advisers took center stage.

"What can I do for you, Detective?" Jonny asked him.

Watson looked down before meeting his eyes. "First of all, I'm really sorry about all that. I did my best to avoid . . ." He flicked his fingers toward the animated discussion happening at the pavilion.

Jonny brushed it off with a wave of his hand. "I saw you get cornered. It's not your fault."

Watson nodded, then cleared his throat. "My superiors want this tied up all nice and neat. Stuff like this doesn't happen around here. You know this, sir. The only real crime I ever deal with is small-time robbery. Occasional trespassing. Parking tickets, when it's slow."

"That's putting it mildly," Jonny muttered.

"They're keen for the show to go on, but I fear . . ." He straightened. "I am not nearly as convinced as they are that it was an accidental death, but I cannot be seen to be investigating where there is technically no crime. I wonder if . . ." He trailed off and looked at Claire with sudden interest. "I may have need of you after all, Miss Walker."

Her heart leaped in faint excitement, her fingers tingling in anticipation. "What do you need, Detective?" Claire asked in as firm a tone as she could.

He twisted his lips a little. "I need you to help me figure out what happened to Ms. Kemble. I think it could be murder."

Claire and Jonny exchanged a look, and Jonny nodded at her slightly. She looked Watson directly in the eye, a weight settling in her stomach. "So do we."

CHAPTER 8

"Some folks say that Viscountess Colburn had a jilted lover who snuck away from Revolutionary France, but all historians agree that is highly unlikely."

"Why's that, Dr. Adams?"

The old woman with short, spiked hair smiled rather indulgently for someone talking about death. "Well, for the simple reason that Viscountess Colburn was a beautiful, charming, accomplished woman, came from a respectable family in France, was a devoted mother of five, and never had a word of gossip said about her in any papers or letters of the time."

"Who is this old bat?" Jonny asked through gritted teeth as he returned to the pavilion with Claire and DS Watson.

"Dr. Adams," Claire murmured with a slight cough, though Jonny thought it might be covering a laugh. "One of our historical advisers. I think she's a local historian, too, or something."

"I've never heard of her," Jonny retorted defiantly.

"And you know everyone in town, do you?"

That was a fair shot, and Jonny accepted it with a half nod of acknowledgment. "It's just uncomfortable, hearing someone talking about my several-times-great-granny like she knew her."

Claire leaned closer and nudged his arm. "How much do historians actually know, anyway? About her and the thing. Family diaries turned over or anything like that?"

Jonny gave her a dubious look. "Regretting missing the beginning of the lecture, Miss Walker?"

"History nerd, remember?" She shrugged, her oversized gray bespeckled jumper making her look more like a teenager than a fully grown adult. "I don't care about the legend, specifically; I just want to know if what they think they know is accurate."

Again, that was fair. Jonny really ought to have less coffee if it was going to make him so snarky. But the mystery was the one thing the family seemed to be known for, and the one thing they really didn't want to be known for. It had hovered over the family for more than two centuries, and it wasn't much of a stretch to say the estate had never fully recovered.

Of course, the estate had managed to make some money off the mystery once the family opened the house up to the public. But there were still no official mystery tours. No ghost tours. No social media posts about the mysterious death of the tenth viscountess. No reminders it had ever happened.

With Lesley's murder now, he might have to consider . . . well, not capitalizing on it, of course, but acknowledging the original murder, at least.

He really didn't want to do that, but he might not have a choice.

"My great-grandfather turned over everything we had on the subject to local historians," Jonny eventually admitted. "Anything belonging to her, actually. Jewels, artwork, letters. The family had kept everything of hers, so there was a lot."

"What was her name?"

Jonny glanced at Claire, not quite processing the question. "Who?"

Claire rolled her eyes, her expression reminding him quite a lot of Gabi. "The tenth viscountess. She's one of your great-nans, yeah? So why not say her name? Make her less of a mystery to everybody, less of a big deal. Then she's a person, not some mysterious ghost or victim or whatever. Lesley is the woman who was killed last night. Lesley Kemble. Not a mystery, not some random victim, not someone related to the legendary viscountess. Lesley, who was a cracking baker and a dedicated nurse with the NHS. Lesley, who loved silk scarves. I knew her, might have been lifelong friends with her, if given more than two weeks with her. She reminded me of an aunt—one of those cool aunts, not one of the boring ones."

She was rambling again, but there was a point somewhere, Jonny was sure of it. There was a dedicated edge to the furrow in her brows. She looked exhausted, there was no question, but there was something else. A light in her eyes that no coffee could have sparked, and a tension in her jaw that almost resembled anger.

But not quite.

"There," Claire said, her brow clearing a little. "I spoke about her. Your turn." She looked at him expectantly, folding her arms and bringing her coffee cup close to her chest.

Oh, for pity's sake . . .

"Marie-Catherine Louise Françoise de La Trémoille," he recited in the most pristine French accent he could. "Went by the name Ree, actually, not that Dr. Snooze will tell anyone that. And she is right, you know. She was loved. Five grandchildren named Marie. First names, mind. Her husband, Charles, never recovered. Went full recluse. Nothing happened at the estate until George inherited." He gave Claire a smug smile. "Happy?"

"Delighted," she replied in the driest voice known to man.

Jonny looked over his shoulder at the detective, who was barely paying attention to the lecture. "Watson, I still don't understand something though, and it's been bothering me all night."

"What's that, sir?"

Setting his coffee down on a nearby chair, Jonny shoved his hands into his coat pockets and turned to face DS Watson and Claire. "Why would anyone kill Lesley? Retired NHS. An amateur baker. Not from here. She hardly seems a likely target for murder . . . and yet . . ."

Claire scuffed her shoe against the ground a few times. "And yet?"

Jonny shook his head, frowning at the other bakers. "Lesley was all alone in the world, right? If that's true, then there is no one to miss her. Is anyone else like that in the group?"

He heard Claire's sharp intake of breath and glanced at her, watching her eyes dart among the other bakers. "No . . . No, everybody else has got somebody, at least. I can't tell you about the crew or anything, but as for the bakers . . ."

"If this was murder, then it was either personal or . . . maybe the killer deliberately chose someone no one would miss," Jonny murmured, surprised by how his stomach dropped at his own words.

"You think it's because of the show . . . or someone with the show?" Claire asked quietly. "Oh, sugar, of course you do. Someone would have been killed at Blackfirth Park before now if it wasn't, right? Local grudges or playing up the ghost idea or whatever."

Jonny smiled a little. "Do you want me to answer either of those?"

Claire turned to DS Watson with a hint of a frown. "Was there any outcry from the town about us coming? Protests or anything?"

"Not at all," Watson said easily. "Everyone was delighted, thought it might bring some spirit and publicity to Blackfirth once the show airs. There was a parish hall meeting, but not a single complaint was raised."

"Are complaints normally raised in parish hall meetings?" Claire pressed in a doubting tone.

"Oh, yes," Watson confirmed with a series of sage nods. "When they wanted to put in an automated car wash last year, half of the room were up in arms against it."

"Brutal, this place," Jonny drawled sarcastically, feeling as though he was living in some poorly scripted period drama set in a quaint little place no one had ever heard of.

Where murders occurred.

Oh, gads, it was exactly that kind of scenario. This was where he lived, and this was real life. He wasn't at all active in the village, his time split between working in London and working from the estate—and working *on* the estate—and there was something odd about being the viscount and showing up at parish hall meetings. Most things that happened in the village didn't apply to him and his life, so he had adopted the distant, reclusive persona long attributed to landowners and peers throughout history.

Probably made him unlikable, actually, to everyone around here.

They'd have thought he was a perfect murderer, actually, since they didn't know him, didn't see him, didn't hear from him. Aside from the people who actually worked on the estate, no one else would know him from Adam. Or know anything about him.

He'd have made an excellent suspect.

He chanced a look at DS Watson, just on the off chance the man might be sizing him up. But he was too interested in the lecture at the moment, or perhaps the coffee on the other side of the lecture.

"Detective," Jonny chanced, "have you helped yourself to the coffee? You're more than welcome to it."

"Thank you, your lordship," Watson replied, pushing past him to head directly to the table.

Jonny sighed heavily as he watched him go. "If we're right—if Lesley really was murdered and if DS Watson's superiors are quietly looking the other way—we could be in real trouble."

"Ugh," Claire groaned. "I wish I wasn't curious and dying to start investigating for him, but I am. I want justice for Lesley."

"Of course you do." He flashed a false, cheeky grin, then sobered quickly. "If I weren't me, I'd say I was the perfect suspect for this. I'm waiting for DS Watson to take me in for more intense questioning."

"You aren't a suspect, Jonny. You've got an alibi."

Jonny rolled his eyes, exhaling roughly. "Yeah, my sister. Great alibi, right?"

"But it's an alibi," Claire pointed out. "Freya's my alibi. Fellow baker. We were just sitting in the Ivy House great room, running through the day together and our bakes, what we could improve. I'm a terrible suspect anyway; I'm not coordinated enough to . . ." She trailed off, her brows bunching together in the most perfect furrow known to man.

"What?" Jonny asked when she didn't go on.

Claire wet her lips, shifting her weight from one leg to the other. "Lesley wasn't all that petite. I mean, she was a grown woman, at least six inches taller than me, and stockier. She was a nurse, so she'd have had to take care of patients of all sizes. Whoever took her down would have to be bigger and stronger, or maybe have a weapon to coerce her. And if we're talking about strangulation by her scarf, well, I think she'd be able to fight a good number of people off."

"And drowning," Jonny said in a low voice. "She's Welsh, right? I know it's not right to assume, but surely she could swim."

"She was from Tenby," Claire told him quickly. "That's a coastal town; I looked it up. She'd have to be able to swim."

"So how does she *accidentally* drown? Your baking friend was right—she could have stood up."

They stared at each other, neither having an answer. Claire looked over at the bakers, her expression turning more sad than contemplative. "She doesn't. She couldn't fight the water. Either she was already dead, or she was unconscious when she went in the water."

"Cause of death is going to be more interesting now," Jonny mused, looking at the faces of those listening to the lecture. "That was the thing with the viscountess: the strangulation and the hanging possibilities. Her neck was broken exactly as it would have been by a hanging, but there were clear signs of strangulation."

"Overkill." Claire rubbed at her brow and leaned her head back against the beam of the pavilion. "I don't know the psychology on that, but it's confusing. And I think we can assume that our killer was mirroring your Great-Nan Ree's murder. But for what?"

Jonny had been thinking the same thing and looked up at his house with a worried frown. "I don't know, but we're going to have to interview my staff. It's entirely possible that it's nothing to do with the show and everything to do with Blackfirth Park."

DS Watson turned from the table of coffee, stirring the cup he held while wearing a bland smile. Dr. Adams was still talking, and her enthusiasm for the topic of Viscountess Colburn's death was evident.

It was eerie, actually. Watching the woman talk about Jonny's family. He'd never even met the woman, and she was positively gushing on the topic. If she had any concerns about Lesley's murder, she didn't show it. But then, she wouldn't be concerned with anything occurring in the present day, would she? Not unless it had relevance in history.

"So, what's next on the shooting schedule?" Mathias asked suddenly, looking over at Mr. Sybil. "Not that all this isn't interesting, Dr. Adams, but I'm more concerned with Lesley, and with baking, if the show is truly going to continue."

"I like that guy," Jonny murmured to Claire.

Claire shushed him, but he caught the slight upturn of her lips as she did so.

"This afternoon, if everyone is up for it," Mr. Sybil told them all. "We'd like to do the episode wrap-up. Get a clean break from the first episode. Then we prepare for the second episode, which we want to film on schedule, next Wednesday."

"What about the ghost?" Benji brought up. "What if it takes someone else like it did Lesley?"

The entire pavilion fell silent at that question.

"And there it is again." Jonny shook his head, closing his eyes on an exhale.

Everyone began to look around, concern and fear blossoming on each face. That was an unfortunate byproduct of all of this. A potentially haunted estate where now two suspicious deaths had occurred, however accidental one might or might not have been.

Of course, someone was going to blame the supposed ghost.

Mr. Sybil stood in front of the group once more. "Any final words for us this morning, DS Watson?"

Watson came over to stand next to the showrunner. "Yes. Make sure you speak to an officer before you return to your current place of residence, and please be careful when you're out alone. Particularly when it's dark."

"Oh, very wise counsel, that," Claire muttered, shaking her head. "Don't slip and fall and strangle yourself. And watch out for vengeful ghosts, just in case."

"Claire . . ." Jonny warned.

She gave him a dark look. "I am well aware that he can't say what he wants to say, Jonny. I agree that we need to be careful, particularly in the dark. But he told you and me that we need to help him. I don't know about you, Viscount Colburn, but I've never solved any crime at all, let alone a murder."

"Right, yeah, but all we have to do is be an extra set of brains," Jonny said with a shrug. "We aren't solving it. He is."

"Then he'd better do something that makes me have some sort of confidence in him because asking me and you to help him reeks of stupid." Claire pinched her nose, exhaling slowly. "Sorry, Jonny. Sorry. I'm so tired, and my head is killing me."

Jonny made a low sputtering noise, shaking his head. "You don't have to apologize to me, Claire. Not about anything, really. I don't know you well enough for you to have to apologize to me. I, on the other hand, am an entitled jerk who could use more apologizing in his vocabulary." He rubbed a hand over his face, exhaling.

"You're not a jerk," Claire grumbled before giving him a speculative look. "Did you tee that up just for me to say so?"

"That would be a classic jerk move, but no." He laughed once and looked at the bakers as they started to leave.

"Miss Walker," DS Watson grunted when he reached them, "did any of the bakers have any problems with Lesley? Wish her bakes would . . . sink . . . or whatever bakes can do?"

Jonny had to fight hard to keep from laughing. Then he realized he had no idea what the right description was either.

What did bakes do, exactly? And what were they not supposed to do?

"It's a baking competition, Detective Watson. We all sort of hope that someone does worse than we do," Claire admitted without hesitation. "But there's no sabotage or anything like that. We may not help each other, but we don't actually want someone to do poorly. It's too terrifying a thought, because . . . what if we're next? At least, I thought that's how it was. I guess I can't be sure, can I?"

"Did anyone have problems with Lesley?" Watson asked again.

Claire shook her head. "No. Lesley was actually great about helping everyone and giving advice. And it all checked out, before you ask. Everything she said was a good tip."

Watson nodded as though committing everything to memory. "What's the prize for winning?"

"Fifty thousand pounds and an appearance in the official *Britian's Battle of the Bakers* cookbook with Alan and Dame Sophie." Claire smiled tightly. "It's a good incentive, but not huge. The winner of series six isn't anywhere to be seen, but the third-place finisher has his own bakery in Swansea and a YouTube channel that has been viral for six months running."

"So, you're saying that winning the show is not motivation enough to kill."

"Not unless someone is desperate," Claire said with a grimace. "Fifty thousand pounds doesn't go as far as it once did. I dunno." She threw her hands up. "I've never understood why anybody kills anybody else."

DS Watson heaved a massive sigh. "Neither have I. And I really do hope that I'm wrong about this."

"But you don't think you are," Jonny stated, no hint of a question.

Watson shook his head. "I really don't, sir. I find accidental death a too-convenient assumption, and too many questions remain."

"You said you wanted our help, DS Watson," Claire suddenly commented. "Let's talk after you all have interviewed everyone and gotten alibis from those who have them. Jonny says it could have a connection to the estate, so he'll get you the names of everyone there and make sure they're available to interview. Then we can meet and get everything together, see what pops up. Will that still be considered tying up loose ends for you?"

"Yes, if I don't ask too many questions of the bakers and crew. Since I have to tread carefully about what I ask, I expect they'll have loose alibis, but it will be a start."

Jonny stared at Claire, half in shock and half impressed.

For all her claims of never solving a murder or a crime, she was certainly acting like she could.

He smiled at her. Couldn't help himself. She was unpredictable, this baker, but she was an interesting unpredictable.

She raised a brow at him, a feat that not many faces could accomplish in truth, and Jonny felt his smile fade.

Right. She was pulling him in on this as well. He was going to have to join her in these deliberations with the detective and attempt to solve this crime with them.

Brilliant.

"Um . . ." He scratched the back of his head. "My cousin was up last weekend, and she's coming up this one as well. She wasn't here last night, but she hung around the crew and such when she was here, so she might be able to give us some insight."

Trixie? That was his offer to help? Trixie had been hunting for Alan the entire time she had been with the crew. What could she possibly know?

"Excellent, my lord," Watson said with a nod. "Thank you both. I'll do what I can on my end under the radar and let you know what I find when I can. I doubt it would earn me a demotion to keep going, but it would certainly land me in hot water with my superiors. Wasting resources and all that. Of course, once we prove ourselves, it won't be a waste at all, will it?" He turned and ambled over to some of the uniformed officers.

"Your cousin, Jonny? Really?"

He gave Claire a sheepish smile. "I needed to say something after you turned detective there. I am way too foggy for brilliant ideas, so until you clue me in on this game of yours,

I'm going to continue to look stupid by comparison. Which is fine, but maybe you can help me look less stupid than I feel?"

Claire managed a smile, maybe some silent laughter by the way her shoulders shook. "I have no game in mind, Jonny. I basically told the detective to do what I've read in books and seen done on *Miss Marple* and the like. If he's going to pull us in, at least we can be brains. Your words, not mine."

"I hate my words," Jonny groaned. "Brains are overrated."

"Oh, no, Viscount Brains," Claire told him, coming to him and looking very intimidating for someone shorter than he was. She held up a warning finger, her petite jaw set. "You're in on this, too. I'll be baking half of the time we're doing this, so you'll have to pick up the slack. I can't split my brain that many ways."

Jonny gripped the back of his neck, more playacting now than anything else. "I think you can. You're a baker, after all. You've made it onto the show, so you've gotta be pretty good. Pretty organized. I don't think you need me at all."

Claire huffed, not falling for his act. "If you want me to stick around the show long enough to help solve things, I'm going to need all the help I can get. The good baking keeps me here, not the case."

"Yeah, but you're only delivering mediocrity, right? Your words, not mine." He frowned in consideration. "How are you going to convince them to let you stay? You're gonna have to do a lot better than mediocrity."

"I will bake like my life depends on it," Claire vowed with a smile. Then the smile faded, and she looked into the now mostly empty pavilion. "After all, it just might."

CHAPTER 9

"I've never heard of *mille-feuille*, Charlie. Have you?"

"No, Lindsay, never. Sounds like a rash."

"Well, you do need cream for both."

Charlie looked at the camera with an open-mouthed grin, waiting for some sort of drumroll and cymbal crash, which wasn't going to happen.

Claire shook her head as the show hosts filmed their bit, grateful that they weren't by her station to distract her. She was only on her fourth turn of the dough for her mille-feuille, and she had to do two more. At least while the dough was chilling before the next two turns, she could work on her filling and toppings.

The show had provided them with historical iceboxes that resembled rudimentary coolers for chilling purposes, but rules were rules: No use of standard refrigerators and regular ovens, as well as only using pre-1900 ingredients. No amount of practicing had prepared Claire for the stress, and as soon as the timer started and cameras were rolling, it was like she forgot everything she had ever known about baking.

Not good.

Her clear and concise typed instructions were all she had to go on, and so long as she heard her nan's stern but loving voice in her mind as she read them, she felt some sort of anchor amid the madness.

"Done," she muttered to herself, wrapping the dough back into muslin cloth and taking it over to her assigned icebox.

She groaned as she saw the hosts and judges coming to her station, cameras in tow. The instructions for these moments were clear as well: Keep it brief, act confident, smile, and accept advice, even if you don't heed it.

Claire was not an actor; she hoped to be a baker. And if that came true, no one was going to stand over her shoulder and watch her make items.

"Hello, Claire," Alan greeted in his gravely showtime brogue. "What are you planning for your mille-feuille?"

"I was looking into popular flavors of the Victorian era," Claire recited, just as she'd practiced in the mirror last night, "and I decided to use lemon and raspberry. So my pastry cream has lemon zest and a bit of lemon juice, and then I will layer fresh raspberries between stripes of cream between the pastry layers."

"How are you making the pastry?" Alan pressed.

Claire swallowed, suddenly nervous. "Full puff. I found that it layers better than rough puff."

Alan gave her a nod of consideration. "Takes longer too."

"Are you concerned about the combination of two tart flavors?" Dame Sophie asked in a prim, almost trilling voice. "It can be quite a collision if you are not careful."

Claire nodded. "I tried a number of combinations, and this cream should have enough sweetness to counter the lemon. And fresh raspberries, I find, gave a better mouthfeel than freeze-dried or using an essence in the cream itself."

Lindsay leaned on the counter, her expression playful. "Tell me about the chocolate, Claire. C'mon, tell me you're using good chocolate."

"Of course I am," Claire told her with a laugh. "I'm doing a dark chocolate icing and marbling with the vanilla icing, instead of the other way around."

"Daring, Claire," Charlie praised, smiling in his usual would-be devilish way. "Turning history on its head, innit?"

Claire made a show of exhaling. "I'm going to try, Charlie, and hope not to offend history or the judges in the process."

"Good luck, Claire," Sophie told her with a polite nod, while Alan only knocked his knuckles on the counter.

Once they were away, Claire let herself breathe and shook her head to refocus on her cream filling. She'd been honest about her many trials of flavor combinations, and Mrs. Comer had been very generous in letting her spend extra time in the kitchen than what was originally slated. Claire would have loved to have someone other than herself to test each flavor, but with the only people in the inn being fellow bakers and Mrs. Comer, it just wasn't feasible. The other bakers weren't supposed to know what she was doing ahead of time, just as she had no idea what they would be doing.

It wasn't a perfect system, as they usually had some idea just by living under the same roof, but it worked well enough.

Dr. Adams, as the designated authenticity expert, came over to her station to look over her ingredients. She was supposed to be ignored, but it was impossible to completely ignore someone who was examining everything you were using to make sure you weren't cheating. She made some soft sounds of ambivalent consideration and walked away without a word. Which, Claire supposed, was the best she could get.

Claire poured a third of her allotted cream into a bowl, then went to work on separating several egg yolks from the whites, adding the yolks to the cream and mixing thoroughly. Adding cornstarch—and feeling grateful cornstarch was invented before 1900—she stirred the entire mixture together before setting it aside. Next, she added the rest of her cream to the saucepan on the stove, followed by sugar, lemon juice, and the rind of three lemons, and whisked until the sugar dissolved.

There was something rather blissfully mindless about the task. A moment to breathe, a bit of ASMR, a simple action that only required observation. After being questioned so intently about her impending creation, she needed this moment of decompression, and it wouldn't impact her timing or process one bit.

Lovely.

When the sugar was dissolved, she let the entire mixture come to a gentle boil, which made her think of all the times she had called her nan to ask her how milky consistencies were supposed to boil without ruining. Her nan had always taken time for those calls, and never once made Claire feel silly for needing to ask.

Her timer dinged, and Claire reached for the slotted spoon, dipping it into the mixture on the stove to remove the lemon rinds. Then, with the most intense concentration yet, she slowly poured the egg mixture into the pot on the stove while consistently mixing. She had curdled this cream twice in her practices, and she could not afford to do so now.

"Slowly," she murmured aloud. "Slowly . . ."

There was an easier way to make pastry cream, she reminded herself. She could have saved herself all this trouble. But no, she wanted to go the entire way, as it was the better version of the cream she wanted to use.

Stupid baking hubris.

When her mixture began to thicken, with no sign of curdling, she removed it from the heat and poured the entire thing into a bowl. Were she doing this at home, she would have put cling film over the bowl to prevent a skin from forming on the cream. But cling film did not exist before 1900, so a muslin hand towel it was.

Then the mixture went into the icebox, and Claire returned to her baking station to check her list, exhaling in satisfaction as she ticked off the cream steps.

She glanced around, ready to pull her dough out for the fifth set of folds, and got a brief jolt at seeing Jonny leaning against the entrance of the pavilion, well out of the way of any cameras. He seemed to not be looking at anything in particular, but Claire had heard him say before that he had no interest in the show or in baking. What would bring him down here, then?

His eyes immediately darted over to her, and he did not seem surprised to be spotted. Or even bothered, really. He gestured to her, mouthing something she couldn't make out. *Can I come over*, maybe?

She checked the positions of the cameras, then nodded, hoping that was, in fact, what he had asked. Sure enough, he pushed off the wall and came over to her.

"Stay far enough away that it's clear you aren't helping," Claire instructed in a low voice. "Maybe on the opposite side of the station."

"Can do," he replied simply. "I'll even follow suit with the others just to cover me."

Claire looked up at him as she moved to her icebox. "Cover you for what?"

Jonny shrugged. "Checking in on you, of course."

Claire tripped slightly, glancing down to check for cords or a bump in the fake carpet beneath their feet. Of course, there was nothing, but she could swear something had caused her to stumble.

"I'm fine," she ground out. "Just baking." She dusted her countertop with flour and unwrapped her dough, placing it on the surface. She grabbed her rolling pin, flouring that as well.

"Why do you flour both?" Jonny asked as she began to roll the dough.

"Stops the sticking."

"Why is sticking bad?"

"Because it is."

"How many more times do you have to do this?"

"One, after this."

"How annoyed am I making you?"

"I'm not annoyed." She set the rolling pin aside and turned the dough before rolling it again. "Just focused. Did you need something?"

Jonny gave a small scoff, but she didn't dare look up to check his expression. "Need. No, I don't need anything. I'm just updating you."

"Update away." Claire continued rolling out her dough, keeping her lines as straight as she did when she hoovered her carpet at home. It was a strange thought to have while baking, but there was something just as comforting in seeing the lines in her dough as there was in seeing the lines in the carpet.

Also she couldn't bear to look Jonny in the face when she was feeling frantic and covered in flour.

"Can you listen and successfully roll at the same time?"

"Yep. And I can think too. Don't freak out."

He whistled as though impressed. "Look at you. Right, so Watson came by and said we should have the autopsy results by tonight. His bosses think neat and tidy, but they aren't going to push for detail like he is. So far, all alibis are checking out, but there are five or six who have no alibi. He's having Lesley's scarf analyzed for foreign fibers, just in case."

Claire stopped rolling and looked up at him with a frown as she folded her dough. "Just in case what?"

"Well, that bit he didn't tell me," he admitted, tilting his head as she continued her absentminded folding and patting. "He said something about hiding something with it, and I figured he could tell me when it pans out."

Grabbing her muslin, Claire spread it out and moved her dough onto the surface. "Fair enough. What are the odds that this is local?"

"Not much," Jonny replied as he followed her to the icebox. "Benji wasn't too out of line when he mentioned the ghost the other day. Loads of locals believe that the place is haunted and are too scared to even come to the estate, but we've never had actual issues before."

Claire closed the icebox, turning to face him. "So you definitely think it's something to do with the show."

Jonny twisted his mouth in thought. "I do."

"Okay." Claire returned to her station, pulling the bowl of raspberries close and beginning to pluck out the best ones. "Strange timing for anyone to have done it, though. I mean, the mill has been here for ages. It's not some special anniversary coming up, is it?"

"Nope, nothing monumental." Jonny heaved a sigh and looked over at the other stations. "I better move or people will ask questions. You don't need questions."

Claire gave him a clipped nod, her mind running through her list of tasks for the mille-feuille, despite having instructions before her. "Nope. Plenty of those already."

"About me?"

She looked up at him in surprise. "Why would I be getting questions about you?"

Jonny immediately shook his head. "No, right. Sorry. Train of thought on the wrong tracks. Will you be free to come by tonight? For DS Watson's update, I mean."

"Should be," Claire told him with a quick look around. "Tomorrow is Occasion Bake, but I think I've got that squared away. Got a time?"

"Not yet. DS Watson will tell us."

"Fair enough. Are all your people cleared?"

"I think so, but he hasn't specifically said. Maybe a grounds worker or two are disgruntled, who knows?"

"Which makes it the show. And quite possibly a baker." Claire smiled tightly. "Do you know how many implements of death there are in this place, Jonny?"

"I don't—"

"Twenty-nine. More, if Anthony's stupid healthy herbs turn out to be something that could kill someone if prepared incorrectly. Has Dr. Adams checked to see if his grass is actually historically appropriate? Is it necessary to have so many hefty historical pots and pans hanging everywhere? Any one of them could easily be taken down and swung into my head,

THE CRIME BRÛLÉE BAKE OFF

in case someone decides the cleaver they're using on their nuts isn't good enough. Do you know what baking is distracting me from today, Viscount Colburn?"

"Erm—"

"I'll tell you," Claire went on, knowing full well she was panic rambling and half-hating herself for it. The other half was relieved to get it out. "It is distracting me from the very clear and terrifying fact that this pavilion is a tent of death!"

Jonny cleared his throat. "Eyes up here, Miss Walker."

Like an obedient student, Claire looked at him, her heart flying in its beats that had nothing to do with his attractiveness.

His eyes were steady, his expression calm. "No one is going to be foolish enough to attack anyone with this many people around. If you're that freaked, don't eat or drink anything anyone else gives you. But remember that a lot of thought went into the attack on Lesley. Enough that Watson says murder, while his superiors say accident, and other people think it's the ghost. So I don't think whoever did this is going to act on impulse, especially with cameras around. Now, back to baking. Not to distract you, but because that's what you're here for, right?"

"Right," Claire echoed, nodding her head quickly. "Right. No death, just baking." She blinked hard. "We need a code word for when we need to talk the case. Or when I'm freaking out about it, as it were. If I say 'Chelsea buns' will that clue you in?"

"Yep, got it." Jonny tapped her counter again. "I'll see you tonight. Good luck."

Claire gave him another tight smile, dipping her chin once as she returned her attention to her work. It would have been easier to not be thinking about a murder while she was trying to make the best mille-feuille of her entire life, but there wasn't anything to be done about that. If DS Watson didn't think he was up to solving the case on his own and wanted Claire and Jonny to help him, who was she to argue? It made no sense to her, but maybe she could help with the problem-solving or thinking through issues.

She had always been a thinker—her dad had joked that maybe they had taken the wrong baby home from the hospital—but it had served her well in her life.

The only real question she had was how much of a distraction would the murder case be? It was unfair to Lesley that they were doing this, and a rather shady form of justice as far as an investigation went, but Claire was under contract to the show and, as such, had no recourse for leaving if they were not shutting down. Without a complicated medical issue appearing, she had to stay.

They all did.

So she was trapped here in Oxfordshire in this tiny town with a murderer on the loose, and somehow, she was supposed to help the police uncover them.

And bake mille-feuille in the meantime.

No pressure.

CHAPTER 10

How in the world was Jonny supposed to help solve a murder? He was an investment banker, for heaven's sake, and a viscount trying to revitalize his estate. The smartest thing he had ever done was choose George Linley and Clive Franklin as study partners for their GCSEs, and he would stand by that statement until his dying day.

His curiosity, on the other hand, wanted to be smack-dab in the center of the whole thing to figure out the identity of the killer like some secret detective who had spent his life in the wrong career. Never mind that he barely managed word puzzles and sudoku some days and had never successfully completed the Friday crossword in *The Guardian*. But somehow, some portion of his brain actually thought he would be useful to the investigation.

Delusional fool.

"Are you providing dinner tonight?"

Jonny glanced up from his desk to frown at his sister in the doorway of his office. "No, I wasn't planning on it. It's just an update from DS Watson, not an invitation to dine."

Gabi leaned against the doorway, folding her arms. "Trixie

will be coming over from Holding Cottage, and Claire will be dropped off by one of the cars. You sure you don't want to have a meal?"

"What are you trying to say?" Jonny asked, leaning back in his chair. "That somehow learning the details of an investigation will make us hungry?"

"No, you goose, that you might want to be polite to both our cousin and an adorable baker whom I was very impressed by and who actually found the dead body on our estate." She gestured sharply with an irritated flick of her hand, palm up, a very "isn't that obvious" movement that his younger sister seemed to be born with. "Sandwiches, at least."

Jonny did his sister the courtesy of rolling his eyes in a much-practiced way. "Fine, tell Mrs. Clyde to provide something simple after the meeting. I don't care what it is, but if you've suddenly developed an interest in being the hostess of Blackfirth for the evening, be my guest." He swiveled his chair from side to side for a moment. "Why's Trixie coming over? I knew she was up here, but not . . ." He paused and gave Gabi a look. "You told her there would be an update."

Gabi shrugged her slender shoulders. "I might have done. It's a family matter! She ought to be informed!"

"We could tell her after we know," Jonny pointed out. "Honestly, we should keep things as quiet as possible. Trixie can't keep secrets."

"You think she's going to tell her kids?" Gabi retorted. "Or Darrin?"

"Darrin is a vault. I don't care if he knows." Jonny drummed his fingers on the armrests of his chair. "Honestly, she should go back home, with what's going on here. Security on the set is much tighter than it was last week."

Gabi brushed that off. "Oh, let her stay a bit. She'll get her fill of the baking and stalking Alan Gables and then head back home without much fuss. With the added security, she's arguably safer here now than before."

"I don't know about that," Jonny grumbled. "Depends on what really happened to Lesley, doesn't it?" He sat forward, resting his forearms on the desk, and gave her a serious look. "Don't go out alone, Gabs. At all. Light or dark out. Please."

She returned his instructions with a slight smile. "Can do. I'm working from here for now anyway, so there's no reason to go out unless a client wants to see animation proofs in person or something. And I have no problem skipping that for now."

"Thanks." He smiled, then looked at his watch. "Well, Watson should be here any minute, so I might as well head down." He pushed back from the desk and started around it, putting his hand on Gabi's arm as he passed. "Come on in whenever you want, or not at all if you don't want."

"I'll be there," Gabi assured him. "I'll just pop down to Mrs. Clyde first. Sandwiches, and all." She patted his shoulder then headed for the back stairs that led down to the kitchen, where Mrs. Clyde kept her office.

Jonny didn't mind providing dinner, really. It just seemed unnecessary. And, considering Claire was joining them, presumptuous. Not that he wouldn't enjoy having her join them for dinner at any given time. He'd welcome it. Conversation with her was always interesting, no matter the topic.

But what sort of conversation could they have over dinner after hearing an update about a murder investigation? Did Gabi think that they could somehow manage to ignore a proverbial elephant of that size and complexity over sandwiches? Mrs. Clyde was good, but she did not possess magical powers.

"My lord," Clyde greeted as soon as Jonny set foot on the ground floor. "Miss Walker and DS Watson are in the sitting room."

Jonny twisted his mouth in disappointment that he hadn't been just a few minutes earlier in coming down, missing an opportunity to spend some time alone with Claire, but that was neither here nor there. "And Trixie?"

Clyde shook his head. "Not yet, sir."

"Well, she and Gabi can come into the meeting, if they wish to. Just so you're aware."

"Very good, sir."

Jonny nodded once and moved to the sitting room with quick strides, hating that his guests had been waiting on him, even briefly. That wasn't the sort of impression he liked to give to anyone, be it in his career or in his home, and at a time like this . . .

Well, he needed impressions of him to be something beyond reproach at the moment.

"Detective Watson," he greeted as he entered the room. "Sorry to keep you waiting. Miss Walker."

Claire nodded in acknowledgment, looking nearly as focused as when he had seen her earlier in the day. She had changed out of her baking clothes, which, as he understood it, she had to wear for the purposes of the filming. For whatever reason, the bakers were supposed to wear the same clothing for all tapings of the show. Something about continuity, which probably meant the show could use any reaction shots they got from any taping at any time.

Maybe that made sense for the film industry, but Jonny wasn't in film.

He never wanted to be.

Still, Claire looked nice. Flannel suited her, and flannel did not suit everyone.

Why did he know that? Why had it even registered at any point that flannel did not suit everyone?

"How goes the investigation?" Jonny asked, taking a seat and mentally wincing at how much he sounded like his father.

DS Watson shoved his hands into his pockets, his suit coat parting from his girth slightly as he did so. "The official investigation, or the unofficial one?" He shrugged slowly. "It's complicated."

Jonny frowned and looked at Claire in confusion, then back at DS Watson for confirmation. "What's so complicated?"

Claire sat forward in her seat. "What did the results of the autopsy show?"

DS Watson pulled some folded papers from inside of his suit jacket. "Well, it appears that even the medical examiner is a trifle confused. There was water in the lungs, but not a great deal. That doesn't necessarily mean the victim didn't drown, but it is suspicious. There was something called puh-tee-kee-ahl hemorrhaging around the eyes and on the face, and bruising in the internal lining of the throat, which indicates strangulation. The pattern of bruising on the neck also supports strangulation, but it doesn't match with what one would find if a silk scarf had been used as the ligature."

Jonny exhaled, irritated and unsurprised. "So you were right."

"Yes, as it happens," Watson admitted as he scanned the papers. "But we have no proof as to what the actual ligature would have been. The scarf was most certainly involved, but something else was applying the pressure on top of it. And then there's the complication that the hyoid bone and the thyroid cartilage were broken. The cricoid bone, which is somewhere in there, I suppose, is intact, which could suggest suicide, but considering everything else, the ME does not believe that is a possibility."

"I suppose that's a good one to rule out," Claire mused slowly.

Watson gave her a nod, one corner of his mouth curving slightly. "Quite. At any rate, she has decided that the official cause of death is strangulation. Everything else is overkill. There was also a large contusion to the head, but it was not the cause of death, nor did it lead to it." He folded the papers and tucked them back inside his jacket pocket before rubbing at his head.

Jonny whistled low. "Complicated is right."

"And I cannot ask many questions," Watson reminded them with a tight smile. "My superiors are content to believe that Ms. Kemble slipped while out, hit her head on a rock, fell into the brook, and floated unconscious to the waterwheel, where the ends of her scarf were caught up and . . ." He trailed off, gesturing for them to continue the train of thought in their own minds.

"It's not implausible," Jonny had to admit with a wince.

"No, just highly convenient." Watson reached into the other side of his jacket and pulled out another sheet of paper. "We don't have good alibis for Anthony Wright, Benjamin Andrews-Lee, Hattie Barnes, Michael Stone, Grant Sybil, and Alice Young—all from the show. From the estate, just Fred McElroy and David Jeffs." He looked up at Jonny. "Any specific people you'd like to suggest I look at more closely?"

Jonny shook his head and looked at Claire for help. "I have no idea."

THE CRIME BRÛLÉE BAKE OFF

Claire was still looking at Watson closely. "There's something you're not saying. What is it?" she asked him, folding her hands over a knee.

"I don't understand why one of the bakers was killed," Watson said with a deep furrow to his brows. "I can pretend to understand making the murder mirror that of the late viscountess in a way, given it took place on the estate, but why now? We've never had trouble with locals and the estate. On the contrary, we're all quite proud of Blackfirth and try to make ourselves known for more than what happened here all those centuries ago."

Jonny nodded thoughtfully, seeing clearly the direction of the detective's idea. "You think it's unlikely that someone in the town did this. You think we should focus on the show."

Watson gave him a quick look. "I hesitate to narrow complete focus just yet, but . . ." He turned to Claire. "Miss Walker, I think your part in this investigation might need to be larger. I think we may need you to watch for anything suspicious that takes place in the pavilion that we might not be seeing, and let us know about any conversations that your fellow bakers are having."

"I don't know if I can do that," Claire admitted, wrinkling her nose. "I tend to avoid and ignore drama, not force myself into the middle of it."

"I understand," DS Watson told her, his smile seeming genuine enough. "But if we're to make any headway in this investigation, it might be necessary. Might be our best option, in fact."

Jonny looked at Claire, seeing the hesitation and indecision warring across her features. She wasn't great at hiding her emotions, he was learning, which could work against her if she was to be spying, of sorts, on her friends and competitors. But Watson was probably right. This looked like their best option, and it could help the case find its proper direction. Or any real direction, for that matter.

He saw Claire's brow clear and knew she had made up her mind. In fact, he knew exactly what she was going to say, and he had to force himself not to smile in anticipation.

"All right," Claire announced in a firm tone. "I'll do it. We have another bake tomorrow, and I'll keep my eyes open for anything unusual."

"Considering how many potential weapons you spotted this morning, I don't doubt it," Jonny teased, raising a brow at her.

Her cheeks colored as she smiled, dimples appearing in each cheek. "Yes, well, I was nervous this morning, and the murder was fresh in the mind. I will be better tomorrow."

Watson all-out beamed. "That's the ticket, Miss Walker. Right then, I'll pass on a meal this evening, my lord, but with thanks. More to uncover, more to learn." He pushed to his feet and headed for the door, nodding at Gabi and Trixie, who were entering.

Gabi watched Watson go, then glared at Jonny. "How did you scare off the detective before I managed to get in here?"

Jonny rolled his eyes and stood up, more to give his cousin a hug than anything else. "He gave us his update, and decided there was work to be done. So the two of you will just have to stick with interrogating your very own baking contestant on that show you love." He turned to give Claire a teasing look, enjoying her shocked expression.

It was cruel, really, turning them on Claire without warning, but it was better they talk about baking than hear details of a murder investigation. And he suspected Claire would enjoy a discussion of baking more than plotting how to spy on the other bakers.

"Ah, yes," Gabi said with the sort of devious enthusiasm that made Jonny think she would have rubbed her hands together if she'd had less decorum. "Are you up for some questioning, Claire? Oh, this is our cousin Trixie, by the way. She's a big fan of the show, like me. And if I know her, she's dying inside right now."

Trixie's squeak was all the evidence needed for Claire's shock to fade into a rather bemused smile that Jonny found very fetching.

"Of course," Claire said. "I could talk about baking all day long."

The girls dashed to sit near her like kids in a candy shop. "How did baking go today?" Gabi demanded.

"Fine, actually," Claire admitted with a laugh. "It was a Classic Bake, and the theme today and tomorrow is a Victorian ball. My pastry baked well and had all the layers I wanted, and the judges really liked my fillings."

"What did you do?" Trixie asked her, grinning like a fool as her feet seemed to dance against the rug. "I mean, the entire thing. What was the bake?"

Claire returned her smile. "I did a mille-feuille today, with lemon and raspberry as my flavors. Dark chocolate with vanilla marbling on top."

"Mmm," Trixie moaned appreciatively. "And did you get an Alan smile for it?"

"This close," Claire said, holding her thumb and index fingers apart just the slightest bit. "He did hum as he ate it, so if that counts—"

"It counts," Gabi and Trixie said together, including matching nods.

Jonny leaned against the wingback chair near him, watching the interaction with some delight. He could see the relief on Claire's face as her hope was reinforced by the girls, and that was even more entertaining for him. What would they know about baking or the show in general? What could their reassurance possibly be worth?

But he could see how much it did mean, and suddenly he wanted to know more about the demands being placed upon her. About what the show was like for her. About the bakes, even. He wanted to be able to reassure her as well, if she'd let him.

Which meant he'd have to learn what in the world a mille-feuille was, but that was beside the point.

"Tomorrow is the Occasion Bake," Claire was saying, "and there will be a lot to do, but I'm more comfortable now that I've gotten a good reaction. Last week was mediocre, so . . ."

Jonny scoffed to himself, only to have all the ladies look at him in surprise. He smiled, holding up a semi-apologetic hand.

"Can you tell us what you'll do?" Trixie asked, leaning forward and clasping her hands in front of her. "Like, how grand are we talking?"

Claire wet her lips, one of her brows quirking. "Well, there's a three-tiered cake, if I can make it stand. Then there are a few meringues, two different tartlets, and four kinds of jellies."

"Are you serious?" Gabi's blue eyes went wide. "That's so intense! Are you going to have time?"

Claire only shrugged. "It worked yesterday within the time, so fingers crossed."

"You feel good about it?" Trixie pressed. "You're not doing any pastry after a pastry win today?"

"Trix," Jonny murmured, clearing his throat. "She's under enough stress from the show itself. Leave her alone. She's got this. She'll be fine."

Trixie frowned at him. "I know that. I'm just checking in with her. Sheesh, bossy . . ."

Claire's eyes flicked toward him with her own small smile, and he felt his heart lurch sideways against his ribs.

Oddly uncomfortable, that.

Returning her attention to Trixie, Claire nodded. "I don't want to rely on the bake before, good or bad, when it comes to Occasion Bake if I don't have to. I think it helps to show them different skills, you know?"

"Oh, absolutely," Trixie gushed, and Jonny rolled his eyes, sensing what might be coming. "In fact, in series seven . . ."

CHAPTER 11

Kerri had been eliminated. It wasn't that big of a surprise. She had been a mess since Lesley's death, and her bakes had shown it. Still, it was hard to see her sitting around without energy, since she couldn't leave. One of the new perks of continuing the shoot was that all the bakers had to stay until filming was complete, just to make sure no word of the "incident" made it out.

That was what the production team was calling it now. The Incident.

Claire was safe for another week, which seemed amazing. She had been quite proud of her Occasion Bake, and Dame Sophie had even gone so far as to say that Claire might be making her way up to the front of the pack. Of course, she had been taking a second mouthful of Claire's gently spiced Savoy cake, which had indeed managed to reach three tiers, as she'd wanted.

Dame Sophie was a sucker for a structurally sound and still moist cake. Everybody knew that.

Claire's jellies had worked out, her meringues hadn't cracked, and her tartlets had avoided being too thick or in any way soggy. She really couldn't have wished for anything else.

But she was most certainly not the front-runner of the group. That belonged to either Denis or Mathias. What they managed to accomplish in the same time frame as the rest of them was absolutely incomprehensible. Denis had a knack for flavor combinations that Claire could only dream of, and Mathias was earning a reputation as king of pastry among the crew.

And Freya had stunned everyone with the molded jellies she had managed, both in structure and in flavor.

Sighing to herself, Claire pulled on a pair of warm socks and padded down to the great room of the inn where she knew the others would be sitting. They weren't really going out in the evenings anymore, what with the risks and the ghost rumors and all, so most evenings were spent in their rooms or together in the great room.

They weren't quite the baking family she had pictured yet, but they were at least friendly and open, and she would take that for now.

"It's just reckless," Benji was shouting as she entered the room. "Keeping the show going after what happened to Lesley. It's like they don't even care."

Denis gave the younger man a scolding look. "Calm down. They've explained why. Plus, we're escorted everywhere. The town is a small one, and it's basically shut down. What more do you want them to do?"

"Maybe not keep us baking at a haunted house?" Benji argued, not tempering his tone at all. "Haven't you all heard about the ghost at the mill? If Lesley hadn't died, someone else probably would have. Old Lady Colburn obviously doesn't like people so close to her place of death, and I ain't going into those kitchens again unless we're shooting."

"I saw something at the kitchens," Kerri announced, her eyes wide. "Something glowing. It moved past the mill door as I walked by. Freaked me out and I ran all the way here."

Everyone in the room stared at her in shock.

"When . . . when was this?" Freya asked.

"Yesterday." Kerri nodded almost frantically. "I thought it was Lesley at first, come back to give me a chance to . . . Well, I hoped it was her; I was so cross with her, and I have to apologize." Her voice broke into a half hiccup, her lip quivering.

Claire tsked sympathetically as she sat down next to Freya on the sofa. "Oh, Kerri . . ."

"Who was it?" Freya demanded, curled up tightly in a ball. "If it wasn't the ghost of Lesley, who was it?"

"Lady Colburn, I told ya," Benji insisted harshly. "She haunts the place, make no mistake. Kerri, did she have long skirts and a forlorn expression?"

"I didn't stay long enough to see her face," Kerri said with a shudder. "But she was definitely wearing a long gown."

Benji gave them all an utterly superior look. "See? We'll all be dead by the end of this, mark my words."

"Benjamin Andrews-Lee, you stop that nonsense," Mrs. Comer instructed with the firmness of a hospital matron as she entered with a tray of mugs. She set down the tray on the nearest end table, glaring at Benji. "You of all people shouldn't be encouraging this scurrilous ghost talk. As if ghosts could cause anyone to die, even if they did exist. That attitude of yours wants setting right, always has done."

"Oh, shove off, Miz Comer," Benji shot back harshly. "You ain't me mum."

Mrs. Comer was not remotely cowed. "No, I am not. So you will not speak to me the way you do her. I don't care if you're a great baker on this show, you're still the scamp from Murray Street who never minded his temper." She harrumphed and shook her head, walking away while muttering under her breath.

No one said a word for a long moment, nor did anyone move for the steaming mugs. Mrs. Comer had only ever been congenial and practically bubbly since they'd arrived, so the sudden shift in her temperament seemed out of character. Benji ran his mouth from time to time, and his temper was short, but he wasn't a bad sort. Then again, Mrs. Comer almost certainly knew him better than the rest of them. He was a local and so was she.

"Crazy woman," Benji muttered. "Always had it in for me. Ever since I tried to date her daughter in secondary school."

"I wouldn't let you near my daughter either," Mathias offered with a wry smile. "If I had one. Or Anthony, for that matter. With the way you two look, the girl would lose her head and her sense. Freya, don't get any ideas. Denis and I will be your dads here, and you're not going anywhere with them."

"Absolutely!" Denis cried out, laughing heartily. "If either of you boys come near her, you'll find a grand old shotgun in your face. I do have daughters, and I've done it before."

Benji rolled his eyes but seemed to have cooled down. "I'm not coming for Freya. No offense, Freya."

Freya shook her head. "None taken. Both of you are too old for me anyway." She sighed, staring into the fire, and leaned her head against Claire's shoulder. "I miss Lesley. I'm sure she'd have jumped in to be my auntie."

"Oh, she totes would have," Anthony pointed out from

the floor where he was holding a perfect plank position. "She'd have threatened us with more than a shotgun."

Benji smiled a little. "Yeah, and probably would've whacked me over the head with a newspaper for how I spoke to Miz Comer."

"Well, Lesley couldn't have been the intended target," Freya said in a low voice. "She was the nicest person. Nobody would want to kill her."

Claire willed herself to not join in the discussion in any way that would raise fear or increase speculation. There was no benefit in conversations like this, not when they were already under so much stress from the show itself. Why give voice to the worries and anxieties that probably lived in all of them? They didn't need the boost into the realms of terror.

"One question troubles me," Denis ventured with a frown, running his hand into his wild salt-and-pepper curls. "Have there been other suspicious deaths on the estate we should know about? Or just the one?"

"Just the one," Benji answered, sliding down to the floor to hold Anthony's feet as he began to do sit-ups. "Well, two, now."

"There you go, then," Anthony panted between reps. "One and done."

Benji shook his head. "I doubt it. Old Lady Colburn, man. They riled her ghost. The show should have stopped. It's only a matter of time before she gets another one of us."

"Lovely," Claire muttered before she could stop herself. "Thanks for that."

"I'm just saying," Benji protested.

Freya exhaled in irritation. "Well, stop saying! I'm already freaked and not going out after dark; I don't need you making me unable to sleep in my own bed."

Benji rolled his eyes and looked away, muttering under his breath as Kerri shook her head and left the room.

"Ignore him," Claire murmured to Freya. "He's probably got cabin fever along with everything else. And he had bad bakes, so stress . . ." She widened her eyes meaningfully, holding her hand out, palm down, and then shaking it to show unsteadiness.

Freya nodded against her shoulder, stifling a laugh in her sleeve.

Anthony continued to do his sit-ups, his forehead creasing as he moved, though that could have been either with thought or with effort. He laid down on his back and looked beyond Benji toward Mathias. "What do you think, Poirot?"

Mathias continued reading, turning a page without paying them any attention.

Anthony frowned, then looked at the rest of them. "Come on, I'm not the only one that's seeing that, right?" He sat up and mimed a grand mustache.

Claire clapped a hand over her mouth to keep from bursting out laughing. How had she never seen that before? Apart from not having a particularly thick Belgian accent, Mathias was certainly a walking impression of the famed Belgian detective, Hercule Poirot. Agatha Christie herself couldn't have picked a better example.

Benji snorted a laugh, watching the oblivious Mathias continue reading. "Oy! Poirot!"

Still nothing.

Denis took pity on their fellow baker. "Mathias."

"Hmm?"

"They're calling you Poirot."

Mathias looked up from his book, glancing over. "They're what?" His eyes darted from face to face, comprehension slowly dawning. "Poirot? Seriously?"

Anthony gestured a full mustache again. "Seriously, mate. You should be solving this ghost mystery."

With a short exhale, Mathias snapped his book shut. "Mate, I may be Belgian and have a mustache, but I've lived in Croyden for the last seven years. Other than knowing who Hercule Poirot is and seeing the movies, I've got nothing to offer up that would help. I'm an architect and a baker, nothing more and nothing less."

He nodded as though that settled things, then sat back in his chair and opened his book.

"Right then," Denis chirped in his optimistic way. "That settles that. Ghost or no ghost, we're all going to be fine. Right, Claire?"

All attention shifted to Claire, even from Mathias.

She fought the instinct to swallow dramatically.

"Me?" she asked weakly.

"You talked to the detective the other day, I saw."

"You've talked to the detective?" Freya demanded, straightening and looking at her with wide eyes. "Why didn't you say anything?"

"Does he think we are in danger?" Benji folded his arms. "Because I certainly think we are. No matter what Mrs. Comer says, there are ghosts."

Mathias cleared his throat loudly. "I don't think Denis meant for us to interrogate Claire—"

"Certainly not," Denis agreed. He did his best to make a calming gesture, though only Claire was looking at him. "Let her speak, please. Apologies, Claire. If you have something you can tell us, please do."

Something she could tell them? She couldn't tell them anything, not if she wanted to keep the integrity of the investigation.

"The last time I spoke with DS Watson," Claire began slowly, her mind spinning on possibilities, "he said something about tying up loose ends and keeping the higher-ups happy."

"No surprise there," Mathias muttered, to the nods of the rest.

Claire racked her brain for more to share, wondering how far she dared go. "He didn't give me any indication on specifics," she hedged. "It seemed pretty straightforward." She looked at Benji almost helplessly.

He didn't seem to like her answer, standing up and beginning to pace moodily.

"Benji, mate, what gives?" Anthony asked from the floor.

"This entire thing is just stupid," Benji muttered. "That stupid DS is just going to sign the papers and we're all going to die, but at least the show will go on." His hands became fists by his sides, then he stormed out of the room without another word.

"Oh, crepes," Claire breathed.

"I was thinking something a little harsher," Freya muttered.

Claire swallowed, nodding quickly. "More like meringue, then."

Freya snorted, then covered her mouth with her sleeves, her shoulders buzzing as she shook with laughter.

It was a dorky thing to say, Claire knew that full well. But she wasn't exactly thinking clearly, and somehow, the stiffness and fragility of a meringue was the only thing coming to mind.

Maybe Freya was laughing out of nerves as much as out of amusement.

Or maybe Claire really was just a dork.

They were all on edge and trying not to be. She didn't know who she could trust, and she figured the others were feeling the same confusion. This wasn't the family atmosphere she had imagined, but they were trying, in spite of it all. Some of them were more trustworthy than others, at least by appearances, but there was no saying that meant anything.

Mathias could have killed Lesley, and no one would have guessed it. Denis could have killed her, hiding a psychopathic nature beneath his congeniality. Anthony could have killed her with his supposedly healthy herbs with no one the wiser. Freya, Benji, Kerri. They all could be hiding something, and Claire, so desperate for the family feeling between them, wouldn't know.

And she was supposed to help solve this case? Had thought her fascination with mysteries and history might make her of some use? It was an even more far-fetched idea than her becoming a baker instead of maintaining the status quo of her life and sticking to the stable and respectable teaching career she had given herself.

Utterly stupid. Benji was right. They could all die here, and there wasn't anything to be done about it until the murderer was caught, if there was one. And, she had to admit, if progress was being made, it wasn't by Claire and Jonny, which left only Watson.

It was too dark for her to go out to try to talk with Jonny or DS Watson, and she didn't have phone numbers for either of them. Which meant that, unfortunately, she was going to have to stay at the inn and stew over the few facts she knew. That or ignore the inkling altogether and try to change the topic of conversation in the room.

She glanced around at the others quickly. Mathias was still reading, Denis was invested in what lay beneath his fingernails, Anthony was doing wall sits, and Freya had pulled out her phone, absorbed in something on the screen.

Stewing it was.

Faking a yawn, Claire got to her feet and headed toward her bedroom, no one making any comment as she left.

There was no reason for anyone to kill Lesley. Nothing else had gone wrong on the show. The murder had been made to resemble a historic event from the estate, but nothing problematic had occurred on the estate lately.

Claire sputtered to herself softly as she closed her bedroom door and sank onto her bed. She'd been laughing off the idea of helping with the investigation before this, so the distance between what was happening and what she knew was wide. But now she needed to close that distance for her own sanity.

She needed to actually join the investigation.

Shaking her head, Claire laid down on her bed and curled up, looking toward her window. She would help solve this case, if she could. If there was anything she could offer. If she had any insight to give.

For Lesley.

CHAPTER 12

Morning walks were becoming a habit of Jonny's, but it wasn't usual for him to go quite so far out on the estate. He'd gone all the way out to the St. Agnes chapel, where restoration work would be well underway in a few hours, and was now on his way back toward the Victoria fountain, but all of it without purpose or pace. He didn't even have particular thoughts floating about his head. He was just . . . walking.

He didn't know how else to describe what he was doing. He was quite simply moving his legs, and they took him from this place to that, sometimes over pavement, sometimes over gravel, sometimes over grass. As yet, they had not put him into water, but he wouldn't put it past his legs to venture there next.

Several topics came and went through his mind. The murder, the estate history, his sister . . . Claire . . .

To be honest, the thoughts of Claire came and went more frequently than that of the estate or his sister, but the murder did cross his mind almost as often. Nothing too great or intuitive about the case or investigation, nothing that was worth pursuing or even mentioning to DS Watson or Claire, but enough to give him some ideas about avenues to go down and possibilities he hadn't considered before. He wasn't going to become an investigator himself, not by a long shot, but he had been asked to assist.

After the fountains, he wandered to the gardens at Holding Cottage, the other family house on the estate, which was where Trixie stayed when she was visiting for more than a night. It was the house her family had spent summers in, not wanting to get too hampered by the constraints of the "big house" or feel as though they had to do everything Jonny's family did. In reality, they had all spent so much time between one house and the other that everything was familiar to all of them.

The gardens at Holding Cottage were smaller than at Blackfirth, but they were also wilder and more natural, less cultivated and pristine, and there was something refreshing about being in them. Holding Cottage had probably been designed as a dower house originally, but it had been a few generations since it had been used as such.

He found himself at the historic kitchens. Which meant he was close to the pavilion. Which meant he would soon be close to the set.

Which meant, fairly soon, Claire would be there.

Was that why his legs had walked him here?

There was no other reason for him to be at the historic kitchens. It wasn't a place he went regularly nor one that held any interest for him. It was just another part of the estate, and a part that the Historic Houses organization took care of.

Historic. All of this was historic, but not to him. It was just life, his family, his responsibility. He had never looked at anything on his estate the way Claire had looked at the mill when he had first met her.

He wasn't sure he had looked at anything the way Claire

had looked at the mill, actually. For being a teacher, she had quite a passion for history. Perhaps she ought to have been a historian like Dr. Adams instead of a teacher, though it might have been harder to find a job that would pay as quickly as teaching.

His thoughts rambled in his mind, rather like his wandering feet, and he wasn't really experiencing much of it in a lasting way.

He was just thinking, walking, and breathing. Half asleep, head pounding, life complicated.

And wanting to see Claire, though he really shouldn't.

"This is a strange place for you to be at this hour of the morning."

Jonny smiled at the sound of her voice and raised his eyes from the path to see Claire up ahead. "I'd say the same for you, but I'm not the one who has to bake today."

"Not here," Claire pointed out, gesturing at the kitchens. "This is just for presenting and judging. If there is going to be a bake there, they're saving that for something else, and they aren't talking. We're in the pavilion, just like before."

"And coming around here early is supposed to ease your nerves about what's ahead of you?" He gave her a questioning look, keeping his smile light.

Claire shrugged, however, and her smiled faded. "I was thinking about Lesley. I came over here to walk through the kitchens and think of her. She nerded out with me about them and helped me see the possibilities in each room. If I make it to another stage in the competition, and do a halfway passable job, it'll be because of her. But we can't talk about her. The show is completely writing her out after the first episode, and they might even decide to replace her. I just . . ."

She folded her arms and shook her head. "We're forgetting her."

That was a sobering thought, and he couldn't argue it. The show was so determined to avoid being shut down that they were moving right along as fast as they could.

Which meant it would be difficult for Lesley to receive any justice at all.

Perhaps ever.

"I'm sorry," Jonny confessed, starting to walk again, pleased when Claire fell into step beside him. "I had forgotten her too. Paying attention to the solving of the crime and not the victim of the crime."

"I wasn't talking about you," Claire protested as they walked. "I just meant in general."

"Well, in general, I had forgotten Lesley, too, so I am sorry for it." He exhaled heavily, then offered a small smile. "And I am sorry for your very intense questioning by Gabi and Trixie the other night. You handled it brilliantly, if it helps."

Claire looked surprised. "No, it was fine. Talking about baking was a welcome change from talking about murder. They're as invested in the show as I was before I joined. I would have asked the same questions if I'd met one of the bakers. It was a strange kind of reality check. Were you bored by it all?"

"Not really," Jonny said simply, shrugging. "The three of you were entertaining. But the investigation wasn't far from my thoughts, so I didn't sleep well. Got up early to walk out here."

Claire nodded, her head bobbing in near-perfect time with their steps. "Being outdoors with my thoughts is usually better for me than being indoors with them. At least, this morning it was." She was quiet for a moment, then looked up at him. "Do you think we'll actually solve this case?"

It was such a frank question, and a partly negative one, that Jonny was almost startled by it. Claire was a fairly optimistic person, he thought, but maybe that was what she liked to portray. Nobody could be the same thing for every minute of every day of their lives, could they?

"I don't know," he admitted. "I'd like to say yes, but until we have more information, I'm not sure we can. I'm not really an optimist, and considering there is no experience with murder solving in Blackfirth . . ."

"Maybe Watson is an optimist?" Claire offered. "Someone ought to be, surely."

"Probably. The more I think about it, the more doubts I have, the more information I want, and the more interviews I want to sit in on. I don't know the first thing about solving a crime." He exhaled in irritation. "Why are there always more questions than answers the further on we get?"

"Don't know," Claire quipped though her tone was soft rather than playful. "It's my first murder."

Jonny snorted a laugh, covering his mouth and nose quickly. He hadn't expected such a frank answer, let alone one without a nudge or a jab to his side in joking. But the simplicity of the answer, the ridiculousness of their involvement, and the heaviness of something as severe as solving a murder all prompted a bizarre form of mirth.

Dark humor, he supposed.

He caught Claire's smile before it vanished completely, which made him feel better about laughing at what could have been an inappropriate time.

"Mine too," he eventually managed to add, keeping his tone as serious as he could manage. "And, apparently, DS Watson's as well. Maybe we'll all learn something for next time."

"Next time?" Claire shook her head quickly. "Nope. Not doing this again."

"What if we're really good at this?" Jonny pressed. "Watson may need us if another murder crosses his path."

She shook her head even more firmly. "No. Absolutely not. I'll leave it to the fiction. I watch some crime shows, read some mysteries, but only the very tamest. You cannot pretend those things are the same as what we are facing."

"No, you're right," he allowed. "It's a different animal together when it is in real life and affecting you in some way, however directly."

"I can't believe the show is going on, even if the ratings are so low," Claire muttered darkly. "From the baking side of things, I'm thrilled the show is happening and that I'm on it, but in every other respect, it doesn't seem right."

They walked in silence for several moments as a light rain began to fall, drops plunking against the fabric of their jackets.

What were they even doing here? Amid a murder investigation, amid a baking show, amid the conglomeration of the two—would the murder have even happened if the show was not here? If he hadn't signed the contract, bringing the show to this historic estate with historic kitchens, would Lesley still be alive?

He wouldn't claim the murder as ultimately his fault, but if he had given things more time and more thought, had listened to his instinct against the show, maybe things would be different.

But what was the use in thinking that way? He hadn't murdered Lesley. He couldn't have known what was going to happen when he'd signed the contract with the show.

None of them could have, least of all Lesley.

"Can you bake something in tribute to Lesley?" Jonny asked Claire, though it seemed like a weak question.

"Can I what?" came her startled response.

He laughed, more to himself than anything else. "Sorry, random train of thought. Never mind. I was just thinking about Lesley, and if there's something you can do for her without being blatantly obvious. Use her recipes or something."

Claire made a sound of indecision that went on longer than he'd anticipated. "Her stuff is still in her room, since the producers didn't want to send anything back, but I can't use her recipes. That's absolutely cheating. Maybe I should do something Welsh or wear one of her scarves. I don't know." She stopped and looked toward the historic kitchens, her shoulders drooping further and further with each breath.

Jonny watched the conflicting but nameless emotions flicker across her face as she stared off, away from him. "What?"

She exhaled, the sound weighted and measured. "The person I really want to talk to about this is Lesley. If she had just been the first to go, that would be one thing. I could call her and get her advice, but she wouldn't have been the first to go anyway. She would have been here, sitting up with me and Freya and talking us through our bakes. Being our mom or our aunt. I didn't know her long enough. I should have known her for years before she was gone." She shook her head, then turned her face away from him.

He heard her sniffle and immediately moved around to face her, his hands going to her upper arms. "Whoa, whoa, what's this? Claire, what's wrong?"

"Other than Lesley being dead?" She swiped at her eyes, still looking toward the kitchens instead of at him. "Other than being trapped here with a potential murderer running around that I'm apparently supposed to help uncover while also making a smashing batch of profiteroles? Nothing, really." She dropped her head, sniffling softly. "I'm sorry. I haven't . . . This is the first time I've cried about any of this. Bad timing."

"Or perfect timing," Jonny offered, stooping to try to meet her eyes. When that didn't work, he did what felt most natural.

He pulled her into his chest and wrapped his arms gently around her. "Come here, it's okay," he said in a low voice. "You're going to be safe. You're going to be fine."

"I need to cry," Claire managed, though her voice sounded tight and high-pitched.

Gabi sounded like that when she was sobbing to him on the phone and needed to cry until there was nothing left. He'd learned all about that when she'd been at university, and he still missed the cues half of the time.

He wasn't going to miss this one.

"Go ahead and cry, then," he encouraged, rubbing her back. "Cry for Lesley, cry for yourself, cry for whatever you need to."

"I have to bake today," Claire choked out, curling against him as though she could ball herself up while still remaining upright. "I need to cry, and I have to bake today. A lot of bakes. How am I supposed to do that? With all of this, how . . . ?"

Jonny put his hand on the back of her head. "I have no idea," he admitted, laughing softly. "I can't bake on a good day. I have no idea how you're supposed to bake at all in this situation. Even without a murder being involved. But a few tears are good for the camera, right? Maybe it'll make you the crowd favorite like Betsy in series four."

"Yeah, she had that effect on viewers. Unlike Bella on series seven, who cried all the time, and then nobody cared anymore." She sniffled, rubbed at her face, then froze. "Wait." She pulled back, looking up at him, suspicion bright in her tear-filled eyes. "I thought you'd never watched the show."

The accusation had the strangest effect of cracking something within Jonny. Not in a brokenhearted sense, but in a sense of his pride being neatly perforated with an unexpected blade. He felt it somewhere around his diaphragm and lowest ribs, and it rippled along each muscle in his torso in a way that made him squirm.

Caught.

He had been neatly and deftly caught, and his entire face filled with heat.

"I, erm . . ." he hedged, chuckling in embarrassment and scratching at the back of his head. "I may have started watching the show after filming started here. Just to see what all the fuss was about."

Claire gaped for a moment, then started laughing, letting her head fall back as she did so, which confined her laughter mostly to her throat, and there was something incredibly fetching about that.

"And how far into the show have you gotten?" she asked through continued laughter. "Series four, at least, unless you skipped around." She raised one of her rather mobile brows, making him grin.

"I finished series four," Jonny confirmed with a nod. "It's inexplicably addicting, and I don't say that easily. I still don't understand Trixie's obsession with Alan, but at least I understand what getting a smile means now. Please, don't tell her or

Gabi that I've started watching. I will never, ever hear the end of it."

Claire put a hand to her heart. "I promise. Not a word." She smiled broadly and only then seemed to realize that she was still standing practically flush with him, eyeing their position as her smile faded.

To be perfectly honest, he'd forgotten how close she was to him as well.

Thankfully, they avoided that awkwardly long moment of staring into each other's eyes that was in every single romantic comedy Gabi had ever forced him to watch by both of them simply taking a cautious step back. And looking away from each other. And clearing their throats at the same time.

Jonny started laughing again, which wasn't awkward or obvious at all.

But it did make Claire laugh again, so he felt less awkward and obvious.

Her renewed laughter also made him wish he hadn't stepped quite so far back, but there they were.

"What time do you have to be at the pavilion?" Jonny asked after he managed to exhale the rest of the laughter away.

Claire looked at her watch, her mouth twisting. "Half an hour. Mostly for continuity checks and makeup, but we won't start filming for an hour at least."

Jonny gestured toward the kitchens. "Time to show me around before you go?"

"You want me to show you around your own historic kitchens?" She scoffed, giving him a wry look.

"Honestly, I have never paid any attention to them," he admitted rather freely. "And I've never asked a baker about them. So, I'd like to see what you think of them, and how they could be used. And maybe we could use them for our case chats, if we need the space."

Claire's face softened, morphing into a sweet smile that crinkled her eyes and caused a pleasant knot to form in his stomach. "You're distracting me, aren't you? From tears, from murder, from . . . everything."

He shrugged. "I might be. I might also truly be interested in what you think about the kitchens. You and Lesley were in them, right? Tell me what she thought of them and paint me a picture of a dinner prep in there."

"You're going to catch the baking bug if you aren't careful," she warned, nodding toward the path and starting to walk.

"I will not," he vowed as he followed, catching up to her quickly. "I will leave all the baking to you, happily and freely. I am well aware of my limitations and stay quite safely inside of them at all times."

"Says the guy who said we could be the brains in the investigation."

"Okay, that was a moment of weakness and bravado, and I will not be held to that for the rest of my life."

CHAPTER 13

"It had to be steamed puddings, didn't it, Claire? You had to have steamed pudding because a regular pudding wasn't good enough. Idiot."

Freya tsked loudly beside Claire. "I wouldn't talk to yourself when we aren't on camera, Claire. People think you're crazy when you do that, not cute and stressed."

Claire gave her friend a hard look. "I don't fake my stress for the camera like Anthony does. I am actually and honestly stressed right now!"

"Why?" Freya gestured down to her oven while munching on licorice. "Your steamed pudding is going brilliantly from what I can see. Jam puffs and macarons looking good. Breathe, for heaven's sake. We've got twenty minutes before cameras roll. Stop freaking out." She patted Claire's back and moved out of the pavilion to wait her turn for her interview while one of the show assistants kept an eye on Freya's baking items.

No interference was allowed from the assistants, but they were to shout if anything disastrous was taking place.

So far, no one had ever needed to shout.

Steamed pudding, of all things. It had sounded like a

great idea for a garden party theme, but it was proving to be the most finicky thing Claire had ever worked with, including any form of pastry she had ever baked.

Despite Freya's confidence, there was no way of knowing if the steamed pudding was going brilliantly. It was in the steamer, and if Claire interfered too much, she could ruin the entire thing. She had at least ninety minutes left on the steaming process, and the waiting between parts of her Occasion Bake preparation was maddening.

If she started her macarons too soon, they would lose their perfect texture. If she filled the jam puffs too early, they would go soggy.

And then there were the cheesecakes. Because she didn't have enough to do. Four items to prepare when she wasn't required to do that many. But she was doing them, and that was that. She just needed things to do while she was in the pavilion because spying on her colleagues was terrifying enough.

Baking would keep her settled. Give her mind something to fixate on besides the idea that any one of her fellow bakers, or possibly a crew member, could kill her as and when they pleased.

Claire sat on the stool at her baking station, drumming her fingers on the countertop as she glanced around the place. It was surprisingly quiet for an Occasion Bake, but given the cameras were off and the crew was working on interviews and the like, why should there be much noise or bustling?

Dr. Adams was going from station to station, examining ingredients and nodding, apparently satisfied with what was being used. Anthony was grinding some herbs, muttering to himself. Mathias, as usual, was reading a book as though nothing was amiss and his bakes were going perfectly. Denis was somewhere outside the pavilion, telling a story, if the entertaining sounds of his voice were any indication. Benji was mixing something at his station, his eyes darting this way and that while his hand moved with impressive speed against the bowl.

No doubt, he would pull off some miracle yet again. He had this unnerving pattern of being positively unimpressive in his Classic Bake, and then doing something extraordinary in the Occasion Bake. He wasn't sharing his secret with anyone, and only offered a tiny smile of pride whenever he was asked about it.

The ability to save himself when he was in danger of elimination no matter the odds. Innovation enough to manage layers of texture that no one else had. It was the strangest phenomenon, and Claire, for one, was wary of it.

Dr. Adams was fairly diligent in checking ingredients, but she could not have eyes on all of them at all times. Could Benji somehow be cheating in a way that they weren't able to detect? Or that they weren't paying attention to? Or was he really just particularly determined and able to mend his bakes every time?

He appeared to be making turnovers at the moment, focusing on his fillings, whatever they were destined to be. She couldn't see the color of them from her position, but she had no doubt they would be marvelous.

Though, now she thought of it, she hadn't seen him working on the pastry. But the puff pastry was cooling; she had seen it carried over. But if he had done any sort of turning and shaving of butter into the dough, she had completely missed it. Was it possible for him to have brought in prepared puff pastry dough and not have anyone notice? That didn't seem at all likely.

She ran through the list of standard ingredients for puff pastry, and there shouldn't have been anything he could have secretly added unless his recipe was very complicated. The fillings were standard as well, and what made them the appropriate texture practically universal. How in the world could he have cheated there?

Oh, she was being ridiculous! She was assuming he was cheating without any sort of proof and speculating on how he was bringing it about.

Helping with this murder investigation was turning her into the most suspicious person known to man.

Suspecting Benji of cheating was not going to help anyone find Lesley's murderer.

Claire shook her head and moved to the corner of her baking station, lifting the muslin cloth from the small pastry cases she had prepped earlier for her cheesecakes. Freya hadn't noticed them on her visit, which meant they would come as a surprise, and that was something Claire was oddly delighted about. Surprises were important, after all. Was there anything worse than predictability in a baker on this show?

While they were on break from the cameras, she got to work on mixing her filling, trying to avoid thinking about the treacle steamed pudding that she desperately needed to go perfectly.

"What are you making?"

Claire jumped almost a foot into the air, and some of the ricotta cheese she had been mixing splattered onto her shirt. "Crepes alive!"

Jonny snorted a soft laugh and held out an apologetic hand. "Sorry, sorry. I thought you might have heard me coming or seen me in your peripheral vision. My fault."

Claire's galloping heart backed up that statement. It *was* his fault. As though she had any power to pay attention to anything while she was in here except keeping herself alive and making sure her bakes were worth something.

"I don't have anything new to report," she said. "I mean, other than I suspect cheating, but I don't know how to prove it, and it hardly compares to Lesley's death, does it?"

"Cheating?" Jonny looked around and leaned on her baking station. "Who?"

With a not-so-subtle nudge of her head, Claire indicated Benji. "I didn't see him work his puff pastry at all, and yet it's over there, ready to go. He bakes something barely passable for Classic and then pulls a pastry rabbit out of a hat for Occasion that gets him through. Every single time."

Jonny hissed under his breath slowly. "But you have someone checking that, right? Isn't Dr. What's-Her-Face looming all the time to find the food problems?"

"Supposedly," Claire muttered.

Her eyes flicked to the woman in question, now examining everything on Anthony's station. She watched Dr. Adams nod, frown, sigh, and yawn, and then, to her surprise, saw her look over at Benji's station with abject disapproval. Yet she didn't go over to him, and she had nothing in her hands that she might have confiscated from his station.

So she was just giving him a dirty look?

That didn't make any sense. As a local, surely she knew Benji was a fireman. Wasn't that something that ought to have rendered him a local hero of sorts? Or at least be considered with kindness or concern.

There was nothing of kindness or concern in Dr. Adams's expression. It was complete and utter disapproval.

"I can hear your trains of thought whistling to each other as they pass on the tracks," Jonny mused aloud, breaking Claire's staring spell and reminding her of the task at hand.

She pulled together her cheeses and other ingredients for her filling and began whisking them together. "What if Dr. Adams doesn't like Benji?" Claire muttered. "Dunno why, but she's glaring at him."

"Well, it might just be something about him. Sounds like a lot of people don't like Benji. Mrs. Comer doesn't. Watson doesn't. I don't."

Claire gave Jonny a hard look, which was difficult when he was looking utterly charming, handsome, and carefree. "You have no idea who he is."

"Nope," Jonny admitted, cocking a crooked grin at her. "But he makes you uneasy, so I don't like him."

Why did that tiny smile make her feel so ticklish? Just behind her sternum, and somehow in the arches of her feet.

She shifted her position quickly, clearing her throat. "Is it bad that I think he's cheating?"

"Nope," Jonny said again, pulling over a stool. "That makes me happy. Let's speculate."

Claire laughed, continuing to whisk carefully. "Here? Now? There are people everywhere."

Jonny gestured around them. "Cameras are off. Denis is entertaining people, Freya is being interviewed, Mathias is nose deep in a book. Plus I heard the PA a minute ago, and Benji is getting interviewed next, so there's lots of time to gossip."

"You are not helping!" Claire insisted with a scolding finger.

"Technically, not allowed to help." Jonny shrugged like a little kid. "Baking competition."

Claire huffed, not nearly as irritated as she had been a moment ago. "What's got you in such a good mood? You're pretty chipper for a brooding viscount."

"I watched a few more episodes last night," Jonny confessed with a quick grin. "Nobody warned me that Rishi was going to actually drop his Gatsby lemon cake on the way to present! I have never actually gasped out loud while watching anything, but I did last night." He shook his head. "Good thing they had all that footage of what it looked like beforehand, right? I swear, the jam tarts on the Classic Bake were the only reason he didn't go home."

Hearing Jonny gush over the show—knowing how brooding and grouchy he'd been about it when Claire and the others had arrived—was one of the most entertaining, if not hilarious, experiences Claire had known in some time, and she was powerless to ignore the rush of her own enthusiasm and matching smiles.

After all, she was a fan of the show as well as a participant.

"Right?" she replied immediately, her eyes widening. "You should have been there for the social media madness that happened when it aired. There were conspiracy theories, Jonny."

"Oh, that Nancy tripped him? I saw the speculation! I looked up the incident when the episode was done. Didn't get to bed until after midnight, thanks to that rabbit hole." Jonny folded his arms and leaned on the baking station, his smile mischievous. "I don't buy into that one, but I do think that Dame Sophie had a crush on Rishi and that's one of the reasons he didn't go home. Alan would have tossed him out without a backward glance."

Claire rolled her eyes in pretended exasperation, though

it was a relief to be talking about something easy while she baked instead of worrying about the knives on the cutting boards at the back of the pavilion, the possibility of poison being slipped into her tea, or the image of being attacked in the dark while she walked back to the inn later. And there was something utterly adorable about having Jonny sitting on the stool opposite her station, eagerly chatting about baking, of all things, and being the most approachable and normal guy she had met in quite a long time.

Was his adorableness the reason her cheeks were heating as she added more cream to the cheese-and-egg mixture of her fillings? Or was it that she didn't think Alan was as much of a jerk of a judge as he appeared and she'd had this argument with her sister before?

"Alan is fair-minded," Claire offered, trying to ignore the increasing heat of her cheeks. "He understands accidents happen."

"Tell that to Jakob in series three."

Of course, he would come back with that argument. Everyone always did, and it was just—

"No, now is *not* a good time!" Benji shouted, his voice filling the relatively vacant pavilion at the moment. "Do you see me working here? I will tell you when it is a good time and do your chuffing interview then! Back off!"

Claire stared at him in shock, along with everyone else in the pavilion. But if Benji cared that the place was almost utterly silent after his outburst, he gave no indication. He simply continued separating his eggs into the mixture before creaming everything together with a wholly unnecessary show of strength.

If the cameras had been on, it would be one thing. He

could be trying to show off for the female viewers, if that was his thing. The footage might not make it into the actual episodes, but many series featured a heartthrob. But this was pure intimidation, if not outright anger. What was so inconvenient about taking fifteen minutes to be interviewed? They had been given a lot of time for their bakes today, and Benji never did anything exceptionally complicated.

And he certainly never yelled at the production staff.

"What's his problem?" Jonny muttered as everyone in the pavilion got back to work, the air of awkwardness still hanging heavy over them.

"Dunno," Claire admitted. "He was bragging about his citrus ginger tart recipe earlier, and that's probably what he's making now. He's being pretty particular for something as standard as a custard, but what do I know?"

Jonny gave her a puzzled look. "A citrus ginger tart, you say?"

Claire nodded as she added elderflower cordial to her own mix. "Yep. And he's doing something strange by not making the custard in the traditional way over the stove, but maybe that's part of the special recipe."

"I wonder where the oranges for his zest are. Or lemons, limes, grapefruit, whatever. I don't see any fruit over there."

Now that was something Claire ought to have noticed, and she looked over at Benji's baking station. There wasn't a single citrus fruit anywhere, and every recipe she had ever looked at for a citrus custard involved putting the zest and juice in early so they could saturate the custard fully.

Benji wasn't doing that. He was adding sugar while he steadily mixed, then a hint of salt, then something orange colored that appeared granulated like sugar. But no zest and no juice.

Very strange, indeed.

"Maybe he adds a concentrated dose later on," Claire murmured, unsure if she was trying to convince herself or Jonny of the idea.

But she was already suspecting Benji of cheating on his turnovers; she was in a very crime-centric and unfair state of mind. It was probably nothing. Dried orange zest mixed with sugar. Cinnamon or ginger or cloves and sugar. Cumin and sugar.

That was a dumb idea. Why would he put cumin in there?

She was rambling in her own brain now, which was surely a sign of something really bad. Or dumb. Or both.

"Good gravy, he's putting a lot of that orange stuff in."

Claire blinked and focused on Benji's station again, eyes widening as more and more of the mystery ingredient was added into the bowl on the scale. It might as well have replaced the sugar in the custard, but he'd already added that.

What in the world was he doing?

"Am I cheating by watching him?" Claire whispered.

Jonny leaned closer across the baking station. "Are you making a citrus ginger tart?"

Claire shook her head quickly. "No, I have no intention of doing that."

"Then, no, you are not cheating by watching your fellow baker do something strange." Jonny flicked his eyes down to her bowl, then met her eyes again. "Just don't mess up because of it."

"Right, yeah. Right. Almost done anyway." She added the last of the ingredients, apart from the rose water, and mixed thoroughly, trying to ignore Benji and his potential cheating for the time being.

Death, ghosts, cheating. This was not the experience she thought she would be having on this show. The family feeling she had hoped for wasn't there, but they weren't at each other's throats. Apart from whoever had killed Lesley, of course. If anyone else died, maybe things would get worse between the bakers, but as of right now, they just kind of existed in a confusing world of driven competition, emotional support, and constant uneasiness.

It wasn't all that fun, to be honest.

The baking part was fine. Stressful, but fine. It was the rest of it that made her so tense. Death hovering over everything, the feeling of being trapped when she ought to feel protected, wondering if the person she was in conversation with was a murderer or the next victim. And she was supposed to help solve this mystery by spying on her fellow competitors.

Definitely not a family feeling.

Claire twisted her mouth as she reached for a spoon, dipping it into the mixture. "Kerri and Benji both swear they saw a ghost at the kitchens." She tasted the mix, then added one more drop of rose water and began mixing again.

Jonny scoffed softly. "Kerri is still traumatized, and Benji likes attention. Did they say what the ghost looked like?"

"Long hair, flowing skirts, glowing aura." Claire shrugged and set her mixture aside, reaching for the cheesecake shells. "Just wondering if there were local legends."

"Loads. Why, did Benji say there were?"

Claire nodded and began scraping the cheesecake mixture into the cases. "He did. Like you said, probably seeking attention. Maybe hoping he can get on camera to talk about the local legends and such."

"Okay, *now* you can interview me," Benji called out, pushing his covered custard mixture to one side of his station. Not cooling it, just letting it sit.

Very odd.

Benji nodded and smiled at Claire as he passed her station. "Looks good, Claire. Great texture."

Claire forced a bright smile. "Thanks, Benji. Have a good interview."

He clicked his tongue with a wink and strode out of the pavilion toward the interview location, now as calm as a spring morning.

"Good acting," Jonny praised softly.

"I'm getting better at it," Claire admitted with a wry note, working on getting the rest of the mix out of the bowl and into the shells. "Lots and lots of practice."

Sighing, she put her cheesecakes into the oven, closed the door, and set her timer, then looked at Benji's empty station.

"Your brows have their thinking furrow," Jonny said. "What's up?"

"Can you keep an eye on Dr. Adams while I go check something?" Claire asked without looking at him. "I don't want her snooping if I'm wrong."

"Sure, want me to wander for a moment?"

Claire nodded and walked to Benji's station. As she passed, she swiped her finger leisurely but directly along a patch of the orange mix that had spilled onto the surface. She popped her finger into her mouth as she exited the pavilion, tilting her face toward the sun, trying to look as though she were enjoying the fresh air.

"Well?" Jonny asked a moment later when he reached her side.

Glancing at him, Claire smiled tightly. "That is Dip Dab. My aunt Shelagh brought them for us every time she visited, and it is not something you forget. He'll claim whatever he wants and there isn't a way to disprove it, but I promise you: That is orange Dip Dab he just put in his custard."

"So Benji *is* cheating."

Claire lowered her chin and folded her arms, glaring toward the historic kitchens and their supposed ghost. "Yes. He most certainly is."

CHAPTER 14

"Are you actually insane, Claire?"

"Not usually, no."

Jonny couldn't believe what he was hearing and rubbed his eyes with one hand. "You want to walk around the estate at dusk. Just because."

"No, not just because," Claire retorted with a roll of her eyes. She turned more fully toward him on the stool in the historic kitchens later that evening, crossing her legs. "I want to see what the killer would have seen the night he attacked Lesley."

"Why?" Jonny asked with forced patience. "What will that do?"

Claire shrugged, which was even less encouraging than her idea. "I don't know. But Watson will be here soon, and—"

"Watson?" Jonny laughed in disbelief. "I thought it was strange enough that you called a Chelsea Bun to meet here, but you actually invited Watson over?"

"I did," the maddening woman said without any shame whatsoever. "If I had your number, I'd have filled you in, but as it is . . ."

Jonny gave her a wry look. "I'll give you my number, if for no other reason than because it will be easier to tell you your ideas are ridiculous via text."

"I don't hear you sharing any ideas for getting this investigation underway," Claire shot back, quirking one of her powerful brows. "Or are you still content to sit and wait for invitations?"

He opened his mouth to offer a retort, then closed it when he realized it would have been a stupid retort, because she was right. Watson might have been a policeman, might have been a detective, which undoubtedly meant experience and exams and the like, but it was his first murder investigation, and he didn't know what he didn't know. And his ability to update them on the progress, despite asking for their help, was seriously lacking.

He scowled, more in protest than in disgruntlement. "So you're actually going to take this on, then? Helping with the investigation."

Claire's smile was quick and impish. "Not by myself. You're helping."

Jonny folded his arms, biting back an impulse to bark a laugh. "Am I?"

"A brain has two halves," Claire pointed out. "I can't be a brain by myself."

"I have every confidence that you would cope extraordinarily well," Jonny said, refusing to be flattered by the joke. "But fine, I'll join in the idiocy."

She matched his pose, folding her arms in return. "It's not idiocy if we get justice for Lesley."

That was also an excellent point.

"True," Jonny admitted. "For Lesley."

Claire's smile softened. "That sounds like a battle cry to be shouted from a horse."

Jonny gestured behind them with his thumb. "Did you want to do that? We have horses."

She gave him a look. "You're not nearly as grouchy as everyone says you are, you know that?"

"Oh, yes, I am." He nodded sagely. "I've known me a lot longer than you have. I'm an absolute jerk."

"Jerks aren't always grouches." Claire's foot began to bounce on the leg crossing her knee. "You have been called a grouch, but I've not really seen that."

Jonny raised a brow. "And you've seen me be a jerk?"

Claire only shrugged once more, looking out the window, her foot bouncing away.

Jonny narrowed his eyes as he stared at her, wondering what had gotten into her to make her so snarky and bright today. She was a fairly vivacious person at any time, but there was something about her today that was different. Some determination mingled with optimism that he hadn't seen in her before, even with the baking show.

Was she confident in their ability to solve the crime? Or just decisive that they were going to try? And why in the world would she want to attempt it with the baking show going on?

"I don't mean to be a jerk," Jonny grumbled, feeling silly even admitting it. "It just happens."

Claire hummed a low laugh. "That's what my dad says about his language. It's why he insisted we use other words for swearing." She looked at him, her smile almost coy. "I firmly believe that nobody really means to be a jerk. They're just impatient or distracted or something of the sort. Ignorant, maybe. So, you know, just try not to be a jerk as often. You'll be fine."

Now Jonny *did* laugh. "Thank you, that's not at all patronizing. Have you been talking to Gabi lately? She's the CEO of Patronizing."

Waving her hand, Claire uncrossed her legs and sat forward. "Stop it, I'm just rambling again. It's what I do when I'm nervous."

"I noticed." Jonny smiled and flicked his own hand in a dismissive gesture. "We're about to be the brains of a real murder investigation. You can be nervous, I guess. I'm nervous about walking around at dusk with you on my own estate."

"Aw, that's sweet. I didn't invite you for my daily evening walk, but thanks for coming along." She smiled and batted her lashes at him.

Jonny's smile faded in an instant. "You were going to go alone? Of all the—" He bit down hard on his tongue, his lips pressing together with enough pressure to make his face hurt.

"Pick different swear words," Claire offered. "It helps."

He exhaled slowly. "Of all the gritty risotto stupid ideas, that is number one."

Claire's forehead creased like ripples on the water. "Gritty risotto? That's what you came up with?"

"It's my first time, don't mock me." He inhaled carefully and exhaled. "You don't go walking at dusk—or any time— alone. That was a rule from the day of the murder. I'm not going to ask you for much, Claire, because I don't have a right to, but for the love of gouda, will you at least stick to that?"

Her mouth opened, and he could tell by the twinkle in her eye that she was going to say something about his choice of word, so he gave her what he could only hope was a warning look.

She sighed, closing her mouth and swallowing. "Yes," she finally said. "Yes, I will stick to that."

"Okay, thanks." He tried to hide his next breath, since his heart was going about a million miles a minute, his head was pounding, and his ears were possibly on fire. But at least he had gotten a promise for that part.

The idea of her walking around in the dark with a murderer on the loose was more than he was willing to bear.

Way more.

"Hello?" DS Watson called from the entrance to the historic kitchens. "Anyone in here?"

Jonny sighed and pushed to his feet, turning toward the long hallway. "In the back, Detective."

DS Watson appeared a few moments later, nodding in greeting and holding out his hand to shake Jonny's. "My lord." He turned toward Claire and extended his hand. "Miss Walker."

Claire shook his hand, standing as well. "Thanks for coming, Detective."

Jonny gave her a bemused look, finding himself grinning at her welcoming the man to a set of kitchens that weren't hers. If she noticed, she gave no indication.

"I'm glad you called," DS Watson told her. "I could use some help getting some traction on this investigation."

"I was afraid of that," Jonny muttered while Claire smiled sympathetically.

Somehow, Claire managed to not look condescending as she gestured for the man to sit on one of the other stools. "Tell us what you know and what you need."

DS Watson looked as though Christmas had come early for him. "Thank you. With the limitations placed on me by my superiors, I'm unable to open an official inquiry. Especially with just the one body."

"Where have I heard that before?" Claire mumbled, resting her chin in her hand as she frowned.

Jonny offered her a sympathetic smile, but she was focused on DS Watson and missed it.

"We know the cause of death," Watson went on with a heavy exhale. "And, after going through all of Ms. Kemble's devices and digital footprints, we know she had not received any threatening messages or communication. The analysis of the scarf came back, and rope fibers were discovered embedded into the fabric."

"Rope?" Jonny repeated, his eyes going wide.

Watson nodded quickly. "Standard estate rope, I'm afraid, sir. Not much to go on, but at least we know it was involved. The scarf was not the ligature, which debunks the theory that it got caught up in the waterwheel. We have not received any strange messages, no witnesses have come forward, and there was nothing under Ms. Kemble's fingernails to lead us to her killer."

"Could you interrogate those without an alibi again?" he suggested. "See if their stories change or improve, go further back with their timeline, anything?"

"No, sir. Discretion, you understand. I really cannot do all that much that appears to be an investigation."

Jonny looked at Claire in exasperation and found shades of her own mirrored back at him. "Unfortunately, Detective, we cannot interrogate," he pointed out. "We can do our best to put pieces together, discover clues, a bit of speculation and observation, but interrogations won't have any legal basis or standing with the pair of us."

The sound of chimes suddenly filled the room, and DS Watson reached into his coat pocket, pulling out his mobile. Holding the phone with one hand, he used the other to swipe and press the screen with the same sort of pointed motions that Jonny had seen in a pantomime. But the detective was not pantomiming anything.

His deeply furrowed brow and repeated attempts to swipe up spoke to that.

"Aha," the detective eventually said, his voice dipping surprisingly low. "Mr. Wright's alibi just cleared. Pity. I was hoping I wouldn't have to focus so much on the local boy, much as it might delight a few others."

"Delight?" Claire repeated in surprise. "Benji?"

Watson smiled tightly. "He is not exactly well-liked, Miss Walker. And he has never been particularly fond of the estate. Likes to spread stories to visitors and such. I'd never let that cloud my judgment or investigation, but it might not look that way from the outside."

"We'll keep it quiet, then," Jonny said simply. "And make sure we look equally at everyone still possible, right?"

"Right," Claire said. "But I think we ought to start with a question I can't seem to answer." She looked at Watson and Jonny in turn. "Why the show? Why the bakers? Why Lesley?"

Jonny rubbed his hands together in thought. "Maybe it's opportunistic?"

"A murder that used such specific details from the legend?" Claire shook her head quickly. "No way. That was pretty precise."

"Although," DS Watson broke in, "there was never any mention of a head injury with the viscountess, as I understand it."

Jonny stared at him for a long moment. "No," he said slowly. "No, there wasn't, was there?" He narrowed his eyes. "Was the blow to the head enough to render Lesley unconscious?"

"Yes, I think." He flipped a few pages in his notes. "Yes. The ME feels the victim was knocked unconscious before her death."

"What are you thinking, Jonny?" Claire murmured.

He looked at her, smiling a little. "Remorseful killer. Or first-time killer. Or not as much of a historical stickler as we thought. What if Lesley was already unconscious when he killed her? Why else knock her unconscious? Everything else was meticulous, but that? It's off-pattern."

DS Watson bobbed his head, scribbling on his pad. "So perhaps he was not trying to replicate the original murder exactly and opted for more of a loose interpretation."

"I was actually thinking of looking over the mill as it gets dark," Claire offered helpfully. "Lord Colburn is going to come with me. Think that could help?"

"Absolutely," Watson said at once. "I would love any insights you can glean from that. Are you sure you can spare the time?"

She nodded, rising from her seat. "I can. Judging is tomorrow, so I won't have any bakes to practice until after that."

"Shall we meet in the morning, Detective?" Jonny asked as he also rose. "Here, if it suits. Or you can come to the house."

"Here would be excellent, sir." DS Watson stood and straightened his jacket. "Please believe me when I say that I do hope that the family and the estate can escape as much as possible from the aftereffects."

It occurred to Jonny then, though it probably should have

earlier, that DS Watson was a local man. Familiar with the village and its people, its traditions, the estate. He was probably well aware of what the estate offered the area and the history of the family, in some respect. And they really were a low-crime area, so it wasn't entirely Watson's fault that his experience in particular crimes was lacking.

He ought to give the man a greater benefit of the doubt.

"Tomorrow morning," Jonny confirmed, nodding once. "Say, nine or so? We can provide breakfast, if needed."

"Coffee or tea will be enough for me, sir." DS Watson smiled and started down the corridor, tucking his phone and his notebook into his jacket pockets.

Jonny looked at Claire and gestured for them to follow. "Shall we?"

Claire gave him a half-hearted smile. "Not exactly the evening stroll I was planning on, but it'll do. Shall we investigate, Brains?"

It was impossible to not smile at her adorable dorkiness, and Jonny nodded evenly, not bothering to pretend he wasn't enjoying this.

"I missed the end of the bake today," Jonny began as they headed toward the entrance. "How did it go?"

"Great, actually," Claire admitted with a grin. "After you left, the steamed pudding came out beautifully, and the treacle syrup was spot-on. I made some sweet whipped cream, not quite as dense as ice cream, and Alan said it was the perfect addition. The mini cheesecakes were really good, according to Dame Sophie. She actually asked for my recipe."

"Claire!" Jonny laughed in pride, wishing he could throw his arms around her and sweep her off the ground or something. "That's fantastic!"

She shook her head as though she couldn't quite believe it herself. "I've never had such good comments, Jonny. Never. Judging is tomorrow, so we'll see if that sticks, but it felt so good. And I was so wigged-out the entire time I was baking, I don't even know how I managed it."

Jonny scoffed loudly as they stepped out into the open evening air. "Oh, I do."

"How could you know?" Claire demanded. "You weren't there the whole time."

He gave her a smug look. "It's because I know the kind of baker you are. And it is definitely not one who only does mediocre bakes. In fact, I don't think you're capable of anything resembling mediocrity, but the fact that you think you are means you are always wanting to push further and work harder. You're never going to be content with what you produce, and it only makes you better."

Claire's green eyes were bright as they searched his. "Really?" she asked in the smallest, most wishful voice he had ever heard.

The moment suddenly seemed to be about more than a bake, more than a show, investigation, or simple walk to a mill. Jonny didn't know what to make of it, or what to even say about it, but his chest tightened, and he struggled to swallow.

"Yep," he replied with too much lightness and not enough sincerity. "Really. And I have no vested interest in this series, so you can trust me when I say that."

Claire burst out laughing, breaking the tension in his chest and somehow removing his kneecaps at the same time. "You are totally biased! Very kind, but totally biased. And I can't take anything at face value. You're so deep into earlier series that you're analyzing everybody still on now, aren't you?"

Actually, he wasn't, but he'd let her pretend he was.

It was easier than letting her believe he was spending more time analyzing her than anything else.

"Could be," he hedged, sliding his hands into his pockets. "I'll have to attend the elimination tomorrow to see if I am right, but . . ."

"Tell me what you're thinking!" Claire begged as they turned onto the path toward the mill. "I want to know what you see and think of us."

Did she, now? Well, he could tell her *some* things, but he was certainly not going to give her the details on one baker in particular.

"To be fair," he started, giving her a warning look, "I didn't show up for the first two episodes, so I have no take on Lesley or Kerri."

"Understandable," Claire replied with a quick nod. "You weren't interested then, and certainly not invested."

"Nope. That's pretty recent." He let his eyes hold hers for a moment or two longer than he might have done otherwise, then focused his gaze ahead of them, smiling a little.

"Our Belgian fascinates me," Jonny mused in a playfully formal tone as they walked. "He's quiet and determined, surprisingly creative in his combinations, and always cool and collected. I've seen him read no fewer than three different books while waiting for his bakes, and I have no idea how he can manage that. So I conclude that Mathias has a system only he understands, and none of it makes sense until he presents. He could go pretty far, but I don't peg him as a winner, sadly."

"Poor Mathias," Claire sighed. "He had a rough day today. Caught the edges of his tart, flavors were too rich for a garden party, missed the mark on his syllabubs. Minor things, but might be enough to cut him. Who else?"

"Anthony," Jonny went on, "is utter chaos. He is so in his own head and so obsessed with trying to make things healthy that he loses ingredients on the regular, and he's lucky if what he presents actually fits the brief without extensive explanation. He is silent in his bakes. Incredibly focused, looking at no one and nothing, saying nothing for the cameras, and actually looking fairly angry for whatever reason. One would hope that such healthy aims would lead to a better attitude and demeanor, but alas . . ."

Claire snorted but said nothing about his bakes of the day. So Anthony was probably safe to healthily bake another day, unfortunately. Or maybe that was Claire's way of saying she didn't care one way or the other with Anthony, which might have been an interesting avenue to explore.

But not right now. Not on this walk.

"My theatrical friend Denis—now there's a creature of habit for you. Everything in its perfect order and place. He knows his attention span is a weak spot, so he has trained himself to make up for it. He knows exactly how his flavors will combine and how to make the most of them. He considers his bakes an expression of artistry and has practiced every aspect until he cannot get it wrong. Which is why he can step away and tell stories that entertain to such a degree. It's less confidence and more experience with what one."

"He told me once that he practices voices along with audiobooks on his long drives in his lorry," Claire confessed with a quick laugh. "I would go on a trip with him just to hear that."

"So would I," Jonny echoed. "Though he'd probably make me join in, and that would *not* be happening."

"Tell me something I don't know," Claire quipped. "Now, what about Freya?"

CHAPTER 15

This was an experiment in the effects of silence and coldness.

The elimination and judging scenes, that is.

Well, the beginning of them, anyway.

The bakers stood in a line just inside the Great Kitchen at the back of the building, while the judges and hosts stood behind long, elm wood tables, the surfaces marred with scorch marks, knife marks, and faint stains of meals of yore.

No one said a word while the cameras panned and crossed, zoomed and focused, and whatever else cameras did while the contestants were required to stand, stare, and remain soundless. Normally, the elimination part of the show was a simple snap of the judges returning to the pavilion and the hosts relaying the decision. There was minimal fanfare and absolutely no fuss.

But this series, apparently, was to be different. Historic Bakes and historic kitchens were apparently meant to give the feeling of the gallows to the bakers each and every time.

It was a waste of this space, but Claire would leave her opinions unspoken.

For now.

"And greeting from Lindsay in three, two, one . . ." one of the assistant directors called out.

Lindsay began to look along the row of bakers, Charlie smiling sadly beside her. "Bakers, welcome to the elimination. Thank you for your hard work on the Garden Party bakes. Dame Sophie and Alan debated endlessly on this one, as you all did so very well. The level of bakes is improving all the time, and your innovativeness and skill are very impressive, to say the least."

It was hard to believe anything said in the elimination speech, as it was all more or less the same from week to week. They all did well, it was a hard choice, something was impressive.

At least the producers weren't making the hosts do a review of what had been said about each baker's work. That would have made something already uncomfortable be unbearable.

"But someone must go," Lindsay went on, clearing her throat as though she were emotional. "And this week, the judges have determined that the baker leaving us will be . . ."

Claire held her breath, more out of instinct than fear.

"Mathias."

At least three bakers exhaled heavily, and Claire found blinking difficult. She had known Mathias would be a likely candidate, but he was so good. So, so good. How could he really be done?

"We're so sorry, Mathias," Charlie told him, coming around the table and opening his arms for a hug.

Mathias accepted the hug without much emotion, patting the smaller man's back. "It's fine, mate. It was not my week."

"Who is going to give me book club reads now?" Lindsay cried with a laugh, coming over to hug him as well.

"Denis reads, try him," Mathias suggested with a more genuine smile.

Freya, standing beside Claire, shook her head. "How can he go home and we stay?" she whispered.

Claire took her hand, squeezing a little. "He's not going home; he's got to stay, remember?"

"You know what I mean." Her grip on Claire's hand tightened. "I can't believe it."

Dame Sophie and Alan gave Mathias their condolences, the cameras catching whatever emotions and words were exchanged.

Then Charlie cleared his throat. "Congratulations to the remaining bakers. Next week, you will be baking for Christmas. Your assignments will come in due course. Good night."

They all stood where they were, however they were posed, with their arms around whoever they were next to, and waited.

"And out," the AD called. "Thanks, everyone. Clear out, and we'll get the empty kitchen footage and wrap."

Claire and Freya didn't bother waiting for the others and started down the corridor toward the entrance of the kitchens. The cameras posted in the nooks and crannies of this main thoroughfare were off, as indicated by the lack of their little red lights, so there was no need to force their faces into some semblance of calm or emotionlessness, as they were encouraged to do when they started the walk into the Great Kitchen. They were recorded as they walked from the pavilion to the kitchens for judging and every step they took once within. Once the elimination was done, however, there was nothing left to film.

Which meant Claire could let herself appear as tired and irritated as she presently felt without someone getting after her for it.

"I can't believe they're getting rid of Mathias," she grumbled, gripping the back of her neck as they moved past some of the camera crew. "Benji's Classic Bake was so bad, but because he pulled off a miracle yet again in Occasion, Mathias has to go? And what about Anthony? His explanation of those tarts took five years to make sure it fit the brief."

"It's not quite as fair as it looks on the telly, is it?" Freya replied with a heavy sigh. "Christmas bakes will be fun, though. Can't see how Anthony will make those healthy, but you never know. Do you think Mathias might help me prep mine? Guaranteed he has some great ideas."

Freya continued to ramble about Christmas bakes, about how she might use Mathias as a source, spewing ideas and plans as though she'd been thinking about Christmas bakes for ages. Which she might have. They had been given the schedule of themes months ago so they could submit their recipes, but they had to act surprised for the cameras.

Claire didn't want to think about her Christmas bakes at the moment. She wanted to go for a walk and then go to bed. The filming had taken longer today than planned, and she didn't have much of an appetite for supper.

Her bed at the Ivy House was a comfortable one, and, at the moment, that was more appealing to her than a meal. Yes, a walk and an early bedtime would be just the ticket.

Solitude and rest. Was that really too much to ask?

Out in the evening air, Claire took in a deep breath and exhaled on a sigh. "Why do the kitchens feel so oppressive when we're all in there?"

"Because they're crammed with cameras and staff and someone is going home?" Freya quipped.

"Guess so," Claire grumbled, tugging the scrunchie out of her hair and running her fingers through the tresses to try to relieve the stress that had gathered in her scalp in the last few hours.

"Ah, ladies. Elimination over?"

Jonny's voice immediately made Claire smile. Seeing him striding in their direction, navy jacket over gray trousers and a peek of a cream Henley at his throat, caused something between her heart and stomach to purr.

"Lord Colburn!" Freya greeted with enthusiasm, giving him a high five at once. "Fancy seeing you here. Yeah, we just finished, so I need some chocolate to get my happy tank filled up. Zaps the joy out of you, those kitchens. But apparently there's a ghost, so maybe I'll pop down after supper and see if she knows any baking secrets."

If Jonny was irked by the mention of a ghost, he gave no indication. Instead, he grinned at Freya like she was a younger sister or cousin he was particularly fond of. "If she's the ghost of my great-grandmother, make sure you ask about the egg tartlets. No one seems to remember how to make them the way she did."

Freya cackled. "Perfect, will do."

Jonny glanced at Claire, his blue eyes seeming particularly bright at the moment. "I found out the details about the St. Agnes chapel renovation you were asking about. I can walk you over there and show you—if you aren't too exhausted or depressed after having the joy of baking sucked out of you by Alan."

The subtle invitation to walk together, hidden by some

historical aspect she had never once asked about, was as attractive as his smile.

"Oh, that would be perfect! There's still enough light to see everything, right?" She turned to Freya with an apologetic look. "Would you mind if I go? I can catch up with you tonight."

Freya didn't seem quite as naive as she'd thought and squeezed Claire's arm. "Go be a nerd, my friend. I'll see you later." She nodded at Jonny, and quite possibly winked at him as she walked by. "My lord."

"Freya."

Claire did her best to hide her smile as Freya left, but Jonny's eyes on hers were making it insanely difficult. He just made her whole body tingle, from the tips of her toes to the hairs on the back of her neck, and her cheeks were beginning to heat from the force of restraining her smile.

"You knew we were about done," Claire stated simply.

"I might have," he admitted, hands sliding into his jacket pockets. "Decent guess based on previous occasions. But I know how you like to walk in the evenings, and walking alone is discouraged, so here I am."

Cakes and a custard, he was attractive. She finally let loose her smile and found a hint of a laugh on her next breath. "Fair enough. Let's walk."

Jonny's smile in return curled her toes like the burning wick of a candle, and he nudged his head toward the path. "St. Agnes is this way. Not far, and a nice walk."

"Sounds perfect." Claire moved beside him and started walking, suddenly unsure if her hands should also go into her pockets, though it would be her trousers and not a jacket, or if she should just let them swing aimlessly by her sides.

When had walking become such a complicated thing?

"So who's going home, so to speak?" Jonny asked once they were far enough away from the kitchens. "Can you say?"

Claire nodded. "Mathias. Sad, really. He'd have been great for the rest of the themes. Just not a great bake this weekend. Is it weird that I'm glad nobody is actually going home and that we all get to stay? I like Mathias; he's a calming presence. Nice to have him around with everything else going on."

"I think that's fair," Jonny allowed. "If, for example, a certain baker I know were to be eliminated before her time, I would certainly appreciate having her stay in the area for the remainder of the show. I might lose interest in the entire show altogether if she were to leave right away."

Something hot and tingling shot down through Claire's legs as she walked, and she managed a quick look at Jonny, shock and hope warring within her gut. "Really?"

Jonny nodded, though the nod was markedly slow and his eyes were fixed on hers. "Absolutely."

Crepes alive.

Claire pointed toward the split path ahead of them. "Which way, Viscount?"

Jonny chuckled low and warm behind her, stepping closer and tapping her right arm. "This way, Baker."

With a light skip, more to distract herself than anything else, Claire started down the path, Jonny coming to her side.

"So what's the next theme?" he asked.

"Christmas," Claire recited like an obedient student. "Because why not?"

Jonny chuckled. "So the Classic Bake is . . . ?"

Claire made a face. "Mince pies. I don't even like them, but that doesn't matter. For my Occasion Bake, I've submitted a raised game pie, a Twelfth Night cake, marzipan, and ginger-bread biscuits."

"Marzipan?" Jonny repeated in a tone of clear disgust.

"Henry VIII," Claire explained, laughing at his expression. "Marzipan constructions were all the rage. I'm making a marzipan Nativity."

"Of course, you are." Jonny shook his head, laughing. "And how much time do you get? At least twelve hours, surely?"

Claire nudged him hard. "No! Don't stress me out! We have one hour of prep the night before and five hours on the day of. It'll be fine, I've been practicing."

"Your marzipan Nativity can't be very extensive, then. Are you skipping the Wise Men? The cows in the stable? Did the shepherds come without sheep?"

"Stop!" Claire laughed, shoving at his arm. "It's going to work out!"

Jonny faux stumbled to the side, joining in the laughter. "If you say so. You're the one who told me you were mediocre when I met you, so I'm just trying to take you at your word."

"I was nervous!" she protested. "We're all nervous. I don't know who was practicing this morning, but someone had such a bad bake that the entire place reeked of burnt pastry. It was absolutely awful. Like gag-inducing. I haven't done *that* in practice yet, thankfully."

A small church appeared in the distance, looking at least five hundred years old with a matching graveyard to one side, gravestones leaning in places and scattered with wildflowers. The church's stained-glass windows glinted in the sunset and created such a charming, quaint atmosphere that Claire actually found herself stopping to stare at it.

"Is that St. Agnes?" she asked, pointing toward it.

"Yep. We can't go in right now, not with the renovation work, but it's really in excellent shape for its age."

Claire shook her head, her history-loving heart swelling with delight. "It's adorable. Do people get married in this chapel? Or do they choose the Blackfirth village church?"

"Depends on who it is," Jonny replied as they started walking again, taking the path that led away from the graveyard and church. "The St. Agnes chapel is small but holds a lot of tradition. The village church is grander and larger, so there are perks there as well."

Humming to herself, Claire clasped her hands behind her back as she walked. "I hope the show takes the entire estate into account for their content and not just the kitchens and the mill and the viscountess's murder. There's so much more to this place, isn't there?"

"I think so, but I've been told I'm biased," Jonny said with a playful nudge. "And speaking of Christmas bakes, they really ought to talk about the history of Christmas balls at Blackfirth. Massive, elaborate parties, they were. Huge. People from London, Edinburgh, Paris, Dublin, Swansea. Royalty, aristocracy—everyone who was anyone wanted an invitation."

"You aren't serious," Claire said, looking at him with wide eyes. "That huge?"

Jonny nodded rather sagely, his smile almost smug. "The parties ended after the First World War, but before that, they were the event we were famous for. Queen Victoria and Prince Albert came at least once, as far as we know."

"No way!"

"Absolutely way," he retorted with a laugh. "The rumor is that they wanted to come every year, but that could be family propaganda. So maybe you should throw Queen Victoria in your marzipan."

Claire sputtered a series of giggles at the unexpected suggestion. "Why would Queen Victoria be at the Nativity?"

Jonny shrugged. "Knowing her, she probably demanded to come down as one of the angels to see it for herself. I'm sure that's in one version of the Bible somewhere."

"You're such an idiot!" Claire laughed, shoving him again. "I'm not risking the wrath of Dame Sophie by putting a character in the Nativity that wasn't there, even if she was the Queen of England! I have quite enough to be getting on with!"

"Question: Do they play that really intense 'time is running out' jingle in the pavilion to set the mood?" Jonny asked as he returned to her side. "Loudspeakers to add to your stress? Cameras zoomed in to catch every glistening drop of sweat?"

Claire was laughing too hard to answer straightaway, her chest and stomach tightening with each racking laugh, practically doubling over as she tried to walk at the same time. "Cakes and a custard, Jonny . . . I can't breathe."

"You're going to fall into the stream if you can't get it together," he told her, grabbing her arm gently and holding her steady. "I'm not about to rescue you from the water. It's not deep, but in your hysterical state, you might not be able to get up for a while. And I am just going to stand here and laugh at you."

"I believe it," Claire gasped between giddy giggles. "You'd hate to be the hero." She took a deep breath and sighed a few times, trying to get rid of the last of her laughter. Then she turned to him, placed both hands on his arms, and looked into his eyes, unable to keep from grinning. "But you'd still walk me back to the house and make sure I was dry and warm before I went back to the Ivy House, wouldn't you?"

Jonny smiled back, giving her a wry look. "Is that a question or a statement?"

Claire shook her head, feeling lighter than she'd been in days. Weeks, even. There was something about walking with him, laughing with him, that lifted her burdens and lightened her pressures. It was easy to be with him, every single moment. Well, apart from those first few, but even then, she had begun to feel the easiness that first day.

There was just something about him.

"Statement," she said firmly. "I know you would."

Even in the darkness, there was a new light to Jonny's eyes, and he shrugged, sniffing once. "Maybe. If I felt sorry enough."

"Liar." Claire released his arms and started walking again. "Liar, liar, apron on fire."

"Apron?" Jonny repeated. "I would never be wearing . . ." He trailed off, his steps slowing.

Claire looked up at him, wondering if he was setting up another joke, but froze, seeing his clenched jaw and narrowed eyes. "What?"

"The lights are on at the mill," he told her in a very low, very soft voice. "It's been shut down since the murder. No one should be there."

Ice raced through Claire's veins as she looked toward the mill, seeing the same thing. "You don't think . . . ?"

They shared a quick look, then bolted in that direction. Jonny was much faster than she was, though she didn't mind. If they were about to come upon another victim, she could do without being the first to see them dead. Again.

Racing over the footbridge, Claire followed Jonny, trying

to see if there was a body in the same place where Lesley had been. Jonny rounded the corner of the mill and stopped, which made Claire's stomach drop as she reached him.

But there was no body.

"Stay with me," Jonny ordered, pointing to his side. "Right with me. I'm going to check the water." He dug into his pocket and pulled out his phone, turning on the torchlight.

Ignoring his order to stay with him, Claire began to look around for herself. She found herself wandering closer and closer to the mill, but despite being all lit up, it was as silent as any other time she had been there.

Eerie.

"*Claire!*"

Jonny's bellow made her jolt, and she looked around in terror, half expecting someone in dark clothing to jump out at her.

"He's in the water, Claire! Help!"

Claire raced back to where Jonny had been, only to find him gone. "Where?"

"In the water by the wheel!" Jonny yelled from the far side of the mill.

She sprinted around the building, still not sure who he was talking about. "Are they floating toward it? Are they in danger of hitting the wheel?" she asked when she reached the bank where Jonny stood.

Jonny shook his head, flinging off his jacket and shoes. "They aren't moving. I need to get down there. It's a steep bank. Don't follow me. I'll swim them over to the brook's edge. It'll be easier to get them out." He started down the sharp incline with more haste than caution, but Claire supposed that couldn't be helped.

"Oh, baguettes, this is cold," Jonny said as he stepped into the water and waded quickly toward the body.

Claire hadn't seen it before, but now she could.

Face down, hovering in the water lifelessly, was the form of a man, but it was hard to tell much else in the dark and with the limited exposure. She wasn't sure if she was seeing legs extending out from the body or if they were tucked under the torso. There was just not enough light.

"Light, Claire!" Jonny called as if he had heard her thoughts.

Right. The torchlight had been on when he'd dropped his phone. She scrambled for it and did her best to shine the light down on the water, but the range was not great.

"I'm sorry! Can you see anything?" she asked loudly, the sound of the wheel almost drowning her out.

"Just enough!" came his reply. She watched as Jonny reached the body and, with all the skills of any pool lifeguard she had ever seen, turned the figure onto its back and began swimming toward the bank, the victim's body half covering him. "Who is it?"

Claire moved around the wheel, trying to follow Jonny's progress as he swam along the brook. She held his mobile out further, squinting at the waterlogged body Jonny held onto as he swam. "Oh, sugar! It's Benji!"

"That explains the weight." Jonny coughed. "I can't tell if he's breathing or not, but there's definitely rope around his neck."

"Crepes, crepes, crepes, crepes," Claire muttered as she almost tripped over her own feet, her trainers slipping in the grass at the bank of the brook. "Can you get him out here?"

Jonny nodded. "Just a bit further. Slopes naturally. Come close if you can. I'll need help."

She nodded and crept as close to the water's edge as she could, shoving Jonny's phone into her back pocket.

With deft, powerful strokes, Jonny brought Benji to the edge and stood, adjusting his hold to heft the man onto the bank as far he could. "Grab his arm. Under the armpit if you can. Hold him and I'll get out."

Claire did so, her pulse thundering in her throat and her fingers suddenly feeling weak.

Jonny climbed out of the water and sniffed, turning to grab the other arm in exactly the same way. "Ready? Together. Pull!"

They heaved together, dragging the unconscious Benji up the bank of grass until he was safely out of the water.

She looked at Benji more closely and inhaled sharply. The angry, raw red marks around his neck beneath the rope were absolutely horrific, and she covered her mouth and nose as she stared down at him.

Jonny reared back suddenly, drawing her gaze. He looked at her with wide eyes. "Claire, call 999. He's alive!"

CHAPTER 16

Jonny paced the room with almost frantic steps. He wasn't one to pace usually, but after what he had been through, pacing was absolutely warranted.

They had saved Benji's life.

That was what the paramedics had said. Those exact words.

He and Claire had saved Benji's life.

And now he couldn't stop shaking. Or pacing.

Thankfully, he could pace and shake in his own home, as there had been no reason for him to accompany Benji to the hospital. DS Watson had said he would meet the ambulance at the hospital and call them with an update.

That had been two hours ago.

Claire was curled up in a ball and dozing on the sofa in the sitting room, and Gabi had come down with a blanket for her. She was sitting by the bay window, staring solemnly out at the night sky.

"They're going to have to cancel the show," Gabi announced in a soft voice. "Two bodies now, even if he did survive. There's no way they can go on. They'll have to reopen the investigation into the first death."

"They'll go on," Jonny assured her, barely sparing her a glance. "Benji's not dead, and they'll find an excuse. One body didn't stop them."

Gabi turned toward him. "They have to do something. Postpone or move to a new location. Give the bakers a ruddy hazard pay, if nothing else."

Jonny laughed without humor. "The bakers don't get paid. Claire told me it's just a per diem for their ingredients and housing while they're on."

"Of all the—" Gabi slapped the cushion beneath her. "Then we need to insist that they start getting paid now! The show is paying for Lesley's funeral expenses—even though you offered to handle it—probably to make sure they look good when it comes out, and I'm sure they'll *generously* cover Benji's medical expenses." She snorted in utter derision. "But this is our estate, and I'm pretty sure the contract you signed never mentioned murder. So demand that they pay the contestants, even if they decide to postpone, because the bakers deserve something for risking their lives over a blasted batch of quiche."

He stopped pacing and looked at his younger sister rather fondly. "Did you want to be the one to tell them? Why should I have all the fun?"

She smiled flatly back at him. "Lady Gabriella Ainsley doesn't hold quite the same amount of power as the viscount, but thanks. I'm going to do something about this, Jon. I really am." She looked at Claire, her expression softening. "What if it had been Claire this time?"

Jonny's throat constricted as though he had been stran-gled instead of Benji. "Don't," he ordered roughly, which is what he had ordered his mind when the same thoughts kept trying to invade every few minutes or so. "It wasn't Claire. I was with her."

"But it could have been," Gabi said knowingly. "You think she'll never go anywhere alone while she's here?"

That was just it—he knew she would. She had planned on going to the mill alone that night after dark to see what the murderer would have seen. She very well could have been the next victim, and he would have been tucked into his high tower, so to speak, completely unaware that the woman he . . . That the person he . . .

He liked her. He liked Claire, and not in a "she's really good company" way, though she certainly was. He liked her in the "he liked looking at her" way, or the "liked laughing with her" way, or the "lost track of time when he was with her" way.

It was a strange feeling. Minutes usually crawled by when he was in the company of most people, and the exceptions to that unofficial rule were few and far between. And nobody had ever given him these extremes in emotion before. Hilarity until he almost cried. Fear that could keep him awake at night. Anticipation that made his legs buzz in the strangest ways. Curiosity that made him go where he hadn't ever intended on going. Investment that made him watch hours of a baking competition he had happily avoided all these years.

He genuinely and thoroughly liked Claire.

So the idea that she could have been killed that night made him want to sleep on the floor of her bedroom and never let her out of his sight.

Ever.

But that was just another wave of intense emotions in a night full of intense emotions.

It would pass.

Surely the hospital would know something by now. Surely Watson had some information he could pass on. Surely—

The sudden buzzing sensation in his right back pocket jolted him out of his thoughts, and he belatedly fumbled to get his mobile free. He tapped the screen and was speaking before the phone had reached his ear. "Hello, Watson."

"My lord," Watson replied rather formally through the phone. "Apologies for not calling sooner. The hospital would not permit me use of my phone in certain areas."

"It's fine," Jonny insisted as he moved to the couch and nudged Claire's feet, trying to jostle her awake without too much abruptness. "What do you know?"

Claire stirred and raised her head, looking around with bleary eyes. "What is it?" she asked in a sleepy voice.

"Watson," Jonny whispered, holding up the phone to show her.

She sat up quickly, swinging her legs down, and rubbed her fists into her eyes, nodding.

Jonny put the phone on speaker.

"Mr. Andrews-Lee is awake and alert to his surroundings," Watson told them. "He did not see who attacked him. He only felt something go around his neck and tighten fast. He says he was soon unconscious, and the next thing he recalls is waking up in the ambulance, soaking wet and with searing pain about his neck."

Claire frowned at the phone. "That's not a lot to go on. Did he say what he was doing down by the mill?"

Watson made some kind of a hemming noise, and the sound of rustling pages blared through the speaker, making them all wince. "He said he'd had a bad practice bake earlier and had gone for a walk after the elimination filming to clear his head. It was later than he'd realized when it got dark, and he was headed back for the inn when the attack happened."

"Someone did have a bad bake," Claire spoke up. "The smell of burnt pastry is pretty strong. And he has been pretty stressed lately. I can understand needing a walk."

"He needs to prove himself on the show to stay in?" Jonny asked her.

"Possibly," she said with a nod. "Maybe he's afraid of being caught cheating too."

"Cheating?" Watson repeated. "Did I hear that right?"

Claire hissed softly. "Yeah, you did. I'm fairly confident he's cheating in the Occasion Bakes."

"Now that's interesting."

Jonny tsked loudly. "Going to be hard to compete with a ring around his neck."

Claire gave him a scolding look.

Watson cleared his throat. "It may be that the two of you interrupted the course of the crime. That may upset the murderer, and they may seek out another of the bakers soon."

Jonny exhaled slowly, shaking his head. "They can't stay in the village anymore." He looked directly at Claire, his stomach practically exploding into his chest. "You can't stay in the village anymore."

Claire smiled slightly, a somewhat sad, almost helpless smile, the unspoken words clear as day. *Where would I go?*

"Everyone should stay here," Gabi announced, reminding Jonny rather suddenly that she was still there. "We have plenty of rooms that are never used, and it would be easy enough to make them habitable for a temporary situation. If everyone is here, it'll be easier to keep everyone safe."

Jonny looked at her with an impatient frown that she

blatantly ignored. He wasn't keen on having *all* the bakers in his house, but if it meant keeping Claire safe, he'd hold the door open for them himself. Each and every one.

"That would make it easier to interview everyone this time," Watson mused through the phone. "It is an excellent thought, my lady. I will be meeting with Mr. Phipps as soon as he arrives at the hospital. Might I pose the offer to him?"

"He's not already there?" Claire buried her face in one hand with a groan.

"No, I'm afraid not. We haven't seen anyone from the show here."

Jonny covered the phone with one hand, looking between his sister and Claire. "What are the odds that one of the show higher-ups are in on this?"

Gabi's eyes widened, and she looked at Claire.

Claire, on the other hand, did not look remotely surprised. "I'm torn. They're keeping everything so quiet to protect the show, but they could also be storing it up to share all at once when the show goes to air. I think most of them are too squeamish to kill anyone, or to have it done. I'm willing to bet they just needed to figure out how to protect themselves before they say anything."

That made sense to Jonny as well, but he would still keep the suspicion about the show's involvement in the murder in a corner of his mind.

"My lord?"

Jonny knew what the detective had asked, but he had hoped the man would forget about it. But if having the bakers at his house would mean that Claire would be able to stay safe from murder and harm, he would endure it.

He'd have to.

"Yeah, all right," he said into the phone, exhaling heavily. "Tell them the estate can house them, if they are determined that the show must go on, or whatever it is that they say."

"Oh, it'll go on," Claire muttered. "You heard them after Lesley. Benji was attacked, but he's also known for being dramatic, so they'll write this off too. We signed contracts, and they can't afford to shut down if they want the show to continue for any further series."

"What's next for Benji?" Jonny asked Watson. "Have they mentioned tests?"

"I believe a head CT is taking place now, and an EEG will follow. There is some concern for whatever length of time he was unconscious, possibly without air, so they are testing for brain function. Chest radiographs to examine the condition of his lungs from being in the water."

The sound of pages turning could be heard again, and Jonny tried not to smile.

So old school.

"Ah, yes," Watson grunted. "Some bloodwork, though I didn't write down for what. Something called a pulse oximetry saturation? No idea what that's for. And an MRI of the neck to examine the throat region for internal injuries. More tests may be required, obviously, but Mr. Andrews-Lee seems in good spirits, considering. Very lethargic and cold, but I am assured that his vital signs are promising. He does not remember the rescue, but he did ask that I pass on his thanks."

Jonny shifted uncomfortably. As much as Claire had joked only hours ago about Jonny not wanting to be a hero, it was actually true. He didn't want attention or praise for something he had done, especially when it had been something he had done without thinking. Surely anyone else would have tried to help Benji in that situation, so it ought to have nothing to do with Jonny at all.

He didn't mean to dismiss the man's gratitude; he just hoped the one acknowledgment was it.

"Consider them passed," Jonny mumbled, rubbing at the back of his neck.

Gabi made the situation worse by coming over to him and pinching his cheek like an over-affectionate aunt.

He slapped her hand away, glowering up at her, which made her laugh uproariously.

Jonny shifted the phone off the speaker setting and put it to his ear. "Right, so anything you need us to do before you're back?"

"No, sir. Though I might recommend preparing those rooms you've so kindly offered. It would not surprise me if the show has the bakers on your doorstep for breakfast."

"Thanks, Watson," Jonny told him, pinching the bridge of his nose. "Coffee on the estate tomorrow if you need it. Cheers."

"Thank you, my lord. Good night."

Jonny set his phone on the armrest of the couch before slouching back against the soft cushions. "I suppose we can't even speculate until we know how Benji's tests turn out. But I thought the police said that Lesley was dead before she was drowned."

Claire tucked her feet up beside her and leaned on her own armrest. "I think that was a possibility, but it was tough to say. Drowning doesn't always require water to be in the lungs, or something." She suddenly tutted, shaking her head. "It would be hard to overpower Benji so suddenly."

Jonny rolled his head on the couch to look at her fully. "What do you mean?"

Claire's mouth twisted to one side as she thought. "Well, he's a stocky firefighter. In good shape, by all appearances. Taking him down, let alone by surprise, would take a lot of work and effort. So that may eliminate quite a few people from the list of suspects."

That was a valid point, and one Jonny truthfully hadn't considered even in the process of getting Benji out of the water. Lesley hadn't been a petite woman, but he would hardly have called her stocky. Benji, on the other hand . . . Claire was right; it would have taken a great deal of effort to render him incapacitated.

Who in the world were they dealing with here? Could it have been a team effort? That would make more sense in the case of Benji, and there were any number of combinations of people that might have been able to pull it off.

The police would have to collect alibis all over again in the morning. So, in a sense, they were back to square one, but with two murders now. Well, one murder and one attempted murder.

Would it make that much difference to the case that the second attempt had not been successful?

"Why was the mill all lit up if no one was in there?" Claire said suddenly, her fingers twirling slowly in her hair.

Jonny stared at her, waiting for her to go on.

She looked at him, leaning her head on the hand entangled in her dark hair. "I almost went into the mill while you checked the water. There's not a ton of dark spaces in there when the lights are on."

"They probably ran away when you guys were running

for it," Gabi suggested, plopping herself down on a large otto-man nearby. "Did you call out before you got there?"

Jonny thought back, then shook his head slowly. "No. They would have heard our feet on the gravel, which is loud, but . . ."

"Maybe they weren't in the mill at that point?" Claire suggested. "I mean, Benji was in the water, so the killer could have been out there too?"

Gabi shuddered and rubbed her arms quickly. "Don't say that. It means both of you were right there by the person."

It was a sobering thought, there was no mistaking it. Either of them could have been mere meters, even closer, from the murderer and not known it. They'd been so focused on finding whoever the victim was, if there was one, that the idea of being in danger had been on the back burner of Jonny's mind. What if the killer had been hiding or coming up with something more to do? What if Claire had gone right into their clutches? What if . . . ?

What. If.

Yeah, there was no way Claire was spending one more night at the Ivy House. Even if no one else came over to Blackfirth, he wasn't going to let her leave. He might be over-bearing, overprotective, and a several-tiered cake's worth of over the line, but he would do it.

"Why don't you stay here tonight?" he suggested, trying to force his voice to remain steady. "It's too late to go back to the inn, and if there's already been trouble tonight—"

"Sounds good," Claire said with a yawn and a wave.

Oh. That was easy.

Jonny looked at his sister, who was watching him with the sort of incredulous mockery only a younger sister could bestow. "Gabs, would you get her settled tonight? I'm going to go check on the rooms and see how much work needs to be done for the rest."

"Sure thing," Gabi drawled, shaking her head at him as she rose. "Claire, I've got a few pajama options for you. Come on, the room next to mine is always set for Trixie, so you can bunk out there."

"Thanks." Claire got up and followed Gabi toward the door. "Night, Jonny."

Jonny watched them go, waving a little. "Good night, Claire. Good night, Gabi."

Gabi turned and pointed at him with a dramatic wink. "Good night, Jon."

He gave her a warning look, which she ignored as she whirled around and looped her arm through Claire's as they turned for the stairs.

Alone, Jonny groaned and rubbed at his face. How in the world was he going to keep Claire safe? And having his quiet house filled with people he didn't know well or care much about was only going to add to his stress and discomfort. It was not a great time to be taking anyone in, or accepting responsibility for them, but what choice did he have?

Someone was trying to kill off bakers on his estate.

How was he going to help any of them?

CHAPTER 17

"Are they serious? A buddy system? I've never felt more like I was in primary school in my entire life." Freya folded her arms with a huff, hair piled haphazardly atop her head, a dash of flour dusting her cheek from her practice session that morning.

Anthony was not sympathetic. "Primary school was like five years ago for you. Calm down."

Freya glared at him. "Really? Three days in this house, and now they're telling us we can't go anywhere anytime without someone else with us? You're okay with that?"

"It's better than death, innit?" he shot back. "If they can get Benji, they can get any of us without a problem."

"Don't say that," Denis groaned. "First of all, it's terrifying. Second, we're safer here than at the inn. Third, if they won't let us go home without being in breach of contract, we really ought to do what they suggest."

Anthony rolled his eyes. "Grow a spine, Denis."

"Leave off him," Mathias scolded, his tone harsh. "What's he ever done to you?"

Kerri cleared her throat. "Why can't they just let me and

Mathias go home? We're not even competing anymore, and we won't say anything."

"They're way too protective of the show for that," Denis told her sadly, his expression full of sympathy.

Anthony huffed and craned his neck from side to side, eliciting cracking sounds. "I just think it could be worse. We could be dead. So I'll stay in the house and like it, but not because the show tells me to."

Freya burst into laughter. "Oh, that's rich. You're choosing to do exactly what you've been told to do, but not because you've been told to do it. Your entitlement is astounding. Tell you what, bruv, take a hike on the estate tonight. Alone. Have fun." She stormed out of the room, and Kerri followed at once.

"What's gotten into sis?" Anthony asked the others, smiling crookedly. "Think it's the pressure?"

"Unbelievable," Denis mumbled, following the others with a shake of his head.

Mathias said nothing as he also left the room.

Claire, sitting silently watching yet another tension-filled meeting of the bakers, pursed her lips, unsure what to say or do in this moment. Anthony had been different since they'd all moved into Blackfirth House: less of the warm and friendly, exercise-obsessed man and more of the on-edge, arrogant, argumentative one they'd been seeing since the murder occurred.

No one wanted to be in his company now, and, as far as Claire knew, they were all actively avoiding him. The only reason they'd been with him now was because one of the production assistants had come to tell them the new rules. It hadn't gone particularly well, obviously, but it was nobody's fault. Not only had the bakers moved into the estate house, but most of the remaining production crew had as well. The show had cut down numbers of their staff for their own safety, but the bakers were not receiving any such consideration.

Gabi privately insisted that she was working on getting financial compensation for the bakers with all that they'd had to deal with on the shoot, but Claire wasn't holding her breath.

There was a brief pause, and then Anthony said, "Sounds like Benji's doing well."

"Sounds like." The fact that Claire knew so much more about Benji's state than any of the others, including most of the production staff, would remain a locked secret for her entire life.

It was safer that way.

"Well, I'm going for a run," Anthony announced unnecessarily. "I'm gonna hit up Hattie from props to join me. She's fit, yeah?" He quirked his brows and strode out of the room, leaving Claire to her solitude.

It was all she could do to avoid slumping in her chair now that she was free to do so.

The only reason she hadn't left was because this particular sitting room was next to the main kitchens of the estate, and it was Claire's turn to practice in them for the show tomorrow and the next day. The last thing she felt like doing was making mince pies, so she was going to work on aspects of her Occasion Bake instead. Much more cheerful and jolly, which she could use a dash of at the moment.

Maybe more than a dash.

Pushing herself up and out of her chair, Claire sighed and moved into the kitchen, pleased that either Freya had cleaned up so well after herself or that Jonny's staff had done so. She wasn't quite sure how things worked in this place; she never seemed to see any staff other than the Clydes, but what got done in a house of this size was simply not possible for only two people. She knew that was traditionally how servants at an estate were supposed to operate, but it was quite a different thing to experience it live.

Living in Blackfirth was an experience in many ways, even only three days in. There were no official meals where they all sat down together, but rather an open buffet at certain times. The house was big enough that she could avoid everyone if she wished, not that she did wish to. She'd only lasted a day before she'd begun exploring the entire house from top to bottom. Room by room. Antique by antique. She was absolutely certain that someone knew what she was doing, via cameras or snooping or the like, but she had never been stopped, which only encouraged her to keep looking.

The library was extraordinary, exactly the sort of place she had imagined all historic houses had. The conservatory made her feel as though she was living in Cluedo, but it was a lovely space all its own. The halls had so much artwork that the gallery seemed utterly superfluous, though it didn't stop her from spending ages in there just marveling at it all. There were carvings in wood, murals on ceilings, plasterwork that would make a sculptor weep. Honestly, sleeping in her designated bedroom seemed like a dream, it was so quaint and elegant and perfect.

Had she imagined herself as a woman in one of the great historical eras wandering the corridors whimsically and staring out of the large windows with a forlorn air that spoke of lost love? Quite possibly.

Would she ever admit that to anyone? Absolutely not.

In the kitchen, she looked for the crate of ingredients with her name on it. She snapped her fingers when she found it, whistling tunelessly as she carried it over to the counter and began unpacking what the show assistants had purchased for her practice bakes.

She ought to have Christmas music playing while she worked. She wouldn't be allowed her phone during the shoot—those were turned in until filming was complete for the day—but it couldn't hurt while she was practicing.

She swiped on her mobile to her Christmas playlist and let the music blare into the space, instantly feeling a better vibe. If she focused on just being part of a baking competition at a historic estate instead of a murder investigation that had baking competitors sequestered in the estate for their safety, it could be a stress-free and utterly delightful afternoon. Just focusing on a Christmas bake.

Looking over her instruction page, Claire set herself a timer. She wasn't going to do all portions of her bake, as the raised game pie would require an one hour the night before for the dough to be fully prepared, and she could make marzipan easily enough. But if she could knock out a Twelfth Night cake and gingerbread biscuits quickly and without massive issues, she would be delighted.

She began mixing ingredients for the cake together, dancing to the cheery holiday music, remembering her childhood attempts at holiday baking with her great-granny. The woman could do incredible things with minimal ingredients, and she never minded if Claire or Ellie or any of the other kids helped her out by stirring the mixture or adding the ingredients or making a hash of the decorating.

The woman had been a saint as far as patience was concerned, and her love of Christmas had been palpable. Claire was adapting her Twelfth Night cake to pre-1900 details, and she only hoped it would do her justice.

"It's the most wonderful time of the year," Claire sang to herself, stirring the dried fruits into her batter. "With the kids jingle-belling and everyone telling you be of good cheer . . ." She spun with her bowl a little, the spoon becoming a microphone. "It's the most wonderful time of the year!"

"What time of year is that, exactly?"

"Crepes alive!" Claire yelped, jumping backward and clutching the bowl of batter to her body.

Jonny was leaning in the doorway to the kitchen, looking entirely un-Christmassy in his cream-colored Henley shirt, sleeves shoved to his elbows. His bemused smirk bore none of the Christmas spirit either, unless one considered the intentional placing of coal into stockings for a laugh part of the Christmas spirit. He folded his arms and raised a brow at her, which, when combined with his almost-smile of a smirk, was ridiculously charming. Unfortunately.

Claire set her bowl on the counter and put a hand to her heart, exhaling as slowly as she could. "You're not going to apologize for scaring the complete and utter life out of me?"

He shook his head rather emphatically. "Nope. It's so rare that I actually get to do that, I'm just going to stand here and revel in it for a moment."

It was one of the most ridiculous things she had heard him say, which had the bizarre effect of making her laugh.

Was cabin fever a thing in a very large house?

"Christmas bakes?" Jonny said as he came into the kitchen.

Claire nodded as she went back to her batter. "Twelfth Night cake. And while that's baking, I'll do the gingerbread biscuits."

Jonny sighed loudly and with much satisfaction. "Gingerbread biscuits are the greatest things. My mum made two batches every year: some for Gabi and me to decorate and some for her to use to build a gingerbread house. Or a village, sometimes. Small village, but nevertheless . . ." He smiled as he picked up the biscuit cutters. "Good memories."

"Did she let you eat the dough?" Claire asked as she turned to her parchment paper and began cutting out a circle for the pan.

"She always told us that if we misbehaved, we'd never get some," he said with a quick laugh. "But we always managed to get some from her." He tapped the counter where she was cutting. "Parchment paper? That's allowed?"

She gave a quick nod and a cheeky grin. "It is. Fudges the rules a little, but I've cleared it. Parchment paper was invented in 1847, so it's fair game. Not sure when they actually used it in baking, but . . ." She shrugged. "Did you need something or were you just wanting to scare me?"

"I didn't set out scouring the house just for the opportunity to scare you," Jonny protested with a quick laugh. "I came looking for you, and when I saw that you weren't paying any attention to anything but your Christmas music and your baking, I took the chance. You're telling me you wouldn't have done the same thing?"

Claire paused, doing him the courtesy of actually showing him that she was thinking about it. "Nope, you're right. I totally would have."

"Thank you." He turned and leaned against the counter, watching her. "Is that the cake that has something in it someone has to find?"

"It is," she replied, setting the parchment circle into the pan. "And if you behave, you can put the bean in the batter."

He snorted softly. "Thanks very much."

Claire focused on pouring her batter as evenly as possible into the pan. "So you were just looking for me for kicks and giggles, or . . . ?"

"Do I need a reason to find you?"

Her eyes flicked to him, then back to her batter, her cheeks flaming. "Guess not. Your house, after all. You can do what you want."

"So can you. If you want me to go, I will. You're baking; tell me to get lost if it will distract you."

It *would* distract her, there was no question about it. Jonny was charming, attractive, funny, engaging, witty. He was always good for conversation, and comfortable even in silence. She liked being with him, liked looking at him, liked . . .

Him. She liked him.

And that was distracting.

But she didn't want him to go.

"You can stay," she said simply, grabbing a spoon and scraping the rest of the batter into the pan. "The bean's on the counter there. The white one. Go ahead and put it in if you want."

"Okay, then." He pinched the bean between his fingers and plopped it into the mixture.

Without looking up, Claire smoothed it over, hiding the bean within the depths of the batter. "Great. Now we bake." She picked up the pan and turned to the oven, tucking the pan safely onto its rack and closing the door. "Timer. Timer, timer, timer . . ."

"Up here," Jonny told her, suddenly behind her and pushing the button to bring up the digits on the screen.

"Fancy." Claire typed in the numbers, ignoring the scent of whatever Jonny was wearing and the warmth of his arm being quite literally beside her face.

Cakes and a custard, he was more than distracting.

She cleared her throat and turned away from him as she walked back to the counter. "Have you heard from Watson today?"

"He's supposed to call, actually," Jonny replied lightly as he ambled back to the counter. "Thought it would save time if we were together when he did."

Why was that the most disappointing thing he could have said? It made sense, and he was right in that it would save time. But why did that have to be the reason he'd sought her out? Why could he not have just wanted to spend time with her?

Then again, why hadn't Claire sought *him* out if she wanted to spend time with him? This street went two ways, and she couldn't be the person standing at the crosswalk and looking in only one direction.

That was how someone got hit by a car.

Metaphorically speaking, anyway.

On cue, Jonny's phone rang, and he pulled it from his pocket, tapping the answer and speaker buttons in quick succession before putting the phone on the counter. "Watson."

"My lord," DS Watson greeted, sounding slightly out of breath. "Is Miss Walker with you by chance?"

"Hi, Detective," Claire replied quickly. She started gathering her gingerbread ingredients, trying to keep it as quiet as possible.

THE CRIME BRÛLÉE BAKE OFF

"Oh good," he said, relief clear in his voice. "There has been a lot happening."

"Really?" Jonny folded his arms, his brow furrowing. "Like what?"

Watson cleared his throat. "Is there anyone else that can hear you?"

Claire looked at Jonny in surprise. "No. It's just us."

Jonny's eyes were wide, and he glanced at the phone intently. "What's going on?"

"The injuries Mr. Andrews-Lee sustained don't quite match what Ms. Kemble endured," Watson told them, his voice low. "We already knew that his oxygen levels were good, that his neurological tests were normal, and that his bloodwork was looking good. There was minimal internal bruising of the throat. No signs of petechial hemorrhaging. No head trauma. The head CT and MRI were normal and clear."

"I don't understand." Claire drummed her fingers on the countertop, feeling like her mind was working backward.

"It would appear Mr. Andrews-Lee had only momentarily been strangled by the rope and rendered unconscious. Perhaps it was the means of incapacitating him, but there is no proof that he was as powerfully strangled as Ms. Kemble was. Not an iota."

"He wasn't strangled? But we saw his neck. The bruising and the marks from the rope . . ." She trailed off, looking at Jonny in bewilderment. "What is going on here?"

"Maybe we've got the order of events wrong?" Watson posed cautiously. "There's no mistaking the injuries to his neck, and he was unconscious in the brook, so the drowning was in progress . . ."

Jonny pinched the bridge of his nose. "Does that mess up the timeline?"

"I don't think so," Watson said, turning pages near the phone. "For this incident, we don't have an alibi for Anthony Wright, Bob Helms, Anna Patton, or Gertrude Adams."

"Gertrude Adams?" Claire scoffed. "She couldn't take down a mouse by herself. She's tiny and frail."

"Which would indicate she'd need a partner, if she was involved," Jonny pointed out. He exhaled heavily, shaking his head. "I hate thinking this way."

Claire nodded, swallowing with difficulty. "Me too." She returned to her ingredients, trying to make sense of the entire situation.

"The rope used was the same," Watson went on. "We are going over the mill again forensically."

Jonny nodded a few times. "Good. There's gotta be something to find there."

"What do you both think is next?" Watson asked. "We have to wait for the rest of the results, of course, but is there anyone else we should be questioning harder or questioning again? Anything strange happening in the baking?"

"We're all on edge right now," Claire admitted, thinking back to the earlier discussion. "Kerri doesn't come out of her room if she can help it, Anthony is cranky and outspoken, Mathias spends more time in the library than anywhere else, since he's been eliminated. I don't know, Detective. I have a hard time pinning this on Denis or Freya."

"Might I suggest we increase security on the estate?" Jonny offered. "Cameras, lights on a timer, patrols."

"Excellent thoughts. I will review my options and let you know what's available."

Jonny nodded and smiled. "Let me know if there is anything the estate can do to help, Watson. I know the restraints you are under."

"Thank you, my lord. My superiors are still considering Ms. Kemble's death as an isolated incident, and the producers are happy to agree, so it is a battle."

"Understood. Take care." Jonny hung up the phone and rubbed at his face, chuckling softly. "What is wrong with us, Claire? I don't think we offered anything useful in that investigation call."

"Probably means we're out of our depth and improperly equipped to be involved," Claire told him with a shrug. "Easy enough."

Jonny tsked loudly. "So much for us being the brains." He sighed and looked at her barely-in-process gingerbread biscuits. "I wish I could stay down here while you bake. Not just because it's gingerbread, but because it's you. How can it be so hard to spend time together when we're in the same house?" He huffed, shaking his head. "There are too many people here, Claire. Just too many."

Well, how was her heart supposed to react to that?

Settling for feeling fluttery and warm, Claire found herself smiling in a way that made her cheeks hurt. "Well, if I decide to eat dinner on the terrace at six . . ." She flicked her gaze at him. '

"I might have some time free to stop by," Jonny finished with a sage nod, his blue eyes twinkling. "We shall see." He knocked on the counter, smiling at her as he backed away. "Merry temporary Christmas."

"It's *always* Christmas for some people," Claire shot back

as she began to measure out her flour. "Not temporary. Bye now."

She heard his laughter as he left, and she bit her lip at the flush of heat his laughter caused.

Oh, crepes alive, she was in trouble.

Adding her flour into the batter, Claire had a thought. She pulled over a small bowl and set it beside the stand mixer. She didn't need all her biscuit dough for today's bake. Why not leave Jonny a Christmas message only he would understand?

Maybe she didn't have to be in trouble alone.

CHAPTER 18

It was, without a doubt, the strangest gift he had ever been given.

It was also, without a doubt, the sweetest.

Not just because it was dough.

Claire hadn't said a word about it when they'd met by chance on the terrace yesterday pretty much right at six, dinner plates in hand. She'd simply chatted away with him without hesitation, without discussing the murder, without discussing baking.

It had almost been like a date, except neither of them had paid and there was nothing going on after the dinner.

And there was a house full of people who could walk out any time and join their conversation.

So not like a date at all, really.

Except it had felt like one.

After enjoying himself immensely talking with Claire, he had finished up some work before going to his room, where he found a small bowl wrapped with cling film. He'd stooped and picked it up, startled that it was chilled, and peered inside.

Gingerbread biscuit dough.

It had been a good thing for everyone that Claire had not been there. If he'd been able to speak, he would have rambled like she did. He'd probably have hugged her at the very least, and, quite possibly, have kissed her.

Which, of course, meant that kissing Claire was all he could think about now.

He imagined her kisses tasted like gingerbread.

But today was a baking day for the show, so he wouldn't get to see her much. He couldn't remember how long the mince pie bake would take, but he'd learned that whatever time the bakers were given, they would have an additional hour before and after for filming extras. And then, if he recalled what Claire had told him, they would be working an extra hour to prepare things for the Occasion Bake tomorrow.

There would be no time to talk today unless he went to the pavilion during filming, which was always a risk. He had yet to make sense of when they took breaks from filming, what was noticed by production assistants, how carefully observed any of the bakers were when the cameras weren't rolling. And he certainly didn't want anyone to think that he and Claire . . . That they had . . . That they . . .

Well, that there was something there.

Murder investigation or otherwise.

He stared out of his study window, just as he had the first day the crew had arrived, his view obscured by the green-and-white canvas of the pavilion. He couldn't see what was inside, but he could picture it. Freya's station would be a mess, scattered ingredients everywhere, and somehow she would present something virtually pristine, despite her constant anxiety about it all. Denis kept a spick-and-span station and presented perfection, usually with an accompanying story, impression, accent, or a scene from a play or movie where he played all the parts.

And then there was Claire. Somewhere in the middle in the neatness of her station, usually strapped for time, her bakes always fitting the brief, but never quite confident in her skills, keeping her cool anyway. She always knew when there would be something for the judges to nitpick and was always surprised by their praise.

He knew far more about her than he did about the others, and what he knew about them was mainly from what he had seen in the pavilion and what Claire herself had told him.

Did he care who won the show? Not really. If Claire was in the finale, he would root for her. But he would not pretend to understand what set one baker apart from another, or what the judges were looking for, or why in the world there were multiple kinds of buttercream. Even in watching previous series of the show, he still didn't understand. He wouldn't claim to have any more insight into baking now than he had before, except now different terms were in his mental vocabulary.

He had no reason to go down to the pavilion and watch the baking. There was nothing new to tell Claire about the case, no new insight he'd had about anything, no spectacular ideas he needed her opinion on.

But he really didn't have anything better to do. There were other things he could have done, of course, and plenty of them.

Just nothing better.

With more of a mental shrug than a physical one, Jonny turned from the study and grabbed the coat he'd tossed on a chair earlier. His security pass was already in his pocket, and the slight rain they were experiencing that morning wouldn't have too much of an effect on him. The temperature was down, which made the rain worse, but it could help the bakers in their endeavors.

As he understood it, baking was better on a cold day than a hot one.

Whether that was true for mince pies, he couldn't say. He'd never even eaten a mince pie before. Didn't particularly care to, either. Nor did it matter. Mince pies were the object of the day for Claire, with preparation for the Christmas Occasion Bake afterward. Maybe the colder temperatures would help her stay in the right mood for it.

He could always offer to sing some Christmas carols.

Picturing the way Claire had danced around the kitchen yesterday to the Christmas music, Jonny smiled to himself. She wouldn't do anything like that when the bake mattered so much and especially not when she was on camera, but knowing she had that inside her made her even more interesting to him.

The camera crew were set up both inside and outside the pavilion, and he could hear the sound from the microphones on the hosts and contestants from the outside. If the Christmas songs Charlie and Lindsay were singing were any indication, there would be no need for building up any of the Christmas spirit.

He winced at a particularly sour note that Charlie hit and thought the bakers might actually wish for a less vigorous attempt at the Christmas spirit.

He showed his badge to security and ducked into the camera-safe corner of the pavilion, scanning the room.

"Half an hour left, bakers!" Lindsay called out, fingers in her ears as Charlie finished his song.

"Right, we'll cut there," Mr. Dean announced. "Everybody's pies are in the ovens, right?"

Bakers nodded all around, and he gave a double thumbs-up. "Take ten minutes. We'll roll with reactions."

"Mine will be out in seven," Denis called out in a slightly apologetic tone.

Mr. Dean sighed heavily. "Fine. Dave, can you get Denis taking his out? Everybody else—ten is safe?"

"Yes," the others called.

Makeup artists and prop masters began moving about the pavilion, so Jonny seized the chance to wander while he could. As it happened, Claire's station was at the very back this time, so he had to look as though he was observing stations like one might browse the shelves at Waterstones or a local used bookshop until he made his way to her.

She sat on a stool behind her station, swinging her legs like a little kid, her content expression marred by a deep furrow between her dark brows.

What had put that there?

"Hey," he greeted softly as he reached her, making sure to keep his stance and his tone casual.

She jumped a little, then smiled quickly. "Hey."

"How are the Christmas pies going?" he asked, tucking his hands into his trouser pockets.

"Fine, for now." She raised her shoulders, holding them up a long moment. "We'll see." With a heavy exhale, her shoulders dropped. "I did what I could, and I won't know more until they come out."

It was exactly the sort of even, almost ambivalent answer he'd expected from her, as though she truly didn't feel the stress or pressure of the competition. But he knew better; she was just as stressed as everyone else, if not more.

Jonny gave her a steady look. "So what's with the frown?"

"I wasn't frowning," Claire protested, tilting her head in confusion.

He drew a vertical line between his own brows. "Right here, you were. What's up?"

Claire pulled a face at that, and she twisted her lips to one side, saying nothing.

"Claire," Jonny said simply, "it's me. What?"

She swallowed, and then nudged her head toward her left. "Over there."

Jonny looked, not seeing anything wrong for a moment. Then it hit him like a ruddy great gong. "What in the actual tart is he doing here?" he whispered, returning his attention to Claire to keep from staring.

"I don't know," she whispered back, keeping her lips from moving as much as possible. "He said he left the hospital against medical advice and was determined to bake, but Mr. Sybil said he was going to be excused for being unwell. They were going to let us all through this week with a double elimination next week."

Jonny glanced over again, quickly.

Benji Andrews-Lee was sitting on the stool behind his baking station, his throat covered by a high-necked jumper. Two production assistants were around him. One had water, and the other . . . well, it wasn't particularly clear what the point of her was, but Benji didn't seem to mind her presence.

"How's he been doing?" Jonny inquired, turning his back toward Benji and making it look like he was staring out of the semi-clear panels of the pavilion.

"Perfectly fine," Claire told him. "You'd never know he was in hospital for four days or whatever it was."

Jonny found himself frowning. "But he's playing the noble martyr? Or victim?"

"He's not exactly drawing attention to himself," she admitted in a low voice, "but he isn't pushing it away either. It's weird."

"Very weird," Jonny agreed. "What's the other assistant for?"

Claire leaned her hip against her baking station to look over at them. "Ah, looks like she's dispensing medications for him."

Jonny scoffed. "She'll be dabbing his brow with a damp cloth next. Anyone offering you water?"

"Not even once. I had to make my own tea when I got here." She growled under her breath, and he turned to see her putting both elbows on her station, her head in her hands. "He's been attacked and in hospital. Why am I suspicious?"

"Because Benji isn't a noble anything and would absolutely have taken the week off without punishment if it would have helped his cause?" Jonny suggested with a cheeky smile.

She removed her hands and glared at him. "You don't know him well enough to know that."

Jonny nodded slowly. "Oh, yes, I do. I know the type well. If he's here instead of taking full advantage of his time away, there's a reason. You're a good person, Claire, and you've got good instincts. If you think something is off, it probably is."

"It's not victim blaming?" she asked with a wince.

"Do you think he sought out his attack? Caused it? Did it on purpose?"

"No."

"Then I think you can be suspicious that he's acting out of character until you know otherwise. We're talking about one murder and one attempted murder, after all. It doesn't mean we have to like Benji."

Claire snorted a laugh at that, covering her mouth.

That made Jonny rather satisfied to hear. His visit was worth it, then.

"So do us all a favor," he whispered, leaning close for a minute, "and crush him."

Claire clamped down on her lips and nodded, giving him a tiny salute.

He winked in return and turned on his heel, going back to browsing the stations. "And the dough was perfection," he said over his shoulder. "Utterly."

He didn't need to see her reaction, but he sure hoped that she blushed. That would be an interesting continuity issue for the cameras. Or perhaps they could work the angle to suggest she had been spending too much time close to the oven.

His smile faded slightly as he returned to the safe corner of the pavilion. Why *was* Benji there if the show had allowed him time off? Had the hospital been concerned about him leaving early? Could they somehow gain access to his records due to Lesley's murder?

From what he'd heard so far, Benji's injuries hadn't been nearly as bad as they had originally feared. Had they missed something?

What if there was something in the historical Blackfirth murder details they were overlooking? The first murder had been modeled on it, and Jonny would be the first to admit that he had avoided learning any more about the original event than he'd had to. Perhaps they'd missed something significant that he would have known had he been paying attention.

The hosts were suddenly there, preparing to go back on camera.

Jonny took his chance and approached. "Lindsay? It is Lindsay, isn't it?"

Lindsay looked at him in surprise, then smiled slightly. "It is. And I promise not to get too personal."

Ooof. Right.

He grimaced in shame. "I am so sorry for that. It was ridiculously ill-mannered of me."

"Don't worry about it," Lindsay said immediately, her smile spreading. "It wasn't exactly great timing on my part. What can I do for you?"

It was really good of her not to hold his words against him, and he'd be sure to thank her somehow later. Or have Gabi think of something, which would probably go over better anyway.

He let himself smile back. "I'm looking for the historian who knew so much about the estate. Dr. Adams, I think?"

"Oh, sure," Lindsay said quickly. "Gertrude will be over in the greenroom helping prep some dialogue for Charlie and me as we highlight the estate."

"Greenroom?" Jonny repeated, hoping he looked as lost as he felt.

She grinned knowingly. "Yeah, sorry. The other small pavilion set up just down the way. She'd love to meet you officially, honestly."

"That's kind of what I'm afraid of," he admitted as he scratched the back of his head.

REBECCA CONNOLLY

Lindsay patted his arm a trifle patronizingly. "You'll get through it."

"Thanks." He nodded and left the baking pavilion, looking around for a smaller structure that would be considered the greenroom. He had never really noticed another one, but he hadn't been looking that carefully. He'd been trying to avoid the entire area unless he was looking for Claire.

But surely it would be right in front of his face. Any structure that wasn't original to the estate eight weeks ago was part of the show, and if he would just open his eyes—

Ah. There it was. Just to his right was a smaller version of the pavilion, though without the green-and-white-striped canvas.

This one was just green canvas.

That same awful, ugly, moss-shaded green. Is that why they called it a "greenroom"? He shuddered and ducked into it, looking around the mostly empty space. The older but well-dressed woman who sat at a card table didn't look up as he entered and continued to edit the document in front of her. With an actual red pen, it appeared.

Classic.

"Excuse me," Jonny ventured, wishing there was something nearby that he could knock on. "Dr. Adams?"

She turned in her chair, readers perched on the bridge of her nose, looking over them like a school professor. "Yes?"

Jonny stepped forward, oddly delighted she had no idea who he was. "Jonathan Ainsley. I wonder if you might have a moment for me."

Dr. Adams grabbed her readers, pulling them down around her neck, the beaded strap holding them in place despite her

208

tight grip. "Lord Colburn! Oh my days. Oh, sir, it is an honor. Please, please sit if you have the time."

Biting back a sigh that would absolutely have been full of irritation, Jonny moved to the table and pulled out a chair. Perhaps a little further than might have been strictly polite, but he suspected she wouldn't care. She fidgeted with her papers, clearing her throat repeatedly.

Eventually, she settled and smiled widely at him, her cheekbones almost hiding her eyes entirely. "How might I be of service to you, my lord?"

He needed to weigh his words carefully if he was going to survive this interaction. She could assume a great many things about the estate and the family name if she was as intense a fan as she appeared to be.

"Our family donated everything about the tenth viscountess to the historical society in the area," Jonny began in a light but even tone. "As such, I am not as familiar about the details as I ought to be, both as a descendant and as the viscount."

"It's understandable, sir," Dr. Adams broke in gently, putting her hand over his. "Such a tragedy for your family, and one that extends through generations. It was a kindness your great-grandfather did in donating everything for the good of the area, but also to spare you."

He did his best to keep a straight face. "Rest assured, I've no interest in asking for any of the items back, but I was wondering if there were detailed reports or histories I could read to know more than the average person doing a Google search."

"Oh, yes, my lord!" Dr. Adams cried with more enthusiasm than he'd expect of anyone her age. "I have several of them that I could send to you very easily. They're all in my computer database in my office. I am not actually needed here at the moment, so I can take a car to the office and send them right now!"

It was on the tip of Jonny's tongue to politely inform her that she did not have to do it at this moment, but he bit back that impulse. This was a murder investigation, after all, and he needed the information as soon as he could get it to try to make any headway in this thing.

So he only smiled indulgently. "I would be most appreciative, Dr. Adams. Here is my card." He pulled one of his business cards from his wallet and slid it across the table, nodding once. "Much appreciated. And might I reply to your email with any particular questions that the reading may bring about?"

"Please do," she gushed. "It would be my pleasure to assist you in any way."

Jonny pushed his chair back and stood, extending a professional hand toward her. "Thank you. I very much appreciate it."

She clutched his hand in both of hers, shaking firmly. "My honor and privilege, sir. Truly."

He nodded again and did his best to smoothly and neatly retrieve his hand from her grasp. Then he moved past her and exited the pavilion, making a beeline for his house and barely resisting the urge to bolt the doors behind him. If there had been a drawbridge, he might have ordered that raised too.

There was something unnerving about a stranger being more passionate about his family and their history than he or any of his relations were.

And he had just asked the most passionate Ainsley family fan for help.

Desperate times were truly here.

CHAPTER 19

Claire rubbed at her eyes as she heaved an exhausted sigh, making her way up to Blackfirth House after her hour of preparation for tomorrow's Christmas Occasion Bake. She had everything set for the morning to her exact wishes and needs, and to the best of her abilities. It was the best possible preparation she could have asked for. Tomorrow would bring its own problems, but she wasn't going to waste tonight's remaining thoughts worrying about them.

Tonight. She scoffed loudly to herself. It was half four.

It ought to have been bedtime, quite honestly. That was how much stress and effort had gone into the day's activities, not even accounting for the mental hurdles she'd endured.

Benji showing up at the pavilion had thrown her for a loop. It was astonishing that her mince pies had turned out to be well-baked, let alone palatable. But she'd received promising remarks, which also set her up well for tomorrow.

As long as she wasn't distracted by Benji.

Something wasn't right, and she didn't know what.

Anthony hadn't seemed surprised that Benji was there, which made her instantly suspicious of both of them. The two men had barely exchanged three words, but they had done some combination of a high five and a semi-hug when Benji had come in. Everyone else was just floored he was out of hospital. Nothing made sense anymore, and, once again, Benji's bake had gone surprisingly well for him.

She'd have thought that result absolute pity, had she not known that Alan and Dame Sophie were not the sort to treat anyone that way. Lindsay and Charlie had avoided talking to Benji on camera at all, which was interesting. Perhaps he was going to be edited out of the final product of this episode anyway? For the optics?

The high-necked jumper was out of Benji's usual wardrobe style, but with only two other episodes to reference, the television audience wouldn't know that.

Something was prodding at her, but she was too tired to consider it clearly. Bedtime was not for a while, and she needed to decompress somehow. No baking, and nothing to do with Benji or his injuries, if she could help it.

Mr. Clyde opened the door to the house for her, smiling blandly but not unkindly. "Miss Walker."

"Hi, Clyde," she offered with a return smile. "Is his lordship around?"

His smile turned a trifle more mischievous, which made Claire's cheeks warm. "In the historic kitchens, actually, Miss Walker. Do you know where that is?"

Claire nodded quickly. "What in the world is he doing there?"

"Waiting for you, I believe."

There was something both ticklish and ominous about that. "Okay. Well, I need to change and wash these for tomorrow's episode, so I'll have to meet him after."

Clyde bowed slightly, clearing his throat. "Leave them outside your door, Miss Walker. We'll have them clean and pressed before you need them in the morning, I assure you."

"You are a wonder, Clyde, you know that?" Claire said with a laugh.

He chuckled with a wheeze in his voice. "I am merely the conductor, Miss Walker. But I thank you all the same."

Claire trudged her way up the stairs, mentally shaking her head. The man might as well have been snatched from a bygone era and plunked into the present. He could have been a butler in the Victorian times without having to adjust a thing. Depending on how he liked wigs, even earlier.

What a strange world the estate-dwelling people inhabited.

Claire changed in her room, left her clothes outside her door, and made her way out of the house, doing her best to avoid seeing any of the other bakers. She didn't have anything against them and would probably see them at dinner, but after having spent all day with them, she was desperate for some different company. Her own, if she could manage no one else, but she much preferred the idea of spending time with Jonny.

His quip about her gingerbread biscuit dough had flustered her just enough that Charlie had come over and teased her out of her apparent stress for the camera. Hopefully, she had played the part well and not looked like someone who couldn't handle being flirted with.

If she had been flirted with.

Ugh, liking someone never got any easier.

She did her best to make the walk to the historic kitchens quickly, as she wasn't using the required buddy system. But if Jonny was waiting for her at the kitchens, it meant he had something to share about the investigation, and no one else could know about that.

She started along the corridor, glancing into each of the rooms but finding them dark and empty. They each had the production-added overhead lights, of course, but the crew only lit the rooms they needed when they needed them. So far, the only light she could see was in the back, where presentations were made and, once upon a time, where the bulk of the meal preparation would have been done.

Claire decided to peek in before making herself known. Jonny was standing over a cutting counter that was strewn with papers. Several more papers were on the floor. He had a pen behind his ear and another in his hand, and he was completely absorbed in whatever he was doing, if the furrows in his forehead were anything to go by.

Claire smiled slightly and knocked firmly on the heavy door.

Jonny glanced up and immediately smiled when he saw her.

Why, oh, why did that make her knees want to buckle?

"Hey, come look at this," he said, waving her over.

Claire forced her knees to remain steady as she joined him at the table. "What am I looking at?"

"Dr. Adams kindly sent me some records and reports she had on the murder of the tenth viscountess," Jonny explained, gesturing to the papers.

"Why would she do that?" Claire asked, eyes widening at the sheer volume of information.

Jonny snorted softly. "Because I asked." At her questioning look, he shrugged. "I wondered if we were missing something about the original murder that might help piece things together. I've spent so long avoiding it that I don't know the specific details, so I decided to ask her. I thought I'd get twenty pages, maybe. She sent me a hundred and forty-seven, and it's all her work."

"Cakes and a custard," Claire breathed. "She's obsessed."

"Pretty much, yeah," he agreed, nodding repeatedly. "But there are some useful things in here." He tapped a page in front of him that had a few things underlined. "Analysis of the coroner's notes, carefully reconstructed timeline of events, the viscount's journals during the investigation."

It was an impressive array of information, no question. Dr. Adams had clearly devoted her life and her educational career to this murder, and she was likely the foremost expert on the topic. But the idea of going through page after page of someone's life work to find clues to Lesley's murder felt daunting.

"Please don't tell me you need help reading all of this," Claire muttered as she took in all the pages on the floor, realizing how deep the layer on the table was. "I've spent all day in the pavilion and trying to process—"

"I wouldn't ask anybody to wade into this mire with me," Jonny cut her off with a laugh. "This is entirely my own fault. The ones on the floor are all biography, so I'm ignoring those for now." He heaved a sigh and craned his neck, eliciting a couple of soft pops. "I don't even know what I'm looking for in this. Anything that gives us a clue, I suppose."

Claire smiled, folding her arms and nudging him with her elbow. "You've marked things. What stood out to you in there?"

He returned her nudge with a knock of his hip against hers, then tapped at the paper with the most markings. "The pattern of bruising. It didn't have an upward slant, so Dr.

Adams concluded that strangulation was not part of the hanging. It was a level ring about the neck, indicating an even pressure of a certain height."

"Practically confirming Lesley's cause of death," Claire murmured, twisting her lips in thought. "Does it mention any other rope marks anywhere else?"

Jonny glanced at her. "What are you thinking?"

"Something with the waterwheel. I don't know how, but that's gotta be involved with the drowning. I have a hard time believing they just tossed Lesley into the water like they did Benji. I think I'll ask Watson if the same thing is in Lesley's report."

"Right, right." He reached toward the back of the table for a neat stack of pages and pulled them over, flipping through. "This is Dr. Adams's transcription of the coroner's report. So if we look for the notes on . . . Here—'Deep abrasions were noted on bilateral wrists, as well as bruising. Indication of binding. Unclear if premortem or shortly antemortem.' That's something that wouldn't have anything to do with strangulation, but it could be the hanging. 'Abrasions noted across torso. Faint, likely due to layers of fabric. Possible match to rope marks elsewhere.'" He tapped the page and looked at Claire with a frown. "We have to know if Lesley had those. And Benji was awfully close to the waterwheel when we found him, which doesn't feel like an accident. I've never heard anyone mention the waterwheel, so maybe it isn't common knowledge."

Claire had been wondering the same thing. "How difficult would it be to access this information?" she asked him. "General history search? Maybe university archives? But wouldn't you need a membership for that?"

"I got these directly from the source," Jonny reminded her. "I have no idea how anyone else would get them."

She pulled out her phone and opened the internet app. "Okay, if I search Blackfirth murder and waterwheel . . ." She typed quickly and waited for the results to populate. "Stuff about Blackfirth having a waterwheel, stuff about the murder, but nothing about both. And I'm not seeing any historical papers on any of it. Let me add 'records' to the search." She waited again, then nodded slowly. "A few historical reports, but I think . . . Yep, you have to have a login and subscription to get it. Probably university based."

"Could we find out if anyone on the crew has access to Dr. Adams's work?" Jonny asked, folding his arms as he leaned against the table. "That's the only way someone could know those details."

Claire looked up at him from her phone. "I think we need to consider that Dr. Adams might actually *be* in on this. She's not strong enough to have done the murder herself, but details like this . . ."

Jonny's expression was full of warning. "Careful. I looked her up, Claire. She's a local historian as well as university royalty. Her connections are deep, and they get important. Like political important. Like 'the last Prime Minister listed her as favorite professor' important. She's retired from the university, but still. What would she want to murder people for? And why did she give me all this information if she had anything to do with Lesley's death?"

"I have no idea," Claire admitted, setting her phone on the table. "But Watson said that she didn't have an alibi for the attack on Benji."

"But did she have one for Lesley?"

They stared at each other for a long moment, questions hovering between them with no answers to be seen.

"I'll call Watson," Claire finally sighed, grabbing her phone again. "We'll need him here."

"I'll ask Mrs. Clyde to have some dinner brought over to us," Jonny said as he reached into his back pocket for his own phone. "This is going to take a while."

DS Watson happened to be able to come rather quickly, and the three of them sat among papers for ages, going through details that only the murderer and Dr. Adams would know. Matching elements of the original murder with Lesley's as well as the attack on Benji. Discussing possibilities and speculating to see if anything plausible came out of the exercise.

Running over every single detail of things together again and again.

And again.

Claire was sitting on the floor between Jonny and Watson, flipping through more papers, when Mrs. Clyde brought dinners in for them.

"Oh my," Mrs. Clyde murmured, her eyes wide. "Is everything all right?"

"No, not really," Jonny quipped as he stood up and came to take one of the plates from her. "We're talking and thinking in circles, and now we're just confused and dizzy."

Mrs. Clyde tsked sympathetically. "You poor things. I insist you all step away and eat your dinners as though it were any ordinary Friday. Separation will be good for the lot of you. Detective, you must be exhausted. You must take a break as well."

Claire scooted over, leaning back on her hands. "I can get behind that. I'm starting to forget who the victim was and when. It might as well be the eighteenth century right now, and I'll have to go get dressed for the ball."

DS Watson chuckled at the idea, clambering up from the floor. "I'd not be invited to the big house for a ball, Miss Walker. My people are staunchly working class, so I'd probably be driving your carriage."

"I'm a terrible dancer," Claire admitted with a laugh. "So this would be my one and only invitation to a ball at Black-firth."

He held out a hand to help her up and walked with her to the other side of the room where Jonny and Mrs. Clyde had their plates. The aroma of roast chicken and root vegetables filled the room, and the salad and rolls made Claire's stomach roar with forgotten hunger.

"It looks and smells amazing, Mrs. Clyde," Claire gushed. "I may need seconds."

Mrs. Clyde patted her back fondly. "You won't, dear. I'll be bringing dessert shortly, and you will want to keep space for that." She winked and left the kitchens with her usual short and quick paces.

"I don't know how I feel about her seeing what we're working on. Or that I've involved you two," Watson murmured.

"She already knows you've been to the house to see us," Claire pointed out.

"True, but this is different. What do you think, my lord?" Watson asked Jonny as he picked up a plate and sat on one of the wooden chairs nearby. "Not that we've let her into the actual information, but . . . Well, can we trust her to keep quiet?"

"We can." Jonny smiled fondly after his housekeeper. "She'd only tell her husband, and he's a vault. They love the estate more than I do, pretty sure. Could run it in their sleep. Besides, we're not rolling around in any answers here."

"Very true."

Claire said nothing, far more agreeably focused on her meal and its utter deliciousness. For someone who had spent her entire day around food, and would again tomorrow, she was feeling more and more like she hadn't eaten anything worthwhile in weeks. Maybe it was the stress of the competition combined with trying to solve a murder, but the comfort that was a good roast dinner simply could not be underestimated.

"How was the baking today, Claire?" Jonny asked from his own chair, not nearly as voracious with his food as she was.

Recollecting that there were others in the room, and that she vastly liked one of them, she tried to remember her table manners. "Not bad at all," Claire told him, covering her mouth as she finished chewing. "I got good remarks on my mince pies, and I'm well set up for tomorrow. I'm really glad today is over, though. Mince pies are not one of my favorite things, to make or to eat."

"I love a mince pie," Watson admitted good-naturedly. "Could eat them all the time. Me mum used to make them and sell them at the market during the holiday season. She said it was tradition, and that one of her great-grandads was a cook for the big house, which was where the recipe came from." He shrugged and took a bite of vegetables. "We've never proved it, though."

"We have records of staff here going back generations," Jonny said, crossing an ankle over his knee. "If you have the name, we can look it up."

Watson brightened considerably. "Would you, my lord?

That would be a fine thing. I'll check for the name at home and let you know. Very kind."

Jonny nodded, returning his attention to his food.

Claire watched him for a moment, finding herself smiling for no particular reason. Jonny had been so irritated by Watson when they'd first met him, but now he seemed almost fond of the man. Claire was glad for that; he was a good sort and had a real eye for detail. It wasn't his fault he was limited in resources and experience in the area of murder.

Benji had referred to Jonny as Viscount Grumps when the bakers had first arrived, but no one seeing Jonny sitting here now would have thought him anything but warm, friendly, and engaging. They would have noted that he was a very attractive man, well-dressed, approachable, without arrogance. They would have seen the Viscount Colburn that Claire had been seeing from the moment she had met him.

Well, not *seeing* seeing. Not like that. Although, it would be quite the thing to be able to say that she was seeing him. She wouldn't have complained.

But as of right now, she wasn't seeing him.

She could just . . . see him.

"Anybody have terrible mince pies?" Jonny asked, bringing her attention back to the moment.

Claire blinked, struggling to think back to the bake earlier in the day. "Erm, Benji's were fine, which is not usual for the Classic Bake, and Freya's were okay, I think."

The conversation flowed naturally from mince pies to other hand pies, and it wasn't until Watson got a call on his mobile that there was even so much as a break among them.

As Watson left to take his call into one of the other rooms of the kitchen, Mrs. Clyde appeared, not with her promised dessert, but with several ingredients in her hands as well as a pair of ramekins.

Claire eyed the strange armful, raising a brow at Mrs. Clyde.

"Don't give me that look," Mrs. Clyde said with a laugh. "I've not done this for you. His lordship requested this, and I'll let him explain it. And I'll be telling Detective Watson that he can return to the house with me for some dessert with Mr. Clyde and myself. Good night."

With an airy wave, the woman bobbed out of sight again, practically humming her way down the corridor.

Claire blinked and looked at Jonny. "I've never felt so blatantly manipulated in my entire life."

"Good," he said with a quick grin. "I wasn't going to have us do this here, but since I doubt we'll be back at the house for a while, I figure here is as good a place as any."

"For what?" Claire asked, laughing as she jerked her thumb over her shoulder toward the ingredients. "More baking for me?"

Jonny's look turned quickly but playfully scolding. "Baking for *me*. As it happens, I make a fantastic crème brûlée."

Claire scoffed out loud. "You do not."

"I can assure you, I do." He got to his feet and held out a hand to her. "I learned when I was a teenager, so eager to try to impress a girl. Turns out she hated anything cream, but when she turned me down, I had plenty of this awesomeness to console me." Without letting go of Claire's hand, he led her to the table. "Don't worry, I made these earlier, and they've been chilling for several hours."

"You *what?*" Claire looked again at the ingredients Mrs. Clyde had brought, finally realizing it was only sugar, a torch, and a variety of topping choices. Not the ingredients to *make* a dessert, but to *finish* a dessert.

Which meant this treat had been planned out ahead of time, regardless of where the evening would have taken place.

No matter what the dessert actually tasted like, this was already the most deliciously sweet thing that had ever happened to her.

"Right, then," Claire managed around a strange lump in her throat. "How are we going to chill it after we torch the top?"

Jonny paused in the act of sprinkling sugar over her ramekin. "Oh. Right. I didn't think about that part. I don't actually know how to use anything in here, so . . ."

It was the most utterly perfect thing he could have said, and Claire found herself laughing softly. "That's okay. I can help you there."

His smile made her tingle from head to foot, rather like he was sprinkling sugar over her instead of the custard, but that was a mental image she was going to save for a different time. One when blushing and smiling would be less noticeable, and a bit of shameless giggling might be more permissible.

The surfaces of the custard in ramekins were suitably sugared, and Jonny brought out the blowtorch, refusing to let Claire have any of the fun.

"No," he scolded with a playful batting of her hand. "You baked all day. This is my turn."

"I didn't get to use a blowtorch today," Claire pointed out, rubbing the back of her completely uninjured hand.

He shrugged. "That was a conscious choice you made in baking. Not my fault." He turned off the blowtorch and set it aside, then turned to her. "Okay, so where can these chill?"

Claire rolled her eyes, laughing at him. "*Now* you want me to do something? Fine." She indicated he follow her and moved down the corridor to the third room on the right. She gestured to a series of iceboxes, all queued up for use in the show. "These should do. Might take a little longer than a conventional fridge, but it works."

"Awesome. Perks of having a historical-themed baking show at my house," he quipped, setting the ramekins in the iceboxes. Then he surprised her by turning back to face her and coming to stand close. "I hope you don't mind that I wanted to do this."

Claire blinked. "Do what?"

"Make you something." He made a face that could have been a shrug, really. "It sounds dumb when I think about making something for a baker, but honestly, the gingerbread dough . . . Claire, that was pretty special, and you really didn't have to."

"I was already making it," she pointed out, her cheeks flushing with heat. "And you'd said that stuff about your mum. I didn't mean to make a point of it, or to make you feel like you had to do something in return, and I definitely didn't think you needed to make me something, especially when I'm already staying at your house because of the situation that we're in, so I hope you didn't feel like you had—"

Her rambling stopped as his finger touched her lips, his laughter soft and warm as it wafted across her cheeks.

"That wasn't what I meant, love," Jonny told her in a low voice. "Curious that it sent you rambling, but I like it, so we'll just keep that between us."

Oh, sugar, had he just called her *love*?

"I meant," he went on, blessedly removing his finger

before she could worry about breathing too hard on him, "that I wanted to do something special for you because of it. Not in exchange, but because I wanted to. And I don't do much that is special, but I kind of like this, and since you're a baking fan, I thought maybe you would be too. That's all."

That's all? That was more than enough, and even sweeter than she thought it was going to be.

Cakes and a custard, she'd never make it out of here alive.

"I am sure it will be awesome," she somehow said, hoping the smile on her face wasn't one of delirium. "Now, inquiring minds want to know: Was that white *and* brown sugar you coated the top with?"

"Good eye, Miss Walker. That's the secret to all my success—don't tell." He winked, which just about set her toes on fire.

Her smile was going to be hopeless now. "I won't. But this better be worth it."

And, as it turned out, it was.

CHAPTER 20

It was fortunate that Jonny had a security pass to be on set whenever he wanted, because now that he was suspicious of Anthony, Benji, and Dr. Adams, there was no way he was letting Claire do anything in their vicinity without also being nearby himself.

He was just overprotective enough to be ridiculous, although it wasn't as though he expected anyone to be killed while the cameras were rolling.

The bakers had been working for two hours already, and if Claire was in any way ruffled, she gave no indication. She was an utter machine in this bake, glasses firmly on, working steadily and efficiently, only saying things when the camera was on her. She was marking things off her list constantly, which made Jonny wonder how specific her instructions were.

Benji, on the other hand, was doing everything he could to get on camera. Joking, talking to himself, chatting with others, calling out to the hosts. For someone who had been fairly standoffish and borderline cantankerous since arriving, it was quite the character change. Maybe the repeated dips in the cold water had altered his personality. He'd left hospital against medical advice, so it couldn't be too far-fetched of an idea.

Everything he, Claire, and Watson had right now was speculation and circumstantial, but it was all they had to go on. Watson was doing some digging today, and Jonny hoped he would find something that would give them actual answers to motivation, if not guilt.

Maybe then Jonny would be able to sleep without having nightmares of Claire as the next person to be found in front of the mill.

He ought to have been worried for Gabi, but the bakers were being attacked.

Why the bakers, they still didn't know. There was no power the show held over the estate, no evil deeds to avenge, no scandals taking place. And the bakers hadn't done anything to upset anyone, so there was no reason to target them. None of the candidates rejected for the show had panned out as suspects, even from previous series.

"Cut!" the director called. "Anybody need water?"

A few hands went up, including Claire's. Production assistants scurried out with bottles of water, and a few of the crew went around adjusting this and that on the set. Makeup artists did touch-up work on the hosts, though didn't do anything for the bakers themselves, he noticed. A young production assistant walked over to Benji with a toss of her long, wavy hair, and shook a pill bottle at him.

Jonny watched the interaction with mild scrutiny, which increased when he saw Claire push her glasses on top of her head and walk over to Benji, saying something as she approached.

Benji showed her the pills in his hands and said something,

pointing at one or two before laughing. He tossed them into his mouth and took a long swig of water, winking at the production assistant. Claire picked up something from the ground and held it out to him.

Jonny watched as Benji said something else, his smile shifting as he put a hand on his right shoulder, working it pointedly.

Claire nodded and dropped a pill in his hand, taking a drink from her own water bottle before pointing at something on Benji's baking station and listening to him explain it.

Jonny would have given anything to hear what Benji said about his meds. Claire hadn't shown much interest in Benji's recovery, as far as he could tell, and he knew she didn't have any medical background. Why would she have questions about the medications he was taking? She was a curious sort, it was true, but the middle of a bake seemed an odd time to indulge in a random question.

He watched as Claire patted Benji on the arm, smiling up at him, then moved back to her station, silently drinking her water.

She pulled a bowl out from the cabinet and began adding ingredients to it before flicking her eyes up directly into Jonny's.

He raised a brow, tilting his head.

Her eyes moved down to her counter, then back at him, without a single movement of her chin.

Ah. He was being summoned.

There was a little thrill of delight and anticipation at that, he wasn't going to lie.

Eyeing the crew still making adjustments at a leisurely pace, he didn't feel bad about starting down the line of baking stations. "You're doing great, Freya," he complimented, giving the girl a thumbs-up.

She smiled tightly at him. "Thanks. We'll see."

He nodded and continued past Denis, who had been entertaining everyone in the evenings with his readings, last night's being from A Series of Unfortunate Events and performed with great gusto. Denis grinned at him, waving a spatula. "Ready for the next chapter tonight, my lord?"

Jonny laughed, not entirely forcing the sound. "Only if I don't have to take part!"

Denis saluted at that, going back to his bake.

Once in front of Claire's station, Jonny put both hands on the counter. "What?"

"Aspirin," Claire murmured as she cracked eggs into the bowl.

"So? It's used for pain all the time."

Claire shook her head slightly. "He's been taking it for years for an old shoulder injury that he had surgery for. He dropped one of the pills on the ground, and I gave it back to him."

"Okay, and?"

"Aspirin is a blood thinner," Claire told him, her lips barely moving as she spoke. "My mum had to take it after having her knee replaced to keep down the risk of blood clots. It makes bruising a ton easier and way uglier, which is why doctors don't keep you on it for long." Her gaze flicked toward Benji's station before returning to her bowl. "He's on two other medications from the hospital, one of which I know is for pain. There is no reason why he—as a healthy man and a firefighter—should be taking full-dose aspirin on a regular basis, let alone taking it for years."

Jonny had to resist the urge to look over at Benji's station himself and kept his eyes steadily on Claire. "You're sure about this?"

Claire widened her eyes. "As sure as I can be. Lesley would be the one to ask since she was a nurse, but here we are. Check the hospital reports Watson got. They should list the medications Benji was taking while he was there. If the aspirin was being distributed by a different doctor, they would have had questions. If it's not on the list, it means he's taking it without reporting it, which is stupid as well as suspicious."

"Okay. I can check that easily enough." Jonny waited a moment. "How did you know?"

She shook her head once. "I didn't. I just saw it fall, and asked what all he was on, given his injuries." She paused and met Jonny's eyes with a real smile. "Maybe Lesley's ghost did that on purpose, eh? Flicked it off his palm so I'd see it fall."

There was something incredibly enchanting about Claire's smile, and something equally contagious. Jonny had to smile back.

It was entirely a reflex.

He laughed once. "I'll take all the help we can get." He reached and tapped her glasses back down onto her face. "Good work, Sherlock."

Claire snorted and adjusted her glasses. "Thanks, Columbo."

"Not Watson?" He pouted, batting his lashes.

"We already have Watson," she reminded him. "Besides, you're a detective all your own. We're equals."

Again, his smile flashed across his face without any direction from him. "Then I'll take it. Okay, you shut off that part

of your brain now and knock this bake out. I'll do the home-
work, and we'll chat when you kill it, eh?"

Claire gave him a little salute with two fingers, smiling
just enough for her dimples to appear. "Yes, my lord."

Jonny rolled his eyes and turned away from the station,
filing back to the corner of the pavilion.

"Back in sixty seconds," the director called, sitting back
in his chair and eyeing the monitor in front of him.

Production assistants and set decorators returned to the
production corner, and Jonny stayed just long enough to
watch Lindsay go over to Claire's station and talk to her about
Christmas traditions in her family.

"I grew up in a pub, basically," Claire said with a laugh,
looking as calm and easy as anything. "Well, around a pub,
anyway. Sticky floors and all. We had some different traditions
than other people, but it was really fun for us."

"Sounds promising," Lindsay replied, leaning on the baking station. "I'm listening."

Jonny turned from his place and started out of the pavilion, keeping his pace steady and sedate even while his mind
spun.

Aspirin. If that detail broke the case open, he'd never un-
derestimate the random bits of information that lodged in his
brain ever again.

By his calculations, there were at least three hours remaining in the Occasion Bake, not to mention the judging and
revelation on who would be leaving. Plenty of time for him to
check the hospital records attached to the investigation paper-
work and relay the information to DS Watson. What exactly
he would make of the information, Jonny wasn't certain. He
only knew that it had to mean something.

Once safely ensconced in Blackfirth, Jonny allowed himself to move more quickly, though there was nothing particularly urgent with his timeline. Still, he wanted to know sooner rather than later, and hurried to his study. It was the one place he could guarantee absolute privacy from any visitors—and it happened to be the only place in the house with a safe.

Which was, of course, where he kept all the documents that DS Watson allowed him to.

Door closed and locked behind him, Jonny moved to the safe and punched in the code. He pulled open the heavy door and riffled through the folders sitting inside. The coroner's report and hospital records were in the same folder, which he pulled out, spreading the contents on the surface of his desk.

He turned over the pages of Lesley's reports, since he didn't need them. The records of Benji's hospital stay were next, and he scanned through them, looking for something he would never have believed significant until today. He needed to examine the list of medications reported by the patient and the medications distributed to the patient during their stay.

Some of the things on the list probably weren't even accurate. He hadn't spent all that much time as a patient in hospital, and had certainly never worked in hospital, but he could imagine the tediousness of recording every medication a patient was given. The general public were likely unreliable in reporting what they were taking at home, so it was hardly a declaration of dishonesty if something was missed.

Claire's insight might not actually prove anything—human error was far too acceptable by way of an explanation—but maybe it could lead them to the revelation that would entrap the murderer.

Jonny picked up the pen on his desk and began marking

every incidence of medications being given to Benji in hospital. The first twenty-four hours, no aspirin was given or mentioned. Instances of the patient updating the nurses were scattered throughout the notes, but nowhere was aspirin asked for or spoken of. Aspirin was never prescribed. Other medications and adjustments in medications, yes. But no aspirin.

Every time Benji had been stuck with a needle for an IV or blood draw, the report mentioned a high-level of bruising. He was even checked for clotting disorders, iron and nutrient levels, and, on one occasion, for cancer.

His bruising was a cause for concern, but aspirin use never came up.

Plenty of other items of his personal medical history had been mentioned, but no aspirin. And, as it happened, nothing about a surgery for his shoulder. His appendix surgery, yes. His shoulder?

Not even once.

That seemed a significant omission, all things considered.

Jonny looked over the next few days, and it was much the same. No aspirin, and reports on testing came back normal. Wouldn't someone who took aspirin daily report that to the hospital staff so he could continue taking it with his other medications? He'd mentioned his multivitamin, for heaven's sake, and they'd let him—

What if it hadn't been a multivitamin? What if he had told the staff that his aspirin was his multivitamin? It wasn't as though they would pay that much attention to it. Hospitals did not dispense vitamins to patients, only prescriptions.

And by claiming it was a multivitamin, Benji could conceivably get away with taking it multiple times a day, specifically to increase his bruising.

But aspirin wasn't a crime. Why hide it?

Jonny forced himself to take two mental steps back. He had no way of proving that was what happened in the hospital. And, legally, he couldn't go into Benji's room in his house and look for multivitamins that might actually be aspirin. Well, *he* could, but he couldn't submit what he found to be tested by DS Watson's lab and then have that used as evidence.

He watched enough crime procedurals to know that probable cause was important, even when it was his own house.

Huffing in irritation, Jonny pulled out his mobile and dialed the detective's number, hoping the man would have some ideas for what to do with this information.

If they could do anything.

"Watson," came the clear tone through the other end of the line.

"Detective, Jonathan Ainsley here."

"My lord, what a pleasant surprise!" There were some sounds of shuffling or scuffling and then he went on with, "How can I help you?"

"Well," Jonny said with a sigh, leaning back in his chair, "Claire discovered something, and I just went through some records that seem to confirm it, but it's all pretty circumstantial and won't prove much of anything directly related to the crime. It's just all-around suspicious, and I don't know what we can do with it."

He heard a gravelly rumbling from Watson's end. "That seems to be the theme of our investigation, sir," he replied, lowering his voice. "Nobody is coming up as blatant for this, even Mr. Andrews-Lee. If I didn't really believe otherwise, I'd think we were looking at this all wrong. At any rate, what have you and Miss Walker discovered?"

Jonny ran through the details of the aspirin and the missing shoulder surgery from the hospital records, what the records did show, and what Claire suspected. It sounded so clear and promising when discussed, but when he looked at it from the angle of what could be proven in a court of law, everything became far more muddled.

"I believe the doctors did a drug test on Mr. Andrews-Lee as part of the hospital's usual workup on unconscious victims," Watson said with some thought. "Do you see the lab results in there?"

Sitting forward, Jonny riffled through the medical records again. "Looks like there was a test performed, but it showed no signs of drug usage."

"But not the actual results?"

Jonny shook his head, even though Watson couldn't see it. "No, just what it found."

Watson made a faint humming sound. "I'll call the hospital and see if we can get the full report. If I remember correctly, even aspirin can be found in a drug test. It won't tell us anything criminal, only that it was left out of Mr. Andrews-Lee's medical history by his own volition. At this point, perhaps we gather as much information as possible and present it to the suspect with our theory—see what happens and how he reacts. If it is Mr. Andrews-Lee, he is not a criminal by nature. We ran his background, and he even pays his driving violations in a speedy manner."

"It would be so much better if we could nail him with something, though." Jonny drummed his fingers on his desk, racking his brain for any kind of solution. "Could we administer drug tests on the show?"

"We could, sir," Watson affirmed, "but to what purpose?

To prove he is taking aspirin? He told Miss Walker so today, and that is hardly a crime."

Jonny rubbed at his forehead with the heel of a hand. "I know, I know. And I can't go snooping in his room if I want anything to stick in a court case for you."

"No, sir, that is true."

Jonny thought for another moment, leaning back in his chair again. "Is there enough right now to prove the attack on him was faked?"

"Well, now, let me see . . ." It sounded as though Watson was pulling out his notebook again by the rustling noises coming through the phone, and Jonny smiled at hearing it. "There was no blunt force injury to his head, which is different from what Ms. Kemble's autopsy showed. No internal bruising in his throat to indicate strangulation. No water in the lungs, which cannot prove or disprove drowning. No lowered levels of oxygenation in his blood. No signs of petechial hemorrhaging. In fact, the only things that actually match Ms. Kemble are the marks on the throat. And the water, of course."

"So could we assume . . . ?" Jonny pressed.

"We could, sir," Watson finished quickly. "But let me get a more informed answer from the medical examiner. If she agrees, we might have something to trap Mr. Andrews-Lee with."

Jonny didn't like the sound of that, and he frowned. "What do you mean *trap*? You mean like an interrogation, right?"

"Yes," Watson said, his voice ever so slightly tinged with hesitation. "But also . . . I am afraid we may actually need to trap Mr. Andrews-Lee in order to make any of this work. At the moment, we strongly suspect that his own attack was staged, but we cannot tie him to Ms. Kemble's murder. I cannot arrest him for faking his own attack, especially as he has not pressed charges on anyone. Unless we catch the attacker red-handed, we cannot move an inch."

"You're not suggesting—"

"I am afraid, sir, that we are going to have to use one of the bakers as bait. I welcome any other options, but if my hunch is correct, that could be the most effective way to move things forward. It won't be about the attack at all, but it will provoke a reaction."

CHAPTER 21

Wedding bakes were almost over. Almost over, and then they would know who was in the final.

Wedding bakes were a pain in the pithivier, and Claire didn't care if anyone knew she felt that way. In fact, she'd said so for the camera just a few minutes ago. Baking humor was always appreciated by the fervent fans.

A historical wedding brought its own set of challenges, and she'd spent so long focusing her attention on the fanchonettes for the Classic Bake yesterday that she'd almost completely screwed up her Occasion Bake today by not practicing at all. Well, almost not at all. She had at least done the cake once.

Which was a risk in and of itself since it was a harlequin cake and not a traditional wedding cake, but she was absolutely certain that someone somewhere had used a harlequin cake at a wedding sometime.

But honestly, the fanchonettes yesterday had been perfection. She had chosen chocolate and hazelnut for her toppings, and somehow she had managed to get the tartlet shells perfectly crisp. There was nothing Dame Sophie hated so much as poorly baked tart shells, and Claire would live in the happy place that was the expression of bliss on the woman's face for ages.

Today was a new day, however. There were no guarantees, and their numbers were dwindling rapidly.

Anthony had been eliminated after the Christmas bakes, which was hardly surprising. Christmas bakes were filled with richness and had nothing healthy about them, and there was no way to make it so. He didn't seem to mind; now he could hang around in Blackfirth without doing anything or having any expectations. His only complaint, which he made regularly, was the lack of adequate exercise facilities in the house. Benji seemed to agree with him on that one, though Claire wondered how Benji could have the energy to exercise with all he was apparently dealing with, including the old shoulder injury that required a daily full-strength aspirin.

Benji, Denis, Freya, and Claire were the only ones left now. Baking for their lives, as it were. Perhaps not in actuality, as there hadn't been a hint of a problem since Benji's attack and subsequent hospitalization. But none of them would be getting out until the show was completed, and that was next weekend, if all went according to plan. But then what? The winner would have their moment of glory among the group, and they all would remain quiet until the show aired in a few months, when the internet and social media would take up the charge of their particular favorites with some passion for the duration.

If the series intrigued them enough, of course.

After the disaster of series eleven, there were no guarantees. This could very well be the last series of *Britian's Battle of the Bakers*, and Claire would be on it. Hopefully not one of the dead ones by the time it ended, but as she suspected no one would know the full story, no one would be considered a dead baker for the series.

They would just mysteriously have died of natural causes after the show ended.

Someone started singing the traditional wedding march, and Claire looked up and around with a frown. Charlie had tucked white linen napkins under a headband and was walking down the aisle between baking stations holding a bouquet of wooden spoons. Which meant the cameras were on.

She forced herself to smile at Charlie's antics, shaking her head as she strained her spinach through cheesecloth. "Sweet buttered crumpets," she laughed as a camera panned around her.

"Three hours left," Charlie sang to the appropriate tune. "Three hours left. Three hours left to go in this Wedding Bake."

"Do you, Charlie, take this cake to be your wedded luncheon?" Denis asked aloud, turning his tone as formal as any priest or minister.

Claire heard Freya snort loudly at that, and her smile was less difficult to force.

"Dearly beloved, we are gathered here today to bake our heads off," Freya added to the mix of jokes.

Claire cleared her throat. "Who gives this baker to be married to this madness?"

"Shut up, the lot of you," Benji snapped, not joining in the fun and not pretending to enjoy any of it for the cameras.

Claire glanced over at him, wondering what he would do to cheat his way into the final this time. They hadn't mentioned anything to the showrunner or any of the producers about it yet; should they do so now?

He seemed to be making a pie dough, and, given what she

knew about his methods, she suspected that he was using vegetable shortening instead of butter or lard. She wasn't about to sneak a taste as she had done with his ginger citrus tart filling, but butter-flavored shortening would add a great deal of flavor and stability to the pie crust without requiring the same effort as working with the historic ingredients. But how could he manage that without the hawk that was Dr. Adams noticing?

The bakers were not in charge of bringing in their own ingredients—it would be suspicious if they did—so if Benji was able to smuggle things in, he either had help or was more skilled in sleight of hand than anyone she had ever heard of.

"Good rapport, all!" Mr. Dean, the director, called out. "Take fifteen. If you're putting something into the oven or pulling it out during that time, raise your hand, and we'll get camera coverage for you."

No one raised their hands, so the staff and crew began chatting among themselves. Claire watched a couple of production assistants head over to Benji, but he was apparently in no mood to entertain them and waved them away rather harshly.

For someone who practically demanded such attention last week, it was a strange shift of behavior. But maybe the cheating was starting to eat at him, and he was afraid of getting caught. Not that the production assistants would have any idea about how he would cheat or what he was presently doing that would constitute cheating, but still. Claire had worked with enough cheating students to know how on edge they became the deeper into the hole they got.

Whatever.

It would be lovely to expose Benji's cheating, if she could find a way to do it, but with all she had going on in today's

Occasion Bake, she couldn't risk ignoring her own work to try to get him caught.

She'd need another set of eyes for that, and today was not a day she had them.

As though expecting her thoughts to travel, Claire looked around the tent, hoping to spot a tall, dark-haired man with bright blue eyes and the most charming smile to ever grace a face. But he didn't seem to be among the group today, and her heart dipped in her chest, bouncing off a rib or two in disappointment.

Jonny was her anchor to reality in all of this, her breath of fresh air, her stabilizing chair while she precariously posed in an absurd form of one-legged yoga. He was the only person she knew she could trust utterly and completely, and there was something inherently binding in that. She wanted to trust the others, wanted to trust everyone, but she couldn't. Not here, not now. Not in this tent of death, not in this dysfunctional, very-much-not-family group she was with, not in this prison of a show that wouldn't let anyone leave or anything be cut short.

Was she clinging to Jonny because he was the most normal part of this madness? Or was what she felt for him more genuine than that? Was her ticklish anticipation of seeing him real or simply a strange form of comfort in the chaos of the investigation and competition? Were their walks together enjoyable because of their connection, or was it because she didn't have to suspect anything of him?

Why was liking someone as confusing now as when she had been fourteen?

"Your brows are trying to touch. What's up?"

Heat burst in her stomach like fireworks and spread into

her fingers and toes as she glanced up to see Jonny across from her station, somehow appearing out of nowhere.

"How in the world did you get in here without me seeing?" she demanded before she could stop herself.

Jonny's little smile appeared, curling her pinky toes. "Were you looking for me?"

Claire cleared her throat and focused on straining the spinach juice into a bowl. "Might have been. You're the only one I trust to bring me coffee, so why shouldn't I look for you?"

"Uh-huh. That looks gross, by the way."

The blatant statement made her choke on a laugh. "It's a natural and authentic green food coloring for my cake. I've already done beet juice for pink and the chocolate and cinnamon for brown. This is the last one, and then I can mix the layers—Why am I telling you this? Crepes alive, it's like I'm always on camera."

Jonny chuckled softly and leaned over to dip his pinky in the bowl of chocolate. "You ramble. It's cute and I'm used to it."

Her hands slipped on the cheesecloth when he said *cute*, but she managed to get enough juice out anyway. "It's a frosting nuisance but thank you for being kind. Anyway, did you hear Benji?"

"Oh yeah. Everyone did." Jonny made a show of looking around the pavilion, leaning his back against the baking station. "The PAs were sad he didn't want them around. There's a lot of talk about his mood lately. He's going to have to watch himself; the show might get rid of him out of spite."

"They wouldn't do that," Claire grumbled with a shake of her head, pouring the green coloring into the bowl of white batter she had set aside for that layer. "Everyone likes a villain in a show."

Jonny snorted softly. "But nobody wants the villain to win. So I may need to call a Chelsea Bun myself if you can spare the time."

That brought Claire up short, and she looked around quickly to see if anyone was watching. "What for?" she hissed. "Has something been uncovered?"

"Not really, no," Jonny murmured, turning around to face her. "But Watson and I have been talking about options, and there's really only one right now. I hate it, but it's the only one."

"And it needs me," Claire said without question.

Jonny nodded, his mouth forming a tight line, his own brows furrowing.

She smiled a little. "Now *your* eyebrows are trying to touch."

He cocked his head, his mouth softening. "Yours do it better."

"That's my one true gift," she quipped, oddly not dreading whatever it was he needed to tell her or ask of her. She could see his concern and knew he wouldn't suggest something of her if there was a better or safer way to do it.

He wasn't taking this lightly, and neither was Watson. So neither would she.

"We are due back on in a few minutes," Claire said in a low voice, gesturing around the pavilion. "But after that, we should all be baking, and everyone's cake will take at least twenty minutes to half an hour, if not more. I can get away for at least that long. Mine take twenty; will that be long enough?"

Jonny nodded quickly and started backing away from her

baking station. "Yep. As soon as they call for a longer break, meet me down there."

"Yes, my lord," Claire replied with a curtsy and a wink that she hoped would ease whatever tension he was feeling.

His broad smile told her everything she needed to know, and it was difficult not to dance a little to herself as she mixed up her batter. Lindsay and Charlie caught her and came over to dance as well, the cameras focusing on all of them as they engaged in the sort of frivolity the show was determined to capture for Wedding Week.

"I'm inviting you to my hen do if I ever get married," Lindsay told Claire when they finished dancing. "You're a dark horse, Claire, and I think we'd have a top night."

Claire burst out laughing and shrugged. "You never know. If you get engaged, call me and we'll see what happens."

Charlie pulled Lindsay away to go talk to Denis about his wedding fifteen years before, and Claire wished she could go with them. She loved hearing Denis tell stories, and wedding stories were always worth hearing.

Maybe Wedding Week wasn't so bad after all.

When she started humming the wedding theme, she forced herself to focus, feeling the need to slap herself out of her silliness, but people were always a little silly when flirtation was involved.

The layers of her harlequin cake mixed together well, the colors rich without being bold, and she made sure that each pan was filled to a perfectly equal level.

"Going in!" Claire called, waiting for a camera to be brought over, as they had been instructed from the very first day.

At the camerawoman's nod, Claire opened her oven door

and carefully placed each pan on the racks before closing the door and setting her timer.

The camera always lingered, so she drummed her fingers on the countertop. "Lemon honey," she said to herself, but also for the camera. She reached for the lemons nearby and sliced one in half, grabbing a spoon and pressing it against the soft insides over a bowl.

It took just a few minutes to juice two lemons completely, and then to grate the rind. She'd leave this to sit while she met with Jonny; she'd have time to make the rest of the honey when she returned and the cakes were cooling. But at least this part was done for now.

"Cut!" Mr. Dean called. "Take twenty at least. We're all good for that, yes?"

The bakers all called out the affirmative, and they were dismissed.

With a heavy sigh, Claire took off her apron and tossed it on her station. One of the PAs stood by the pavilion's edge and looked at her expectantly as she approached.

"Just going to go for a quick walk," Claire told her with a smile. "Just to the historic kitchens and back. That okay?"

"Of course! Go right ahead." She waved Claire through, her eyes on Benji alone.

Claire's thanks went unacknowledged, which was fine by her, and she stepped out of the pavilion, making her way quickly down to the historic kitchens.

No one from the show paid particular attention to them unless it was time for judging or elimination, so the kitchens were often empty. In fact, when they were empty, they were remarkably cool and refreshing, and the perfect place to escape from the stress of the pavilion.

Claire practically skipped down the steps and ducked into the corridor, looking from room to room as she walked. "Marco?" she called playfully.

A short laugh came from a room just ahead. "Polo."

She grinned.

She found Jonny in one of the smaller rooms—the scullery, if she remembered her introduction correctly. He was leaning against the stone counter with his arms folded, smiling in greeting when she appeared. He'd pushed his sleeves up to his elbows, and his eyes crinkled, making him look positively boyish and not at all like the brooding viscount one might think lived in Blackfirth.

Quite attractive, this version of Jonny.

Then again, all versions of him were attractive, it had to be stated.

What an inconvenience.

"All right, then," Claire said, rubbing her hands together slightly. "What is this plan you hate so much?"

Jonny's smile faded, and he exhaled, lowering his eyes and twisting his lips to one side. "Watson and I both think that we need to catch Benji cheating on camera. Something that will expose whatever his plan is. I'm starting to think Watson's hunch is correct and that Benji really was involved with Lesley's death, but we still have only minimal proof, given Benji's own staged attack."

"So catching him cheating could trigger him enough to act again." Claire put her hands on her hips and started to pace. "He'd be plenty angry, but would it be enough for him to want to attack someone?"

"He could use the murder, or attempt at murder, to make his cheating seem less serious by comparison," Jonny pointed out, "and heighten the stress of being a victim himself, or any number of other excuses. But he will be rattled, and therefore unpredictable, and I believe that is the point."

Something in his tone caught Claire off guard, and she turned to look at him, narrowing her eyes. "What aren't you telling me, Jonny?"

His attempt to look perfectly innocent fell flatter than a proper crepe, and he scowled. "Watson believes we'll need to use a baker as bait. And he thinks—I don't agree—but he thinks—"

"He thinks it should be me." Claire nodded slowly, pursing her lips in thought. "I can see that."

"How?" Jonny demanded, his tone harsh.

His outrage was cute, she had to say. She gave him a pitying smile. "I'm the only baker who knows about Watson's secret investigation, so I should be the one to try to catch Benji cheating while baking. With any luck, he'll see me as competition to be eliminated, and that means we won't have to put any of the other bakers at risk. It makes perfect sense."

Jonny shook his head repeatedly and slowly. "No, it does not make perfect sense. It does not make *any* sense. The man is probably unhinged, and I don't think risking you is something that ought to be considered."

Claire was silent for a moment, then took two steps closer to Jonny, noting the almost wild light in his bright eyes. "I think it should be considered," she told him quietly. "More than that, I think I should do it. The police can be right there. We can have me wired and protected and whatever else we need to, but it makes sense, Jonny. You don't have to like it. Sugar, I don't even like it that much, but I really don't like the idea of Freya being used. Or Denis. So it has to be me."

She saw his throat tighten, watched a muscle tick in his jaw, caught the slight shaking of his head once more. "I don't like it," he whispered.

Feeling oddly brave, Claire put a hand to his cheek and smiled a little. "That's okay," she whispered back. "You can be the one to make sure they protect me. Okay?"

His eyes searched hers, and then he surprised her by pulling her into his arms for a hug, holding her tightly. "Okay," he grumbled, the words barely audible over the pounding of her heart. "Okay."

CHAPTER 22

Cheating day was here, and Jonny could not have hated the idea more.

Not the cheating part, he would take great delight in exposing Benji as a fraud, but because of what would happen *after*.

Tonight's plan, if they were predicting Benji's reaction right, was what Jonny hated.

He was down in the historic kitchens with the crew and the bakers for the final Classic Bake today, which was being held there for the cameras rather than in the pavilion. The Occasion Bake would be the same, setting it up as the highlight of the series. The tight quarters also meant tensions were already running high.

It was the perfect situation to stir something up.

Maids of Honour were the order of the day, and the theme of a Royal Visit was set for today and tomorrow. More work, more elaborate decoration, and more severe judgment, according to the introductory speech given at the beginning of taping. Everything was being done to add more stress for the bakers, and Jonny was honestly surprised there wasn't any ominous music playing down here.

He watched the bakers work, doing his best not to smile at Claire.

Claire was focused and careful, as always. Her perfectly printed instructions were on hand to guide her every step, though she had a slight furrow between her brows. She was in her own world unless she was required to be on camera for something. She seemed confident today, which he was glad for. If she was going to try to get Benji to admit to his cheating on camera, she was going to need to be confident in her own work. He was concerned about her, not just for that, but with Freya getting eliminated in the previous week and no longer competing, Claire probably felt like she had fewer friends and allies in the pavilion. Freya was still staying at Blackfirth, of course, but it wasn't the same thing.

Denis was whistling while he worked and had some sort of aerobic two-step going on. His portion of the Great Kitchen was tidy but not perfect, and he had already called out three or four iconic lines for the general audience, even if the cameras weren't on. If he was stressed about this being the final, he was not about to show any sign of it.

Benji, on the other hand, was an absolute mess. Ingredients were everywhere, he had yet to smile, and he seemed unable to find anything he was looking for at any given time. It occurred to Jonny that it was a very good ploy for someone who intended to cheat. It would be difficult to catch someone in the act if they were completely discombobulated. There was the risk, however, that he would not cheat today. If Claire was right, Benji only cheated in the Occasion Bake, never in the Classic.

Both Claire and Jonny were hopeful that he would change his patten for the finale and cheat in both.

All the bakers had their pastries in the ovens at this point, the tins filled with baking beans for a good blind bake, and now they were working on fillings, which would be what truly set them apart from each other.

Oh croissants. If he could provide a running commentary on the process without knowing how to actually do a single thing he was seeing, it meant he had been watching too much of the show. This was what the show did to people: They began to think they knew more than they did and became sofa experts, comfortable judging people they did not know who did things they could not do and made things that they would not taste.

How else could he explain his irritation when Greg chose rough puff over full puff in series six? Jonny didn't even know the difference, but he knew the choice had been wrong, and the judging proved that.

"Take ten, everyone," the director called out, removing his headset. "Bakers, if you need to keep working on your fillings, go ahead."

Denis stepped away from his station and moved over to the tea stand that had been set up, pouring himself a fresh cup. Benji leaned against his counter for a moment, looking at the bowl of currant jam that Jonny had watched him make without cheating, then walked to a corner of the Great Kitchen with a bottle of water and popped a few pills into his mouth.

He still wore high-necked tops to cover his bruising, which was probably at the request of the show, but it made it difficult to know how it was healing. If he was still taking aspirin. If there were any ill-effects of his staged attack.

It was difficult to be certain of anything.

Jonny looked over at Claire, who had taken a seat on the stool beside her portion of the great tables, and was surprised to see her staring off into the distance.

It would be more difficult to check in with her when the space was smaller and more crowded, but he needed to find a way to do it.

Glancing around, he saw several water bottles. He picked up three, walking over to Denis first. "Denis, water?"

The man nodded, smiling widely with his salt-and-pepper goatee. "Many thanks, my lord. The sweating will begin soon enough, and hydration is key to maintaining stamina."

Jonny grinned, wondering how many pearls of wisdom Denis had for life, and handed over the bottle. "Well, good luck, mate."

Denis saluted with the bottle and turned back to his tea.

Following the natural flow of the stations, Jonny went to Claire. "Water?" he asked softly, offering it to her.

She nodded, taking the bottle, and then looked up, a slight frown appearing when she saw it was him. "Wow. Didn't expect you to be handing out water today."

He shrugged a little. "Couldn't just walk over here and check on you without a reason, so I improvised."

Claire's mouth opened a little, then broke into a grin. "Okay, that's cute. Ten points."

He pretended a bow, feeling silly that hearing Claire thought he was cute made him want to tap dance, despite having no idea how. "I do what I can. Any thoughts yet?"

"It's been hard to tell," she admitted in a low voice. "He's uncharacteristically messy today, and I'm doing my own thing. Did his jam get made here?"

"Yep, sure did," Jonny vouched, tsking softly. "Step by step."

Claire made a face and took a long drink of her water. "Is he doing a curd cheese?"

Now that was a phrase Jonny had never heard and certainly didn't care for the sound of. "Do I want to know?"

She scoffed. "It means we make our own curd for the filling using whole milk. We're supposed to do that or ricotta, they said. Has he strained anything?"

"No," Jonny said slowly. "But he still could, I suppose."

"Or he could be using ricotta," she replied. Sighing shortly, she pushed to her feet. "I've already strained mine, so I might be able to pay more attention. Take him a water and then look over his station as you walk back. If you don't see ricotta cheese, rub your left eye when you get back to your place. Then I'll watch to see if he strains to make his own. It's a gamble, but it might work."

Jonny nodded and tossed the water bottle to himself in the hopes it would make him look more laid back. "Got it. And he knows the rules?"

Claire grunted once. "He should. We reviewed them several times this week, and he was nodding every time."

"Okay." Jonny started away from her but made sure to brush his fingers against hers before he was completely gone. Why, he wasn't sure. He wanted to touch her, but that wasn't a new thing. He wanted to comfort her, but that wasn't something he could do in an obvious way. He wanted to remind her that he was here, but she could see him, so . . .

It didn't make any particular sense, but it seemed sense was not required when it came to Claire. And he'd felt the way her fingers had flicked against his as he'd touched her, so maybe it had been a good idea after all.

Right. Water to the enemy next.

"Benji," he called as he neared him.

He turned on his heel, as tense as a caged tiger. "What?" he demanded.

Jonny did his best not to react, waving the water bottle. "Wanted to see if you needed another. It's hot down here to-day."

Benji grunted and held out his hand. "Right, yeah, thanks. If they didn't need so many people down here, it might be okay, but whatever." He shrugged and turned his back to Jonny without another word, apparently wanting to brood alone.

Random, but fine. If he wasn't looking, it would make studying his station easier.

Jonny started back toward where he had been, looking over Claire's station first, almost like he had seen Dr. Adams do, and nodding to himself. Then he moved to Benji's, look-ing at every single item with quick eyes. No sign of anything resembling ricotta, and no milk for straining as far as he could see. So what was he doing for the filling, then?

He reminded himself to look at Denis's station as well, needing to keep up appearances for the sake of his own per-sonal continuity and to avoid raising suspicions. Denis was doing an orange filling, and had prepared orange water, it seemed. Random choice, but knowing Denis, it would be well practiced and taste amazing at the end.

Once back in his previous spot, Jonny turned to face the Great Kitchen as a whole, and, seeing Claire surreptitiously looking in his direction, pointedly rubbed his left eye.

Her chin dipped in the smallest of nods.

The game was afoot, then. How she was going to bring it up, he didn't know, and how it was going to be caught on camera, he knew even less.

It was all resting on Claire's shoulders.

And that made him nervous.

"Back on in thirty seconds," the director called.

Benji turned from his corner and came to his station, face set in stone. Denis whistled his way back to his place, taking a long drink of tea. Claire pulled her long hair back in a ponytail, asking one of the PAs if that was okay.

"Charlie, kick us off three beats after on," came the director's instruction.

"Yes, sir," Charlie called back, allowing the makeup artist to dust a brush over his nose before he walked pointedly between the tables.

The light appeared on the large camera, and, three beats later, Charlie looked at each station. "Call me ignorant, but surely Maids of Honour would have been better last week for weddings. But I am not a judge, so there you have it."

Lindsay joined him, and they walked over to Claire's station together. "Claire, what are you cooking up for us?"

"Lemon curd and lemon filling with a Tudor Rose dusted in icing sugar," Claire recited with a bright grin. "It works beautifully with the strained curd cheese filling. I'm so glad they had us do it that way. It really does make all the difference for the filling to set properly."

"Historically speaking or in general?" Lindsay asked, looking interested.

Claire shrugged. "Both. This method works best for this particular recipe, so, historical or not, it's the way I do it.

Ricotta wouldn't work with this one, but I know they're allowing ricotta for recipes where it works. It's just such a classic thing, Maids of Honour. And Dame Sophie *always* strains her own curd cheese. It's in her cookbooks."

Charlie gave her an impressed look and turned to Lindsay. "Did you know that?"

"I did not! We have a true Dame Sophie aficionado here! Have we said that on camera yet?" She turned to the nearest camera and said, "Claire follows Dame Sophie's instructions in everyday life. Someone should hand out extra credit."

Claire snorted a laugh and shook her head, turning to focus on adding butter, sugar, juice, and lemon zest to a bowl that sat over boiling water.

Jonny bit his lip so he wouldn't nod in approval or shake his head in amazement at the neat little trap Claire had set up as the hosts moved along the stations.

If this worked . . .

"Benji!" Charlie cheered as he reached him. "My man, are you a fan of Dame Sophie's methods?"

"Who isn't?" Benji offered without enthusiasm. "She's the gold standard, isn't she?"

Lindsay nodded in approval. "So you prefer the curd cheese too?"

Benji froze. "I . . . Well, yes, when I can. But this recipe doesn't call for that, so it's a risk."

"Oooooh," both hosts said in unison, leaning closer. "Risky bakes for Benji. Are you doing ricotta instead? We've heard that might be inferior, but we can't verify that."

"Erm, yes," Benji said, pointing to his bowl of cheese. "Creamed the ricotta for a nice, smooth texture."

Lindsay looked at it closely. "That's the smoothest ricotta

I have ever seen." She grabbed a teaspoon and dipped it in, then tasted it quickly.

Jonny held his breath, feeling like time had actually stopped.

Lindsay's brows snapped down as she swallowed, her head tilting to one side. "That's straight-up cream cheese. Not ricotta."

Every single camera suddenly fixed on Benji.

"It's . . . a different ricotta," Benji said simply. "More acidic."

Lindsay tapped her spoon into the palm of her hand. "Ricotta and cream cheese taste nothing alike. I grew up on a dairy farm, this one I know. Benji, did you sneak cream cheese in and claim it was ricotta?"

Silence filled the Great Kitchen. Denis stopped whistling, the faint murmur of PAs and crew members faded away, and even the water on the stoves seemed to be boiling silently.

Forget the cameras—at this point, all *eyes* were on Benji.

He looked directly into the camera. "Yes. I did."

And then, incredibly, he ignored everyone and continued with his bake. His mixing was more intense, his breathing turned unsteady and harsh, and he muttered under his breath in a steady stream of words no one could decipher.

Lindsay and Charlie looked at each other, looked at the director, and, at Mr. Dean's ushering, moved over to Denis to question him on his bake.

Rolling right along, then.

But there was no mistaking what had happened, and, if the show had integrity, it would have to intervene.

Ten minutes of aimless chatter and camerawork, and then there was another break. The bakers were still working, but Jonny was watching the crew and staff, all of whom were having some rather intense conversations to one side of the kitchens.

Benji suddenly punched his table and looked at Claire. "Why did you have to talk about the cheese, Claire? What did you know, huh? What were you going for?"

Claire turned to look at him with wide eyes. "Excuse me?"

Benji came closer, towering over her. "What's the big deal, eh? Curd cheese, ricotta cheese, cream cheese—who actually cares? And why did you have to bring it up?"

Jonny moved before he could stop himself, standing in front of Claire and pressing a hand firmly against Benji's chest. "Back up and back off," he ordered coldly.

"Ooh, Viscount Grumps is getting involved," Benji seethed with a hard laugh, taking a dramatic step backward. "Mind your business, your high and mightyship. This is between me and my fellow baker."

"No, this is between you and the show," Denis insisted as he came over. "Claire was filling the airspace, just as we all have done every single day the cameras are on us. You know how they harp on us to give details of our bakes. How was she supposed to know that you were . . . that you . . . You just leave her alone."

Benji looked at Denis the way one might look at a gnat. "Go back to your station, Loony Tunes. Nobody asked you."

"Mr. Andrews-Lee," the low and formal tones of Mr. Sybil intoned from the entrance to the Great Kitchen. "A word?" He gestured with two fingers and did not turn until Benji started walking toward him.

Mr. Dean cleared his throat. "Right, someone keep an eye on his stuff so it doesn't burn or boil or whatever. We've got a tight schedule, and Denis and Claire have bakes on the move. Frank, stay on Claire. Keith, you're on Denis. Hattie, go tell the judges what's happened."

Jonny nodded his thanks to Denis, then turned to Claire, who, miraculously, wasn't shaking like a leaf. "Are you okay?" he asked her softly.

She took his hand, squeezing hard, and only then could he feel the slight tremor. "Yeah, I think so. I didn't think he'd turn like that, but he couldn't do much more in here with everybody." Her green eyes raised to meet his and her full lips curved ever so slightly. "Guess we've got what we needed for tonight, huh?"

Somehow, that made Jonny laugh, even though he hoped the plan for the night would be unnecessary and that Claire wouldn't have to do anything else with Benji ever.

But the wry edge to her words and the even more wry tilt of her lips was too perfect, and if he didn't laugh, he would have been as angry as Benji, but for completely different reasons.

"Guess so," he managed, linking his fingers with hers as subtly as possible. "Now finish today's bake with your usual awesomeness so we can fill Watson in. It's going to be a complicated evening."

Claire laughed. "You can say that again, Columbo."

Now he couldn't laugh. "Only saying it once, because I'm still against it. But kill this bake, Claire. You've earned some serious praise."

She nodded, squeezed his hand again, and returned to her station and her bake while he moved back out of shot, a cold and nagging feeling of dread starting to prickle at the base of his spine.

CHAPTER 23

"Of all the stupid things I have ever done in my life, this takes the actual cake."

The officer fitting Claire with a tracker, body camera, and wire gave her a sympathetic look. "We're all going to be close enough to intervene before anything happens."

Claire looked at her with as flat an expression as she could manage. "Still, intentionally going for a walk so a murderer can catch me. Not exactly that encouraging, Diane."

"I know," she admitted with a grimace. "Sorry. Sergeant Burke will be following you as closely as possible, hidden in the shadows. The suspect won't even be able to hit you, much less anything else."

"Honestly?" Claire found herself smiling a little despite the horde of yellow jackets currently buzzing around and stinging inside her chest. "A blow to the head followed by a nice nap might be great with the stress I've been dealing with here."

Diane laughed and moved to Claire's back, fastening the wire with tape. "Tell me this much: how did the judging go today? I was on patrol here last week, so I know who everybody is."

"Really tough," Claire told her, smile fading. "The Occasion

Bake is going to be key. I don't know who is going to win. Denis did some amazing work, and even Benji did amazing things, cheating aside. I had a great day, but I don't know how tomorrow will go. I don't think I have enough oomph in my plans." She exhaled heavily, surprised that she was able to do so with so much equipment hidden on her body.

Looking over her shoulder at Diane, Claire frowned. "You're intentionally distracting me, aren't you?"

"Could be," Diane said easily as she stepped in front of Claire again. She looked her over and nodded. "Okay, looks good. How do you feel?"

"Like I'm going to throw up." Claire shook her head, trying for another exhale and not finding it in her. "Why did I agree to this?"

Diane put both hands on her shoulders and looked her squarely in the eye. "Because you want this to end as much as we do, and you know that pushing Benji means you'll be targeted, not Denis. Now, between you and me, Viscount Hotsfor-you is halfway to a conniption at the thought of you doing this, so if you look freaked, he's going to pull the plug. Might even get himself arrested for assaulting officers, if I read him right. Now, I'm not saying we live our lives to please the man, but I really don't want to arrest him tonight when we could catch a real criminal. Eh?"

She squeezed Claire's shoulders slightly, and, for a moment, it was as though Lesley were there, squeezing her shoulder and reminding her that she'd done plenty of other crazy things.

Like apply for the biggest baking show in Britain. Like actually agreeing to go on the show once she made it. Like talking to an actual viscount and becoming friends with him.

And then pretty much falling for him.

So she had to help the police catch a murderer by being bait. Watson had asked for their help, and they had agreed to give it. This was just one more way to do that. A big, scary, life-threatening way, but she would be fine.

If the police didn't get to her quickly, then Jonny would.

How did she know that? Diane had said if she had read things right, he would but Claire could see that in him herself. He was protective of Claire, and that didn't necessarily mean . . . They were friends, and she felt something for him, and maybe he could come to feel things for her, too, but he looked out for her. Took an interest in her.

Which meant he would be there. He'd take Benji down himself if he had to, just because that was Jonny.

Claire would be fine.

She took in a breath and released it with minimal trouble. She could do this.

Nodding, Claire forced a calm smile on her face and followed Diane to the door of the room, grabbing her jacket from the chair and shrugging into it.

Jonny was already outside with the others, and Diane had come into the house in plain clothes so no one would know her real job. There were enough members of the crew staying in the house these days that almost anyone could have passed for an employee, and there was tight enough security to even get onto the estate that no one questioned anyone else.

Claire was reminding herself of all these things as she walked the halls of the house toward the southwest door, as she had been directed. Diane would split off at that point and exit another way, and then Claire's mission, of sorts, would begin.

What if no one had gone out that night? Would someone

have been abducted from their bed? Tricked into going out for the night?

Someone else getting killed while they all stayed at Black-firth would be awful for Jonny and Gabi, and that was reason enough for Claire to go through with this.

Without saying another word to Claire, Diane turned down the hall while Claire kept going straight. Every step felt measured, and every breath that passed her lips felt too cold, but the door outside was approaching, and she had to walk as though a solo evening stroll on the estate wasn't forbidden. As though she was fine talking a walk at her usual time even if Jonny wasn't with her.

No big deal.

The first sensation of the evening air made her gasp, but she was quick to swallow it back and push forward. If she looked too freaked, nothing was going to work the way it needed to. People were jumpy enough as it was.

Life was so much easier when she only had to worry about a souffle falling or a student turning in a late paper.

Claire shoved her hands into the pockets of her coat and focused on walking, keeping her attention directly ahead and forcing herself to walk at the most sedate pace she could. She wanted to turn around and check that Sergeant Burke was behind her, though she doubted she would actually be able to see him. She also wanted to spin in slow circles as she walked so she would know exactly when someone was behind her, assuming Benji decided to take the bait and attack her tonight.

But spinning would defeat the purpose, make her dizzy, and probably lead to the greatest risk of bodily harm she'd face tonight.

How was she meant to be calm and clearheaded? She

thought back to her bake earlier in the day and her steady pace that had led to her greatest success so far. She'd received the best feedback of anyone for her Maids of Honour today, and she ought to be riding that buzzing feeling until at least Monday. No matter how things went for the final Occasion Bake tomorrow, celebration ought to have been the order of the day, not walking into a trap on purpose.

Maybe she could finagle some sort of dessert out of Mrs. Clyde later. A big house like Blackfirth surely must have all sorts of desserts at the ready. It wouldn't be the sort of celebration Claire might have expected from her family and friends at the White Fox, but it would do.

"Stop right there."

Claire inhaled sharply at the cold, flat tone behind her and started to turn toward it out of sheer instinct.

"Don't!" the voice insisted at once. "Do not turn around. Just stop."

Her lips were suddenly parched, and she tried to wet them unsuccessfully.

What if they'd gotten this all wrong? What if it wasn't Benji? What if he was just a cheater and not a murderer? What if someone else was behind her and she had missed all the signs? She wasn't a detective, after all. What did she know?

Enough to get caught by the murderer, evidently.

"Okay," she managed to squeak out.

The person behind her grunted. "Walk. Normally. Don't turn, don't speak, don't make any sound at all. Nod if you can do that."

It actually hurt her neck and head to nod, but she managed to do so.

Something prodded at her back, and her feet started

walking of their own accord. The gravel beneath her feet crunched with a thundering volume, ringing in her ears like a lorry dumping a load of small rocks with each step.

Her heart pounded in her chest with so much force it made her ribs ache. A bruise was probably forming with each beat, and she would be black and blue across her entire torso.

That would confuse the coroner, no question.

Her captor sighed heavily. "You are so predictable, Claire. Why? I could have just let today's episode run its course for tomorrow, but no, you had to stick to your walking schedule—"

The owner of that voice suddenly sprang into her mind. "Benji?" Claire asked, more for the wire than anything else. "Is that—?"

"Stop," he retorted, cutting her off. "It doesn't matter who I am. We're going to the mill, all right?"

Claire bit her lip to keep from whimpering. "Do we have to?"

Her voice sounded soft and small, almost tiny, and she felt like a little girl who had wandered into a shady pub after hours. Alone, uncertain, and utterly petrified about what the next few minutes might hold.

"Yes," he said gruffly. "Why mess with a good gig?"

A good gig? Was that how he would describe re-creating the gristly murder on the estate? What was he even saying? Benji was a hothead and a cheat, but she couldn't believe that a man who had dedicated his professional life to saving people was choosing to take a life by his own volition.

Were they going to meet someone else in the mill? Was there more than one person involved? Was there something bigger going on than any of them realized?

The mill was fast approaching, all lit up as it had been

when she and Jonny had rescued Benji from the brook by the mill wheel.

Had that even been a rescue? Could Benji have freed himself? What was the truth in any of this?

"Benji," Claire ventured softly.

"Don't try, Claire," he told her roughly, a slight edge to his voice. "If you'd just let things ride, pretended you didn't know about the cheating, we wouldn't be doing this. I've been cheating all along, and they haven't caught it even once. Don't you think I know that I'm a lousy baker? I've been trying to get kicked off, but then they locked us down. I even attacked myself to get out, but I was pressured to come back for the storyline. It's the show's fault, Claire. Not mine."

Claire shook her head as he pushed her into the mill. "The show? Benji, why did you kill Lesley in the first place? What did that even do?"

He laughed once. "You think I'm going to tell you? You have no idea what is going on here. It was supposed to be just one life. Just hers. This is happening, okay? Just shut up and walk."

"Okay," Claire stammered as cold chills began racing all through her frame. Where were the police? At what point were they going to intervene? No one had really told her what they would be listening for, or what the trigger words might be. Was she just supposed to wait patiently and hope she didn't die in the process? The finality and resignation in his voice frightened her more than the tinge of desperation did. She couldn't convince him if he was already settled on it, and if he was being forced . . .

"Look, it'll be quick, okay?" Benji told her, his voice gruff. "I'm not a monster."

"Please don't do this," Claire whispered. Her throat convulsed for a moment, squeezing her vocal cords like the noose she soon feared would surround her neck. "Please."

"Just close your eyes, Claire." There was a sharp rustling, and she heard something heavy tapping against fabric. "Close your eyes, and it will all be over before you even know it happened."

Obediently, but biting down on her quivering lip, Claire closed her eyes. Her entire body shook, but she felt it most in her jaw and her chest. Her fingers were cold, her toes were numb, and she anticipated everything fading to nothingness very shortly.

Would nothing really be nothing, or would she have some awareness before death claimed her? How knocked out *was* knocked out?

A scuffling behind her made her jump, but she kept her eyes closed for good measure.

"No!" Benji groaned. "No, I have to finish this. *I have to finish this.*"

Claire flung herself to one side, clinging to the nearest stair post while the sounds of punching, kicking, scuffling rose up around her. She didn't want to watch. Didn't dare hope that the police had Benji, that she was safe, that she was going to live.

"Down, down!" a rough voice grunted through the sound of straining. "You're done."

A near-deafening thump behind her and a slight trembling beneath her feet told Claire that, in all likelihood, Benji was now on the ground.

Her life was still flashing before her closed eyes like a recap of every bake in the *Britian's Battle of the Bakers* series, only with less entertaining music.

"Morton!" the officer bellowed, the sounds of struggling still evident. "Cuffs!"

Claire exhaled, but the air was cold. She felt no relief, no relaxation, no emotion, only a mere function of lungs and muscles. She might have watched herself exhale for all the good it did.

Somehow, with all of that, she had almost forgotten that she was being followed. That she was wired. That any of this had been planned. The complete lack of intervention throughout her walk to the mill and her conversation with Benji had replaced the plan with complete and abject fear.

She had truly thought she was going to be knocked out and never know a single moment of life again.

But there had been the police and the plan, and she was still conscious. Alive.

They had Benji in custody, she could hear that. Knew that. She ought to be less afraid, but she stood with her eyes closed, waiting for someone else to knock her out. Her mind and her body were operating on completely different tracks, their trains of thought and action passing each other in opposite directions.

"Claire!"

Jonny's voice broke through the haze of her mind, and her eyes snapped open at the sound of her name. Her trance broken, she managed to turn slowly, her joints actually aching as she did so. The door to the mill was just there, and the police had Benji down on the ground, still thrashing against their hold.

"Claire!"

Her feet moved, and she walked out of the mill, every motion and every breath feeling unnatural and stiff. She peered out into the darkness of the night, unsure what else it might hold as her eyes were slow to adjust, and wondering if she would ever feel safe again.

Jonny was practically flying down the path from the house at her, his face wreathed in a blend of tension and warmth that made her shake all over again. Her hands came out of her pockets, and a dry sob rippled up her ribs until it almost barked from her lips.

His arms were around her before her fingers had uncurled themselves from the fists they had been, and it was all she could do to put her hands against his side and lean into him.

His breathing was hard, and his heart pounded beneath his coat, thumping against her face in an oddly comforting cadence that grounded her to the situation, her surroundings, and him.

She was grounded in him.

"Tiramisu!" he rasped, shaking his head. "Crème brûlée, forks, knives, and the entire ruddy pantry, I don't ever want you to do that ever again."

"You said ever twice," Claire pointed out, her voice muffled by his coat.

Jonny pulled back and cupped her cheeks, a smile in his eyes but not on his face. "Ever, ever, ever. I'm making an ever-loving point, you madwoman."

Then his mouth was on hers, and the entire moment froze, stilling like the fading of a breeze and then warming like a sunrise, turning sweeter by a dusting of new sugar and igniting corners of her soul that had never existed until just then. Numb toes became flaming toes that arched up, cold fingers became latching fingers that anchored her, and a shaking jaw and chest burst into sunlight with glorious brilliance.

Or something equally poetic.

It was a kiss, not the climax of a firework show with an orchestra elevating the entire thing.

But it was a ridiculously good kiss.

And a much needed one.

Claire felt her lips break from Jonny's, not quite sure when she had begun taking an active part in the kiss, but recollecting that there were several police officers, a certain detective, and a suspect in their vicinity, all of whom could probably see everything.

Opening her eyes, she tried not to wince as she looked at Jonny. A wince would definitely send the wrong message, and this was not the time to risk wounding the man's pride, especially when she wanted to kiss him again after this.

Wincing would be bad.

Jonny wasn't wincing. He was grinning.

Oh, blessed sugary crepes, he was grinning, and that made her grin too.

And giggle.

"That," Jonny said emphatically, brushing his nose against hers, "was long overdue."

"Agreed," Claire admitted in a quiet voice. "And maybe next time we can do without the audience."

He laughed once and glanced over his shoulder. "Eh, no one's looking. They've got their man, so we can take a moment."

"I am wired, you know." Claire made a face, shrugging.

"Yeesh. Let's get that sorted, and then we can see if Watson will let us in on the interrogation." He turned, dropping his arm around her shoulder, pulling her much closer than he'd ever done, and pressing a quick kiss against her hair. "I may freak out a little later, once the adrenaline settles. You okay to sit on a couch in my arms until that stops?"

Claire nodded, swallowing with some difficulty. "Yep. I'm definitely going to freak out, so being secure in your hold would be great. Especially if there's dessert."

"Gotcha. Can do."

Watson came over to them, smiling tightly, though there was a distinct air of satisfaction in his person. "Nicely done, Miss Walker. We're not taking him down to the station tonight; we don't want to draw any attention from the house or at the station at this time of night. My lord, I understand there are some lower-level rooms toward the back of the house that were once used for kitchen staff?"

"Yes, there are," Jonny said slowly. "Why?"

"We'd like to interview him down there, and, if the two of you were to, I don't know, be in the neighboring room and hear everything . . ." He shrugged, smiling a bit. "How would I know for certain or the legality be at risk?"

Claire gaped before breaking into a smile. "I would *love* to hear this."

"So would I," Jonny grunted. "Mostly since I didn't get to be the one to tackle him to the ground and rub his face in mill dust."

Watson chortled, nodding once. "Indeed, my lord. We will be down there within half an hour. Should you choose to be nearby." He winked at Claire and strode away, waving a couple of officers nearby to follow him.

"Well, well," Jonny mused as they started toward the house together. "Maybe it really is over."

She may have imagined it, but Claire thought his arm tightened around her further as they walked back toward Blackfirth and the police.

She didn't mind that one bit.

CHAPTER 24

It had been some time since Jonny had intentionally tried to overhear a conversation in his own house, but Watson had been absolutely right in selecting the rooms by the kitchens for his interrogation.

The walls might as well have been paper between them.

Which was probably useful in a bustling kitchen with a large staff, once the historic kitchens fell out of use.

There was no way the cooks, housekeepers, or butlers of Blackfirth in years gone by would have anticipated a police interrogation in that space. But, given how the staff tended to love gossip about the family, it might have entertained them.

Watson stood outside of the room where the officers had stuck Benji and indicated to Jonny and Claire silently that they should enter the neighboring room.

They nodded with equal silence and moved into the empty room, vacant counter space and gaps where smaller ovens had once sat providing enough nooks and crannies for any sort of hiding game anyone could wish. But they didn't need to hide, so Jonny simply gestured to the wall that was shared with the interrogation room, and Claire nodded.

Then she surprised him by sitting on the floor, her back to the wall, leaning her head back and closing her eyes.

It hadn't occurred to him that she would be exhausted from the long day of baking she'd had before they'd managed to trap Benji, and the addition of such an excursion had clearly left her completely devoid of energy. He was still wired with the nerves of watching her walk away from the house in the darkness, knowing that Benji would probably follow, and then being able to hear the exchange through her wire. He wouldn't be tired for a long, long time tonight, that was for sure.

But he still wanted to hold her, and, he hoped, she wouldn't mind letting him. So he sat down beside her, matching her position before snaking his arm around her shoulders and pulling her gently against him. To his relief, she came willingly, almost curling into his side.

He tried not to smile as he rubbed her arm with his free hand, now encircling her with both arms. Surely he ought to be thinking about the interrogation and the ending of this case.

But holding Claire . . .

Well, it was the second best part of his day.

Kissing her was the best. Hands down, no contest.

"Right, Mr. Andrews-Lee," Watson's voice sounded from the other side of the wall. "Would you like to tell us about your attack on Miss Walker first? Or should we start from the beginning we all know about?"

"The beginning, I guess," Benji said, sounding glum.

"I will ask you once more if you are sure that you do not wish to have a solicitor present. That is your right, and we will not begin proceedings until you have one, should you wish to."

Benji scoffed loudly. "No, I don't need or want a solicitor.

Whoever my public defender will be can just deal with whatever I say on the recording."

"Fair enough." Watson cleared his throat. "Starting the recording. Interviewing the suspect, Benjamin Andrews-Lee of the village of Blackfirth, Oxfordshire. Present in the room are DS Watson and DS Brenner. The suspect has repeatedly declined offers of a solicitor."

Images of various crime procedurals flashed through Jonny's mind as he listened to the formality of Watson's voice. It was exactly like he had seen in the shows, which either spoke well of the detail of those shows or to the relative ignorance of Watson in these matters. Whatever it was, Jonny couldn't think of any legal loopholes in what had just been stated.

"Can you tell us where you were on the night of the eighteenth of April of this year between the hours of seven and eleven in the evening?" a new voice asked, which must have belonged to DS Brenner.

"I was at the Blackfirth Mill," Benji admitted on a sigh. "I told everyone at the Ivy House that I was going to bed early. The truth is that I had packed my bed to look as though I were asleep in it under the covers. I even set the white noise on my phone so that if anybody had gone into the room, they would have thought I was there. None of us were close then, so there was no reason for anyone to try to wake me. I'd had a bad bake that whole episode, so I was moody anyway."

"And what were you doing at the mill?"

"I was waiting for Lesley."

Jonny felt Claire gasp more than heard it. There was no remorse in Benji's tone, and barely any emotion at all. The words stated and flat. Facts and nothing more.

"Why were you waiting for Ms. Kemble?" Brenner asked.

"I was going to kill her," Benji admitted. "She . . . she had been the nurse on duty when my girlfriend, Maisy, died. She was fine when she went into the hospital, so Lesley must have screwed something up. Made some kind of change that made Maisy die, and the hospital refused to look into it. They didn't even—" Benji's voice broke off for a moment. "No one was listening, and no one was apologizing, and someone needed to pay."

"Okay, so why get involved in the show at all? How in the world did you even know she would apply, let alone make it?"

A loud screeching sound made Jonny think Benji had scooted his chair back. "I've been stalking her for three years, man. Do you know how easy it is to bug people's phones these days? Hack their email? Especially if they aren't paying attention. I know everything she's been up to. I baked well enough to get onto the show—they wanted a local guy, and most people here can barely make toast. And killing her on this stupid estate? That was just icing on the cake. My aunt's stupid research about Old Lady Colburn made it easy to fuel ghost rumors."

"Your aunt?" Watson asked sharply. "Who is your aunt?"

"Dr. Adams. Great-aunt, technically. She's a bat, and my mom can't stand her, but she tries to support her research and such. You wouldn't believe how much of her research junk we have laying around the house just because she sends it to her."

"Did Dr. Adams get you the position on the show?"

Benji barked a loud, disparaging laugh. "Not a bit. She hates me. She was shocked that I made it on."

"How did you know enough about the murder of the tenth viscountess to replicate her murder on Ms. Kemble?" Brenner asked.

Jonny could easily imagine Benji's look of derision in the pause that followed. "Weren't you listening? My aunt sends *everything* she writes to my mom. I had access to everything the woman has ever done, so as soon as I knew Lesley would be on the estate for the show, I studied up on it. I could have killed anybody in exactly the same manner a week before the show started to film. I was ready."

"Well, you did manage one original thought for yourself," Watson said in an almost musing tone that had Jonny wanting to applaud.

"Excuse me?"

Watson tsked loudly. "You decided it would be best to work on an unconscious victim instead of a coherent one. Minor detail, I am sure, but there was never any proof that the tenth viscountess sustained a blow to the head."

"He's not going to like that," Claire whisper-giggled.

Jonny bit his lip hard, shaking his head.

"So what?" Benji demanded. "I still killed her just the right way. Tell me you didn't look at my aunt for this, honestly, because of the accuracy."

"Actually, the head wound would have ruled her out pretty neatly. If your aunt had been involved in any way with this, she'd have done it in the most authentic manner possible. I'm sure she'll be flattered that you intended her to be a suspect, though."

There was more scraping and scuffling sounds, and Jonny would have paid a great deal of money to know what exactly had happened. But Benji would have been cuffed, and there were enough police in and around the rooms that he wouldn't have been able to breathe in Watson's direction the wrong way without getting taken down again.

Watson was definitely playing with fire, and Jonny had never liked the man more.

"So you killed Ms. Kemble," Brenner went on after the sounds of Benji's reaction settled. "Then what? Thought the show would pause or cancel?"

"They were supposed to shut down," Benji insisted. "And then I'd be free. When they didn't, I just figured I'd cheat along and get eliminated quickly. Then I didn't get kicked off because the cheating worked." He laughed, and it was a raw, grating sound. "With my aunt distracted as all get-out by the historical mirroring of the murder and then my attack, cheating got easier after that."

Maybe Benji was a budding psychopath that had only just begun to bloom. Who knew what he might have gone on to do if they hadn't caught him?

"I knew from the beginning, though," Benji went on, "that it could be dicey. So I started taking aspirin six weeks ago in case I needed to blame the 'ghost' for another attack—with myself as the victim. I know aspirin can make bruising worse by thinning the blood, which means I could make myself look like a plausible victim without actually having to die."

"How could you have known someone would find you during the right window of opportunity?"

"Easy. Claire and her viscount boyfriend usually walked in the evenings. They thought they were so secretive about it, but we all knew. I just made sure the mill was all lit up, got my neck situated with the rope and left myself some good marks, then I waited in the water until I could hear them running. It was ridiculously easy."

"What were you going to say when the hospital tests came back normal?"

"My attack was interrupted, clearly. How could they question that?"

Jonny looked at Claire and found her green eyes on his, the same thought reflected back. It was true. The hospital probably wouldn't have been able to add much insight into the falsification of the attack, since the entire premise was that it had been falsified. If the police had tried to take Benji to court over it, there would have been too many unanswered questions. Maybe the actual strangulation part of the attack was supposed to happen after the water part, so how would the lack of internal bruising be relevant? Could they really prove that he had never been unconscious based on the scans and lab work, or would that have simply been a theory? It would have been a shaky case from go, and shaky cases were not good.

Watson had been absolutely right. They'd needed to catch Benji in the act of attacking in order for any of this to be proven, and if Benji had wanted to, he probably could have come up with a decent defense.

And yet . . .

"Right, so you decided to go along with the show and come back instead of getting out," Watson said on a sigh. "Why?"

"They offered me money," Benji told him, his voice hard. "To come finish the show, I mean. Claire somehow knew that I was cheating and set me up to be caught on camera, which is why I needed to get rid of her. Would it help me in the show, since I was cheating? Don't know. Didn't really care at that point. The show is so interested in finishing—and finishing quickly—that they said they would edit out the cheating and I'd have a chance anyway. Denis did a passable job on his bakes, but he did have some criticisms. With Claire gone, my chances increase. And we play up the mystery more with two deaths, three attempted . . ." Benji laughed a little. "The show should actually thank me for improving their ratings."

"He really is delusional," Claire breathed as she scooted even closer to Jonny, now practically in his lap.

Jonny didn't mind in the least. As soon as Benji had talked about doing away with Claire like she was a gnat, Jonny had pulled her closer anyway.

He couldn't reply to her statement, couldn't look at anything objectively at the moment. The man in the room behind them had tried to kill Claire and had admitted to it like it wasn't a big deal. Like someone had asked him if he'd eaten the last of the muesli for breakfast. Jonny had barely held it together when Claire was literally walking into the trap, but now . . .

If he hadn't been holding onto her, he might have marched into the other room and gotten a few good blows or kicks in before someone restrained him.

It would have been worth it, though.

"Let me get this very clear for the recording," Watson said with a loud clearing of his throat. "You confess to the murder of Lesley Kemble, the attempted murder of Claire Walker, and faking the attack on yourself to make you seem like another victim."

"Yes, I confess. Congrats, you got me. Maybe you can be Sherlock now, Watson."

"That's low," Jonny hissed, shaking his head.

Claire sputtered softly. "I'm sure he's heard it before. He'll be fine."

"Interrogation terminated at twenty-two fifteen," Watson announced. "Brenner, take him down to the station and have him booked. Go out the back with some uniforms so no one else in the house sees. We'll tell everyone in the morning."

"Yes, sir."

The sounds of chairs scraping came from the room, and Jonny finally felt himself relaxing a little. No more shocking revelations, no more murders or attacks, no more investigation.

It was all over now.

"He killed Lesley for revenge," Claire whispered, quick tears falling from her eyes. "For what he thinks she did as a nurse. After all the good she had done in her life, that was what she had to die for?"

Jonny swallowed with some difficulty, realizing that, in many ways, none of this was over. The fallout hadn't even happened yet. The emotional toll on Claire and the other bakers was only beginning to show. There was so much more to be worked through.

He shifted his position beside her, cupping her cheeks. He smiled gently and smoothed away fresh tears. "Don't try to make sense of his delusion, love. You know and I know, as do most other people in this world, that there is more value to a life than any of that. We've got Lesley's killer in custody. She will get justice."

Claire nodded, sniffing softly as her throat bobbed on a swallow. "I know. It just hurts."

Jonny stroked her cheek again and leaned in, but he let his lips hover above hers, waiting. If she didn't want this sort of comfort, this new and still tentative connection between them, he was not about to insist upon it.

Blessedly, Claire tipped her chin up and met his lips gently, gripping his shirt in her hand as she sighed against his mouth.

There was no fervor or haste, just a soft meeting of lips that was somehow familiar and fresh all at the same time.

"I love that I get to do that now," she whispered as she nuzzled against him.

"Oh, believe me, so do I," Jonny admitted with a grin. "Feel free to kiss me whenever you want."

Claire laughed and laid her head against his shoulder, entwining her fingers with his. "I'll keep that in mind."

They heard footsteps in the hallway, retreating and getting softer in their progression. Only when it was quiet again did another set of footsteps start up, slowly and getting louder.

Watson appeared in the doorway to their room, smiling a little as he leaned against the doorjamb and looked at them. "Could you hear it?"

"Every word," Jonny confirmed with a nod. "Nicely done."

"Thanks. I didn't expect him to admit to everything so easily, but . . ." Watson shook his head, shrugging. "I'm not sure what else there is to do at the moment. Some of my team are already quietly collecting evidence from his room and going through evidence we already have." He turned his attention to Claire. "You did make your statement already, yes?"

Claire nodded. "I did, yeah. Should be all set. Have you told the show yet?"

Watson shook his head. "No, they will be my next stop and conversation, if Mr. Sybil is still awake. If I know him at all, and I am beginning to sense I do, he'll start work on replacing Mr. Andrews-Lee right away. No idea how that works, but they will want to preserve the so-called integrity of the show." He rolled his eyes, the hypocrisy clearly not lost on him.

"There's a pair of alternate bakers ready to step in," Claire told him, lifting her head from Jonny's shoulder. "They'll probably just film bits of one of them doing the other bakes and doing a judging and such for continuity. I doubt Benji will even appear in a single episode."

That was an impressive amount of editing to do, but Jonny could see how it might work. That there were contingency bakers in place was something he hadn't considered, and now he wondered if the previous series of the show had involved an alternate baker instead of an original one and the audience had been none the wiser.

Watson turned to Jonny then, his expression forlorn, "I do have some concerns for the village when this news breaks, my lord."

Jonny frowned. "In what way?"

"One of our locals, a firefighter, no less, engaged in a murder for personal gains." He shook his head again, this time with a weariness that was oddly touching. "And on the estate that has done everything for us. The wider news may not make much of the death and attacks, given how under wraps everything has been, but the village does know about them, my lord. It is discouraging, to say the least, and I am afraid it could be devastating. I don't know what can be done about that."

It spoke well of the detective that he felt so strongly about their community and the effect this crime would have on them as a whole. Jonny hadn't even considered them in either the wider aspect or the more general sense. Blackfirth, in his mind, was his estate and not the village around it. But the truth was that Blackfirth was both, and it was high time he started treating it as such.

"Well, I may be able to do something about that," Jonny said slowly, ideas pinging off the walls of his mind in rapid succession. "There has been enough distance between the estate and the village in recent generations, and I have let the historical murder become a taboo subject. While I am not saying we should embrace it, I do think we could stop avoiding talk of it so much. Lesley's murder, on the other hand, should be treated sensitively, and we will ensure that there is a memorial to her on the estate."

"Very sensible, sir. Very kind."

He hadn't been saying so to get the detective's approval, but if the man thought it ought to be given, so be it.

"I will speak to the show's producers," Jonny went on, "but I think, since they'll have to do reshoots anyway, we might make a few alterations. Maybe the final episode of the show ought to be an occasion where the entire village is invited on the estate to celebrate together. We've all been encased in this bubble of sorts while the show has been here, and we can celebrate the end of that bubble together. My sister has been wanting to be more involved in the estate, and she loves a party on any given Thursday. We can create a position of a liaison between the estate and the village. Develop community relations, that sort of thing. Would that help, do you think?"

Watson looked as though he might get emotional, and Jonny was instantly uncomfortable with the idea. Tears were bad enough from his sister or any other woman of his acquaintance, but he had never known what to do with tears from men. Obviously, men shed tears, but in his experience, they did so privately. How did one comfort a crying man?

Jonny looked at Claire in concern, but she was looking rather teary too.

Was it a rubbish plan on his part? Was he showing just how remote a person he was, and they both felt excessive distress about it?

Claire smiled at him through her shimmering eyes, creating a bewilderingly pleasant knot in the pit of his stomach. Was that pride he saw mingled with affection in her expression? It almost looked like adoration, and it instantly became his favorite look for her.

"That would be a beautiful thing, my lord," Watson admitted in a hoarse voice. "It would help, indeed."

Jonny found himself smiling rather sheepishly at the detective, bobbing his chin in a nod. "Very well, then. I'll put the pieces in place as soon as the case is complete on your end."

"Very good, sir." Watson looked at Claire, smiling broadly. "Another chance for you to win this show, Miss Walker. I think I can safely say that the entire force is rooting for you."

EPILOGUE

ONE WEEK LATER

It was done. It was really and truly and finally done.

The Royal Occasion Bake, postponed a week so that Freya could film the Classic Bake of Maids of Honour, had finished an hour ago, and judging had just taken place. Claire's thrill over having Freya back with them had been kept in check—barely—by her own stress over the bakes, but it was all over now.

They weren't waiting a whole day to announce the winner of the show. Not this time.

This time, the hosts would come out to the frantically organized Blackfirth Fête on the lawn, and, in front of all the village, the eliminated bakers, and the Blackfirth Park staff, announce the winner.

The show wasn't done, of course. They had to bring in one of the alternate bakers and get him to film several bakes and reaction shots. No one was quite sure when he would be eliminated or how they would replace Benji throughout the entire series, but apparently the producers had figured it all out and said it would be fairly simple.

It would make watching the show when it aired that much more interesting.

But Claire couldn't think about that now as she sat on the bench with Denis and Freya, waiting for the judges and hosts to appear.

She really couldn't complain about how she had done in the Occasion Bake. Her Charlotte Russe cake had held its shape beautifully and tasted perfect. Her tiny pithiviers cakes had not leaked, and her layers were all cooked. The pistachio dauphines had been a hit, and her Sablé Bretons had just the right snap that Alan was always harping on about in previous series. Alan had bestowed a smile upon her, fully and freely, which had earned her a round of applause in the kitchens.

Claire had no illusions about the judging. Denis had done a perfect Victoria sponge with an homage to the actual Queen Victoria, and somehow he'd managed the most gorgeous array of macarons and jellies and tarts along with a chestnut pudding. He would be nearly impossible to beat. And Freya! Coming back after her elimination in Wedding Week, which had been brutal for Claire, the fact that she had killed truffles with champagne wine, chestnut puddings, a chocolate raspberry Bavarian torte, and Earl Grey tea-flavored macarons was incredible. Dame Sophie had sung praises about her torte in a way that no one had ever heard before.

Claire was not going to win. The announcement hadn't been made yet, but she was fairly positive considering how the Occasion Bake had gone. Good, but not perfect.

And when Denis and Freya had produced perfect bakes, anything less was disastrous by comparison.

But she'd made it to the finale, and there was something to be said for that.

"I'm so nervous," Freya whispered as she sat next to Claire, arms folded and left leg bouncing with barely contained energy. "My torte could have been so much better. It was outstanding in practice. And a tea-flavored macaron is always a risk. Why didn't I go for rhubarb?"

Claire gave the girl a reassuring smile. "Dame Sophie loved your torte. And Alan liked your tea macaron. He said he couldn't fault it."

"That doesn't mean he could praise it either." Freya shook her head firmly, tears at the corners of her eyes. "It's not going to be me, Claire. I know it. And do you know how awful it will be to lose twice?"

It was clear she was in no state to hear any arguments to the contrary, so Claire just put her arm around Freya and pulled her close, rubbing her arm.

She was not going to miss competing, Claire decided. She loved baking—adored it, really—but the stress of baking under strict time constraints and with ultra-critical judges was like writing a thesis on your favorite subject.

Wonderful and entertaining in theory, but soul-crushing in reality.

No, it wasn't that horrible, but it did make baking a little less enjoyable, and Claire was ready for baking to be entirely enjoyable again.

What she was not ready for was leaving Blackfirth. Once Benji had been taken away and his criminal shadow had lifted, being on the estate had been truly a joy and a wonder.

All the bakers had stayed on at Blackfirth House at Jonny and Gabi's invitation, even when the security had lessened. Being in a home had made the entire experience more enjoyable and relaxing. Even if that home was hundreds of years old and decked out in historic art and priceless heirlooms and the like.

And then there was Jonny. The two of them were thick as thieves, and this idyllic interlude with him had been something refreshing, uplifting, and wholly unexpected for Claire. Who'd have thought she'd have found a blossoming romance with the brooding man of the manor hosting *Britain's Battle of the Bakers*? But found it she had, and the idea of going back home to Surrey while he stayed here was depressing. She'd probably look into teaching positions again, just to pay the bills, but she knew it wouldn't fill her soul like baking had and did. Being nothing more than a baker for the past few weeks had lit a fire within her, and she was more determined than ever to find a way to become a full-time baker someday.

But it wouldn't be nearly as enjoyable or fun if Jonny wasn't around for it.

They hadn't put labels on what they were to each other, hadn't even gone outside of the estate for dates, given the restrictions of the show. Would this relationship, if that's what it was, work once it was released from the constraints within which it was created?

How did that conversation even begin? Did he begin it or did she? It wasn't a fling on her part, and she didn't think it was for Jonny either, but did that mean this could be serious?

Why did people make things complicated?

Baking was so much clearer. Flavors could be improved. Ingredients could be added or subtracted or changed. No one asked cherries if they wanted to sink to the bottom of a cake or bread; if the mixture was right, the cherries went where they were supposed to go. Simple as that.

So, was this mixture of theirs right?

Or were they simply a pair who had been tossed together by a murder and by solving a crime, and found a respite with each other throughout?

"They're not having us stay on to film continuity with the new guy—Rhys Whatever—are they?"

"No, you goose," Claire assured her. "We're done. Except for Alan and Sophie, I guess. Do they count?"

"Dame Sophie judges my dreams these days," Freya admitted with a soft snort. "I don't envy Rhys facing her alone."

"Oh, for sure." Claire nodded in agreement, looking toward the pavilion for the judges and hosts to appear.

No one had told Rhys about the murder, as far as Claire knew. Nondisclosure agreements had been given to everyone on the show, preventing them from talking about anything to do with the murder until after the show aired. Benji's arrest had been kept quiet—the investigation was not yet public knowledge—and any conversations about what had happened could only take place in private in hushed tones with those who had been there.

It had been an odd bonding experience for Claire and the rest of the bakers, once the news of Benji's arrest had spread among them. They'd chatted about what had happened, expressed their shock and suspicions, and each of them had told Claire separately that they couldn't believe she had baked so well with all of that going on, given how involved she'd become in the investigation. She had tried to tell them that she hadn't really had a choice and that baking had been her best coping mechanism, but they wouldn't hear it.

Nothing felt impressive to Claire about what she'd done and endured. It had simply been, and she'd done what she could.

DS Watson updated her and Jonny on various details now and again, but he hadn't visited the estate in a while. There hadn't been a reason to, and Claire found she missed him. He really was a good-natured sort, even if he'd been bang out of line in asking her and Jonny to help him secretly investigate the murder. It had all ended well enough, and she wouldn't hold it against him.

His superiors had basically given him a handshake and a biscuit tray for his part in the actual investigation—an investigation that *they* had bungled. For putting him in that situation—and for failing Lesley—she would hold everything against them for a very long time.

"Distract me," Freya ordered suddenly, turning to face Claire. "What would you do with the money if you won?"

Claire sighed a long-suffering sigh, looking at her young friend with a raised brow. "Really, Freya?"

Freya all but stamped her foot in impatience. "Humor me, Claire. Please!"

It wasn't something Claire liked to talk about, and it seemed rude to tempt Fate that way, but since Claire wasn't going to win, there really wasn't any harm in finally talking about it.

Besides, maybe she'd find another way to make it happen.

"I'd open a bakery, which isn't all that original," Claire told her in a low voice, finding herself smiling as she thought of it. "But I want it to be a different kind of bakery. I grew up in a pub, right? So, I want to do a bakery that's more like a pub. A place to sit and enjoy company while you eat the bakes, maybe have a pint on the side, and get that traditional pub feeling, even if the food and drink isn't quite the same."

Freya grinned, nodding in approval. "Love that. What a cool idea! What would you call it?"

"Oh, I dunno." Claire laughed and looked away. "Pubs have the most random names, and it might depend on where it is and what the culture of the town is."

"What a load of waffle." Freya snorted a loud scoff and pointed a finger at her. "You have a name in your head. Tell me what it is."

Claire saw Jonny walking up the path from the house, and her smile grew as his eyes connected with hers. "All right, there is one. It's a joke my dad and I had from when I started baking."

"And that is?"

Biting her lip, Claire looked at Freya with a bit of a playful wince. "The Brass Crumpet."

Freya burst out laughing and clapped her hands. "Yes! Oh my gosh, yes! I need you to do this, and I need to come visit. I can see the place now—kind of an old green as a theme color and dark brown shades of wood inside, sticky floor for ambiance . . . Please make this happen, Claire. Whatever else happens, I need this place to be real."

"Find me some funding, and we'll talk," Claire said, trying to brush the entire thing off to keep her friend from seeing just how delighted she was by Freya's reaction.

No one knew about Claire's plans for a bakery, not even Jonny or her father. It had been a pipe dream, something that lived rent-free in her mind but would never know a moment of reality. Claire would never have the funding for it, and she doubted anyone would want to start a business with her, given her complete lack of experience in that area.

But it was a fun thing to dream about.

Alan and Sophie suddenly emerged from the tent, followed closely by Charlie and Lindsay. Mr. Dean stood from his chair and whistled; his camera crew hustled to get their shots in place.

"Oh, hello," Claire muttered, nudging her head toward them for Freya. "Think they're getting ready to go."

"I'm not ready," Freya blurted, her arms folded so tightly that her shoulders were almost at her ears. "I'm not ready. I don't want to know. I don't want to know. Oh gosh, I'm going to fall over."

Claire rubbed Freya's arms gently. "It's going to be fine, Freya. Come on, let's go stand on our line."

Just then, Mr. Dean announced, "One minute to rolling for elimination! Places, please. Bakers, form your line."

A twinge of nostalgia and sadness prickled at Claire's heart as she and Freya moved to stand on the ribbon that had been placed in the grass. Denis joined them, and they all put their hands on each other's backs for support. It was exactly the sort of family feeling Claire had hoped the show would elicit among the bakers, though it had taken long enough for it to develop. Lesley would have been chief in bringing it about earlier if she'd been alive, and she most certainly would have been here today for this episode, brightly colored silk scarf waving in the breeze.

But they were here now, and Lesley had left a lasting impression on all of them regardless.

Hopefully, they had done her proud.

"Establishing shot in thirty seconds. Silence among the party."

Alan, Sophie, Charlie, and Lindsay stood in the front of the pavilion, presently out of shot, but they would be focused on as soon as establishing was done.

"You've all done brilliantly," Denis whispered to Claire and Freya. "Well done, whatever happens."

Claire smiled at him. "You too."

"Three, two . . ." Mr. Dean shouted, holding up a silent finger for *one*.

The red light appeared on the camera, and all three bakers kept their expressions even as they stared straight ahead for a few moments.

"Camera two, on the judges."

Claire counted to five in her head, knowing the rough timing of the elimination announcement.

Sure enough, Lindsay stepped forward. "Bakers, thank you for the incredible work you brought to your Occasion Bake today, and for all the bakes you have brought to this Historical Bakes series. The judges have had a lengthy discussion, and, after much deliberation, they have decided that the winner of series twelve is . . . Denis."

A massive cheer went up from the crowd, and Claire found herself joining in. Freya turned to Denis with a gaping grin, hugging him tight while the man himself seemed entirely without words as he stared at the judges.

"Are you serious?" he finally said as he tried to hug Freya back and throw an arm around Claire at the same time. "Are you serious?"

"Yes!" Charlie shouted. "Come here, Denis!"

Claire went up on tiptoe and kissed Denis's cheek. "Congratulations! You deserve it. Go get your trophy!"

He put his hands on her shoulders, smiling through tears and shaking his head.

"Go!" Claire urged, patting his arm.

He walked over to the judges and hosts, all of whom

shook his hand and patted his back. Lindsay handed him the coveted crystal whisk trophy while Alan brought flowers over to Freya and Claire.

"Ladies, you did really well," he told them, smiling like a fond uncle. "I couldn't be prouder, given everything."

"Thanks, Alan," Freya replied, her cheeks coloring with embarrassment.

Claire nodded and took her flowers, reaching out for a quick hug.

Alan patted her back. "You did good, love. Really, really good."

Touched, Claire pulled back and grinned. "Thank you. That means a lot."

He nodded and turned to say something more to Denis, who was being mobbed by the other bakers, as was tradition in the series.

"And cut!" Mr. Dean called. "Nicely done, gang. Interviews next."

Claire sniffed back a surprising rise of tears, forgetting that this was all taped and part of a show. It was the strangest existence, having a camera filming everything you did, and she certainly wouldn't miss it.

"Freya, can we get you first?" one of the assistants called. "Youngest baker to ever be in the finals!"

Freya groaned, rolling her eyes. "If she expects me to be peppy, we're going to be in for a long interview."

Claire looked around the green lawn, then toward the pavilion's green-and-white top with a fond smile, relishing the feeling of being in the space without any sort of stress or pressure for the first time. Now it was just a place, but one wherein she had found new versions of herself, new skills, new friends, new hopes. It was a classroom of sorts, and now she was leaving it.

Strange how a place of challenges could come to mean so much.

"I'll stage a revolt if you want. Demand a recount. Form a picket line."

Claire laughed and turned to face Jonny, who stood there looking gorgeous in a burgundy jumper and jeans, hands in his pockets, warmth dancing in his blue eyes. "It's not necessary. I'm good. I think it was the right call."

"Probably," he admitted with a shrug. "Since you do mediocre bakes and all."

She rolled her eyes and closed the distance between them, looking up at him with a quizzical expression. "And what would you know of my mediocre bakes, hmm?"

"Did I say mediocre?" He tsked and shook his head. "I meant masterful. Utterly brilliant, and it is a crime that you didn't win."

"You can start the fan club when the show airs," Claire told him with a prim nod. "I want a large following on social media and some sort of public outcry that means I'll get selected for one of the holiday specials in a few years."

Jonny nodded once in return. "Done. I'll see to it. Shirts and all—we'll make sure everyone knows." He grinned and put his hands on her upper arms. "Can I tell you how ridiculously proud I am of you? Or is that completely and totally patronizing?"

She pretended to consider that. "Not completely and totally patronizing, but if you tone it down a little, you can tell me something of the sort."

"I am so proud of you," he said in a low voice, emphasizing each word. "Seriously, I don't know how you did any of this, let alone doing it so well. You could have won."

Cheeks warming, Claire shrugged, glancing away. "Maybe, if I'd baked better today and throughout, but I didn't, and that's how it goes. I'm still shocked I made it this far."

"I'm not."

She looked at him quickly, his warm smile making her toes curl in her trainers. "No?"

"Not a bit. From the moment I met you, I knew you were way better than mediocre." He chuckled softly and cupped her cheek. "Way, way better."

"You don't know anything about baking," Claire reminded him softly.

Jonny frowned playfully. "I've made it well into series seven, thank you very much. I know more now than I did then. But I'm not talking about baking. I'm talking about you."

Her heart fluttered like a fledgling bird in her chest, and she rocked on her heels, her hands playing with the hem of his jumper. "Are you?"

"Mm-hmm." He cocked his head, his smile going crooked to match. "I know the show is over, and, technically, it's time for you to go home, but do you think you could find a reason to stick around here a little while longer? There are always kids to teach here, or maybe . . . the village could use a new bakery?" He quirked his brows in suggestion, his smile playful but hesitant.

Ticklish did not begin to describe the feeling coursing through Claire, but whatever it was, it was warm, and it was delicious.

She twisted her lips a little, contemplating the idea. "Sticking around, hmm? I think I could probably be persuaded."

The way Jonny's smile grew, the slight air of disbelief in it, and the sweet light of relief in his face made Claire's heart sing, and she linked her fingers around the back of his neck, unable to keep up the playfully coy facade one moment longer.

"Well, luckily for us both," Jonny said, "I am very, very good at persuading."

Claire only got one good laugh out before he kissed her, and then she was quite occupied with kissing him back.

The fact that there were a few claps and whistles coming from the nearby cast, crew, and village only made the thing more entertaining.

And an entertaining kiss must always be appreciated.

CRÈME BRÛLÉE

1 cup heavy cream	1 whole egg
1 cup milk	¼ cup granulated sugar
1 vanilla bean pod	Brown sugar
3 egg yolks	Sliced fruit or berries

1. In a small saucepan, combine heavy cream, milk, and vanilla bean. Heat to boil. Remove from heat, and steep 10 minutes. Divide vanilla bean and scrape bean seeds into the milk mixture, discarding the pod.
2. With an electric mixer, combine eggs and granulated sugar. Add the milk mixture in a steady stream. Strain mixture through a fine strainer. Skim foam.
3. Divide into 4 small ramekins (about 4 ounces each), set ramekins in baking dish, and pour enough hot water around ramekins to come to halfway up the sides. Bake at 325 degrees F. for 25 to 30 minutes, until just set. The crème brûlée should tremble slightly.
4. Top with brown sugar, mixed with additional white sugar, if desired. Caramelize the tops with culinary torch. Decorate with berries.

CHELSEA BUNS

2½ cups lukewarm milk

3 tablespoons + 1 teaspoon dried yeast

8⅓ cups strong white bread flour

½ cup granulated sugar

10 tablespoons butter, cubed, at room temperature

2 eggs, beaten

1¾ teaspoons fine sea salt

Flour, for dusting

FILLING

2 cups butter, room temperature

1⅓ cups granulated sugar

3 teaspoons ground cinnamon

Pinch of fine sea salt

2½ cups currants

SUGAR SYRUP

¼ cup granulated sugar

¼ cup water

Superfine sugar, for sprinkling

1. In a small saucepan, warm milk slightly, then add yeast. Stir briefly and gently to activate yeast. In a large bowl or the bowl of an electric mixer fitted with a dough hook, combine flour and sugar. Add butter on top. Pour half the yeast mixture over the butter and start kneading. When

milk and butter are completely absorbed, add the remaining yeast mixture and eggs. Knead dough for 5 minutes; the dough will be very wet. Allow dough to stand for a few minutes, then add salt and knead an additional 10 minutes, scraping the dough off the dough hook and sides of the bowl, if needed. Dough should be smooth and elastic, not too dry but also not too wet.

2. Cover dough and set aside for 1 hour, until it has doubled.
3. Make the filling by combining butter, sugar, cinnamon, and salt in a large bowl. Whip until creamy. Set aside.
4. On a floured surface, roll out the dough into a rectangle (about 24 x 38 inches and 1/16-inch thick). Cover the top half of the dough with ⅓ of the filling, then fold the bottom half of the dough over the filling. Use a rolling pin to flatten out the dough.
5. Spread the remaining filling over the entire surface of the dough. Dot with currants, then fold dough lengthwise into a long roll. Cut the roll into 2-inch slices and place slices in two 15 x 10-inch jelly roll tins lined with parchment paper. Make sure the spirals are facing upward and there is space between each bun. Bake at 400 degrees F. for 20 to 25 minutes, until buns are golden brown.
6. While the buns are baking, make the sugar syrup by heating the sugar and water in a small saucepan until the sugar has dissolved.
7. Brush hot baked buns with the sugar syrup and sprinkle with superfine sugar.

CLAIRE'S STEAMED TREACLE PUDDING

1¼ cups all-purpose flour

⅓ cup dark brown sugar

2 teaspoons ground ginger

1 teaspoon baking soda

⅓ cup cold butter, cubed

1 large egg

⅔ cup whole milk

6 tablespoons golden syrup, divided

½ teaspoon vanilla extract

1 small orange for zest and juice

1. Grease a medium, 1-liter pudding basin or a heat-resistant bowl with butter.
2. In a medium mixing bowl, add flour, dark brown sugar, ginger, and baking soda. Stir together.
3. Add cold butter, and use a pastry blender until it resembles coarse breadcrumbs.
4. In a separate bowl, mix together egg, milk, 1 tablespoon golden syrup, and vanilla extract. Finely grate in the zest of the orange, then cut the orange and squeeze in the juice.
5. Add egg-and-milk mixture to the dry ingredients. Mix together.
6. Pour remaining golden syrup into the pudding basin, then add the cake mixture.

7. Cover the pudding with a circle of parchment paper, followed by foil. Tie in place with string.
8. In a large pot, place pudding in a steamer. Pour in enough boiling water to reach the base of the steamer. Cover and steam for roughly 1½ to 2 hours, topping up with water when necessary.
9. While pudding is still warm, remove parchment paper and foil, then turn the pudding onto a serving plate. Serve pudding hot with vanilla ice cream.

JONNY'S GINGERBREAD BISCUITS

1¾ cups flour, plus more for
the parchment
1 tablespoon ground ginger
¼ teaspoon ground allspice
¼ teaspoon ground mace

6 tablespoons unsalted butter,
room temperature
¼ cup firmly packed dark
brown sugar
½ cup black treacle or dark
molasses

1. In a large mixing bowl, whisk together flour, ginger, all-spice, and mace. Add butter, and rub it into the flour mixture with your fingers until the mixture is the consistency of coarse breadcrumbs. Add dark brown sugar, and stir with a wooden spoon until fully incorporated. Add treacle, and mix until blended.

2. Knead the dough in the bowl until smooth and evenly dark.

3. Lay a sheet of parchment paper on a work surface, and dust it lightly with flour. Place the dough in the center, and pat it into a thick, flat disk. If using a cookie cutter, roll out the dough a scant ¼-inch thick and cut out as many biscuits as possible. Transfer them to 2 sheet pans lined with parchment paper, spacing biscuits about ¾-inch apart.

4. Gather the scraps of dough and roll out again. Cut out more biscuits and add to the pans.
5. Bake at 275 degrees F. for 15 minutes. Rotate pans back to front, then bake another 15 minutes, or until crisp.
6. Transfer pans to wire racks and let biscuits cool on the pans for 5 minutes. Transfer biscuits to the wire racks and allow to cool completely.

LESLEY'S LEMON
AND LAVENDER LOAF

¾ cup vegetable oil

1 teaspoon lavender, culinary grade

1½ cups granulated sugar

1 tablespoon lemon zest

3 eggs

¼ teaspoon salt

2½ cups all-purpose flour

1½ teaspoons baking powder

⅔ cup lemon juice

¾ cup yogurt or sour cream

LAVENDER GLAZE

1 cup royal icing

1 cup confectioners' sugar

1 teaspoon lemon juice

2 to 3 tablespoon hot water

1 teaspoon vanilla extract

3 to 4 drops purple food coloring (optional)

1 teaspoon lavender, culinary grade (optional)

1. In a small saucepan, heat vegetable oil and culinary-grade lavender until the oil is hot but not sizzling. Cover saucepan with a lid, turn off the heat, and allow the lavender to "bloom" for 20 minutes.
2. Strain oil into a cup and allow to cool. Set aside.
3. In a stand mixer (or using a hand mixer), beat together sugar and lemon zest until sugar takes on a yellow color.

4. Add eggs one at a time, allowing each to incorporate. Beat on high until mixture is fluffy. Add cooled lavender oil in a slow drizzle.

5. Reduce mixer speed to medium, and add salt, flour, baking powder, and lemon-flavored sugar gradually. If the dough starts to look too thick, add lemon juice, followed by the yogurt. Blend until mixture looks fully incorporated and smooth.

6. Line a loaf pan with parchment paper, and grease sides with butter. Pour cake batter into loaf pan and bake at 400 degrees F. for about 1½ hours, or until the end of a skewer comes out clean.

7. While the cake is baking, make the glaze by combining royal icing and confectioners' sugar in a medium bowl. Add lemon juice, hot water, and vanilla gradually—only 1 teaspoon at a time. Do not allow glaze to become too thin.

8. Once the glaze looks smooth and resembles honey, add purple food coloring if, desired.

9. Once the cake has cooled completely, top with glaze and sprinkle with lavender.

DENIS'S VICTORIA SPONGE CAKE

¾ cup unrefined caster sugar

½ teaspoon vanilla essence

¾ cup unsalted butter, softened

3 eggs, beaten

1¼ cups self-rising flour, sieved

BUTTERCREAM

⅔ cup unsalted butter, softened

1¾ cups icing sugar, divided

⅓ vanilla bean, split

Strawberry jam

1. In a large mixing bowl, cream together caster sugar, vanilla essence, and softened butter until light and fluffy. Gradually add the beaten eggs a little at a time to avoid having the mixture curdle. Add sieved flour, and fold together until ingredients have combined.
2. Prepare two 8-inch Victoria sponge cake tins by greasing sides with butter and lining the bottom with a circular piece of parchment paper.
3. Divide the cake mixture evenly, and pour into the prepared cake tins. Carefully smooth mixture to create two level layers. Bake at 350 degrees F. on the middle rack

for approximately 20 minutes, or until the cake appears golden brown and an inserted skewer comes out clean. Remove from oven and allow cakes to cool slightly before turning them out onto a wire rack.

4. While the cakes are baking, make the buttercream by adding softened butter to the icing sugar in a medium-sized bowl. Add the vanilla bean seeds, discarding the pod, and mix until the buttercream is pale and fluffy, with flecks of vanilla seeds throughout.

5. Once the cakes have completely cooled, top one cake with an even layer of buttercream. Add a thick layer of strawberry jam. Place the second cake on top of the jam and gently press down. Dust the top of the cake with icing sugar and serve.

ACKNOWLEDGMENTS

Massive thanks go out to Heather Moore, Jen Johnson, and Hannah Groesbeck for their help while I worked through this brand-new kind of project for me. Thanks to Stephanie Black for guiding me through mystery writing. Thanks to my dad for helping with a great list of baking-related puns. Thanks to Dennis Gaunt for reading the manuscript and giving notes and not taking it personally that Denis is not Dennis. (He's not you!)

(Jason Wright, if you're reading this, no, Mr. Wright is not you either.)

Thanks to Casey Robertson for giving me this idea in the first place so long ago, and to Lisa Mangum for making it into a murder even though I thought it was crazy at first.

Thanks to Lorie Humphreys for her help with the crème brûlée recipe.

Thanks to the whole team at Shadow Mountain for setting me on this new and unexpected course that has given me a legitimate reason to binge crime shows and documentaries.

And thanks to the *Great British Baking Show* for being the perfect inspiration and the single most addictive show I have ever watched.

RESOURCES

Acton, Eliza. *Modern Cookery for Private Families*. 1855. 2nd ed., London and New York: Longmans, Green, and Co, 1887.

Baker, Gerard. *The Great British Bake Off: How to Avoid a Soggy Bottom and Other Secrets to Achieving a Good Bake*. Random House, 2013.

Black, Maggie. *The Medieval Cookbook*. Thames and Hudson, 2000.

Coleby, Georgina. *Mrs Beeton's Guide to Baking*. Amberley Publishing Limited, 2015.

Downton Abbey. *The Official Downton Abbey Afternoon Tea Cookbook*. Weldon Owen, 2020.

Flanagan, Mark, and Edward Griffiths. *A Royal Cookbook: Seasonal Recipes from Buckingham Palace*. Royal Collection Publications, 2014.

———, and Kathryn Cuthbertson. *Royal Teas: Seasonal Recipes from Buckingham Palace*. London: Royal Collection Trust, 2017.

Gray, Annie. *At Christmas We Feast: Festive Food Through the Ages*. Profile Books Ltd, 2022.

———. *The Greedy Queen: Eating with Victoria*. Profile Books, 3 May 2018.

———, and Andrew Hann. *How to Cook: The Victorian Way with Mrs Crocombe*. September Publishing, 24 Sept. 2020.

King, Caroline B. *Victorian Cakes*. Holiday House, 1 May 1986.

Lloyd, Martha, et al. *Martha Lloyd's Household Book: The Original Manuscript from Jane Austen's Kitchen*. Oxford Bodleian Library, University of Oxford [Chawton Hampshire] Jane Austen's House, 2021.

Mervis, Ben, and Jeremy Lee. *The British Cookbook: Authentic Home Cooking Recipes from England, Wales, Scotland, and Northern Ireland*. Phaidon Press, 2022.

Oliver, Charles. *Dinner at Buckingham Palace: Secrets & Recipes from the Reign of Queen Victoria to Queen Elizabeth II*. Kings Road Publishing, 2018.

Rochford, Michael J. *Georgian Recipes and Remedies: A Country Lady's Household Handbook*. Pen and Sword History, 2020.

Rossi-Wilcox, Susan M. *Dinner for Dickens: The Culinary History of Mrs Charles Dickens's Menu Books*. Prospect Books, 2005.

Timberlake, Emily, and Susan Vu. *The Official Bridgerton Guide to Entertaining: How to Cook, Host, and Toast Like a Member of the Ton*. Hachette UK, 2024.

Ysewijn, Regula. *The British Baking Book: The History of British Baking, Savory and Sweet*. Weldon Owen International, 2020.

———. *The Official Downton Abbey Christmas Cookbook*. Weldon Owen, 2020.

ABOUT THE AUTHOR

Photo by Sarah Schroering

REBECCA CONNOLLY is the author of more than two dozen novels. She calls herself a Midwest girl, having lived in Ohio and Indiana. She's always been a bookworm, and her grandma would send her books almost every month so she would never run out. Book Fairs were her carnival, and libraries are her happy place. She received a master's degree from West Virginia University.